# Not Until You

## A Hope Springs Novel

## Valerie M. Bodden

## Hope Springs Series

Not Until Forever
Not Until This Moment
Not Until You
Not Until Us
Not Until Christmas Morning
Not Until This Day
Not Until Someday
Not Until Now
Not Until Then
Not Until The End

## River Falls Series

Pieces of Forever
Songs of Home
Memories of the Heart
Whispers of Truth
Promises of Mercy

## River Falls Christmas Romances

Christmas of Joy

# A Hope Springs Gift for You

Members of my Reader's Club get a FREE book, available exclusively to my subscribers. When you sign up, you'll also be the first to know about new releases, book deals, and giveaways.

Visit www.valeriembodden.com/gift to join!

## Need a refresher of who's who in the Hope Springs series?

If you love the whole gang in Hope Springs but need a refresher of who's who and how everyone is connected, check out the handy character map at https://www.valeriembodden.com/hscharacters

For as high as the heavens are above the earth,
so great is his love for those who fear him;
as far as the east is from the west,
so far has he removed our transgressions from us.

Psalm 103:11-12

# Chapter 1

Nate squinted into the blinding expanse of the parking lot. Had the world always been this bright, or did it only seem that way after seeing it through bars and walls for the past seven years?

His gaze roved the cars scattered throughout the lot. He'd written home to let his parents know today was his release date, but they'd never written back. Not that he'd expected a reply. After seven years without contact, a person kind of gave up.

Still, he'd half hoped, half dreaded that at least one of them would be here to meet him. He had a grand total of ten dollars to his name. Which left him with the options of sleeping on a park bench tonight or hitchhiking the fifty miles back to his hometown.

"Nathan." There was no mistaking his father's stern voice.

Nate turned to find his dad standing several rows away. He probably couldn't bring himself to come any closer to the building that proved his son was the worst kind of screw up. Dad looked older than the last time Nate had seen him, his once salt and pepper hair now all salt, his suit fitting him more loosely than it used to. He stood as stoic and unsmiling as ever, though.

Nate forced himself to breathe as he approached his father. Forced himself to keep his shoulders straight and his chin up, the way Dad had drilled into him.

Two feet in front of Dad, he stopped and held out his right hand. Dad looked at it a moment, then slapped a piece of paper into it.

Nate flipped it over. A slow churn started in his gut.

"A bus ticket?" He swallowed the bile rising at the back of his throat. The only thing that had gotten him through the past seven years was the promise of going home. Of making things right. Of making up for what he'd done.

He'd work the rest of his life to do it if that's what it took.

"Get in the car. Your bus leaves in twenty minutes." Dad disappeared into the driver's door without another glance at Nate.

Nate stood frozen a moment, then moved toward the passenger door. What had he expected? That Dad would welcome him home with open arms like some sort of long-lost son?

The moment Nate closed his door, Dad backed out of the parking spot.

"Can't I at least see Mom first?" He pressed his lips together, trying to push down the emotion building in his chest. "And Kayla?"

"The bus will take you to Hope Springs."

"Where?" Nate had never heard of the place. "Why?"

But before Dad even threw him the dark look, Nate knew. He was being banished.

"We just bought out a property management firm there." Dad's voice, the voice Nate had remembered for its resonance, was flatter than the cornfields that stretched in every direction around them. "It's in pretty bad shape. You're going to make it profitable. I expect weekly progress reports."

"Dad, I don't want—"

"Card's in the suitcase." Dad plowed on as if Nate hadn't spoken. "There's a law office next door. They have the key. At least one of our buildings has an empty apartment. You can live there."

"Dad—"

"There's a bag in the back."

Nate swiveled to look over his shoulder. A small suitcase rested on the backseat, as if Nate were going on some sort of vacation.

"There are clothes in it. Some money." Dad's head didn't move so much as a centimeter.

"I don't want money. I want—"

"Frankly, Nathan, I don't care what you want. This is what you get. You made your choices. Now you have to deal with the consequences."

Nate stared at Dad. Didn't he think Nate knew that? That he'd spend the rest of his life living with the consequences of his actions?

He wanted to argue. To plead. But he'd learned early on that once Dad's mind was made up, nothing was going to change it.

A sharp silence sliced the air between them. It took Nate two tries before he could open his mouth to tell Dad what he'd needed to say for seven years. "Dad, I know it's not enough, but I want to say I'm sorry. I don't expect you to forgive me. But you have to know, if I could trade places with Kayla, I would. I—"

"But you can't. And all the sorries in the world aren't going to change that." Still that flat voice. Anger would be better. Or sadness. Anything but this stony, emotionless man.

"I know they're not." Nate said it so quietly he wasn't sure Dad heard him. He made himself speak up. "Can you at least tell me how Kayla is?" Seven years with no word on his sister's condition had been the worst part of his punishment.

Dad's jaw tightened. "You ruined her life, Nathan. And mine. Your mother's. You expect me to sit here and chat with you like we're old buddies?"

"No, but—"

"You know, Nathan, when I think about how excited we were when we learned your mother was expecting you— We thought you would be such a blessing." He let out a sharp, humorless laugh. "Some blessing. We'd have been better off if you'd never been born."

Nate turned toward the window and scrunched his eyes shut, pinching the bridge of his nose between his fingers.

He deserved every one of those hateful words. He'd told himself the same thing every day for the past seven years. But hearing them from his dad's mouth—the same man who had read him bedtime stories and played airplane with him and told him he loved him—sliced through every vital organ in his body.

Dad pulled up to the curb outside the bus station. Nate mashed his teeth together and grabbed the door handle. "Please, Dad. Just let me say goodbye to Mom and Kayla."

Dad stared straight out the windshield. "Show me you're not the worst mistake of my life, and maybe someday you can see them again. Until then, I'm not letting you near my family."

Nate wanted to say they were his family, too. That he would do anything for them. But his words would never convince his father. He'd have to make a success of this new job Dad had assigned him. No matter how much he hated it.

If it meant he could see his mother and sister again, it would be worth it.

# Chapter 2

Violet eyed the empty boxes she'd spread across the living room floor of her small apartment. She had to do it. She knew that. She'd been putting it off for three years, but it was time.

The Black Forest cuckoo clock on the wall behind her let out a squawk, as if chiding her to get moving, and she jumped.

"Okay, fine."

She picked up the thriller that had sat, unread, on the side table for the past three years. A bookmark stuck out of its pages about halfway through. A stab went through her as she plucked it out of the book. It was a leaf she had pressed for Cade the first year they'd been married. She'd wrapped it in packaging tape to preserve it. But the leaf was faded now, its edges thin and worn.

She put the book in the box she had marked for donations, but she tucked the bookmark into the Bible sitting on the other end of the table.

There. One item done.

Only six hundred and fifty-seven more pieces of Cade's life to sort through.

She moved systematically through the apartment, adding items to the donation box: Cade's jeans and shoes. His books. The collection of baseball cards he'd never been able to bring himself to part with, even though they weren't worth anything. She let herself keep a few of his sweatshirts,

5

the knit cap someone from church had made him, and the ticket stubs to the first movie they'd seen together.

But everything else she put into the boxes. With each item, she felt like she was shoving a needle deeper into her own heart. And yet it wasn't only pain she felt. Somewhere buried under that was a sharp relief. She wasn't sure which was worse, really—the pain or the relief. This was all she had left of her husband. And if she got rid of it, what would she be left with then? Aside from the giant Cade-shaped hole in her heart?

By the time she got to the bathroom, she'd filled six boxes, and she wasn't sure if she could make herself do more.

She glanced at her phone. She had ten minutes before she had to get downstairs and open the antique shop.

*Last room*, she told herself.

She sorted through Cade's stuff, which had been shoved to the back of the medicine cabinet. She tossed the deodorant and razors in the trash. But when she came to the fresh, slightly sea-smelling cologne he always wore, she pulled the cap off and spritzed it in front of her. She leaned forward into the mist, inhaling deeply. She could almost imagine Cade standing next to her, close enough to put his arms around her. But no arms circled her. No one brushed her curls off her face. No one dropped a kiss onto her forehead.

No one ever would again.

She stuffed the ache deep into a corner of her heart as she tucked the cologne back into the cupboard and closed the box she'd filled.

She moved it to the laundry room with the others. She needed some time to get used to the apartment without Cade's stuff before she took the final step of donating everything.

Eventually, she'd learn to live without it, like she'd learned to live without Cade.

*Have you?* a voice in her head taunted.

She pushed it aside and reached to turn off the light, but her gaze caught on her finger.

*It's time.* That same voice.

But this time it was harder to ignore.

Violet had tried to take the wedding ring off before. But her hand had always seemed too heavy without it.

Quickly, before she could change her mind, she slid the ring over her knuckle and dropped it into the palm of her hand. Her breath came in ragged heaves as if she'd just run a marathon.

In a way, maybe she had.

The past three years had been a marathon of grief and anger and regret.

She stared at the ring, lying still and lifeless in her palm, as she walked into the bedroom. Ignoring the trembling in her fingers, she plucked the ring out of her hand, opened her jewelry box, and deposited the ring inside.

Then she fled to the living room.

But without Cade's stuff everywhere, it felt smaller. Incomplete.

Just like her.

# Chapter 3

"This is it." Nate's seatmate nudged him as the bus crested a hill.

"Mmm." Nate turned toward the window to appease the woman, who had introduced herself as Linda or Lucy or something like that. In five hours, she hadn't gotten the hint that he had no interest in talking. She'd even gone so far as to show him pictures of her friend's wedding.

The rain that had started an hour or so ago had slowed, and the sun had pierced through the clouds low on the horizon. Shafts of light glared off the choppy waves at the bottom of the hill. That had to be Lake Michigan. The masts of dozens of boats stabbed toward the sky, where seagulls circled and swooped. Nate's gaze swept down the street, lined with colorful shops.

Great. Dad had relegated him to a tourist trap.

"Oh, look, a rainbow." The woman leaned across him and pointed.

Nate obligingly craned his neck and grunted.

The rainbow stretched above the lake, its far end disappearing into the tree line at the edge of the horseshoe-shaped bay.

Once upon a time, Nate might have convinced himself the rainbow was a sign from God that his new life would be better. But he'd stopped believing in such signs right about the time God had stood by and watched his whole life fall apart.

The bus slowed to a stop. The woman stood and stretched. "It was nice talking with you." She gave Nate a smile without a trace of sarcasm behind it.

Nate almost retorted that it'd been nice being talked at, but he bit his tongue. She was only trying to be friendly. He supposed he'd have to get used to that. Not many people had been kind to him in the past seven years. Which had been fine with him. He didn't deserve anyone's kindness.

Nate followed the woman off the bus.

The air was hot and humid, and the ground was wet. In spite of himself, Nate pulled in a deep breath. The fresh, clean scent of the town made something deep inside him twinge.

"Leah." A middle-aged woman rushed forward with her arms outstretched, and his seatmate—Leah, apparently—stepped into the hug as if it were the most natural thing in the world.

Nate looked away. When was the last time he'd been hugged?

He grabbed his suitcase and riffled through the front pocket until his hand fell on a card.

*Benson Property Management. 1201 Hope Street.*

Wherever that was.

"Bye. Hope you like Hope Springs." Leah and the woman passed him on the sidewalk.

"Thanks," Nate mumbled, stepping out of their way. It wasn't until they were a dozen steps past him that he managed to get his voice to work. "Could you tell me where Hope Street is?"

Leah turned with a smile. "Sure can. It's right there." She pointed across the parking lot to the street that ran parallel to the lakefront.

Nate nodded his thanks. It felt like the first thing that had gone right for him in seven years. Maybe it was the beginning of a streak.

He picked up his suitcase and kept his head down as he directed his footsteps toward the storefronts lining the street. He passed two gift stores, a fudge shop, an antique store, a restaurant, and the post office before he came to 1201. The sleek steel of the building's exterior stood in stark contrast to the old brick storefronts on either side.

The sign on the door indicated that the building held a law office, a dentist, an accountant, and a property management firm. Apparently *his* property management firm.

*Welcome to the first day of the rest of your life.* Nate's lips twisted into a sneer directed at himself.

This was a far cry from where he thought he'd be at twenty-eight. If things had gone right, he'd be cutting records and touring with his band now.

*But things didn't go right.*

No, they didn't. And he had only himself to blame for that.

Nate grabbed the sleek metal door handle and stepped inside. The building was cool and had the faintly antiseptic smell of a dentist's office. He wrinkled his nose. This was where he was going to be spending his days.

A door immediately to the right was marked with the name of the dentist's office. Farther down, on the left side of the hall, was the accountant's office. Which meant his office must be upstairs. Nate followed the long hallway to the back of the building, finally finding a staircase there.

At the top, it opened into another hall, identical to the one downstairs, except with an oversize vase of fake flowers on a small table next to one of the doors. Nate shuffled down the hall.

Of course the flowers would be outside the door to his office. Those would have to go.

He continued to the door of the law office on the other side of the hall.

Thankfully, the lights were still on inside, even though it had to be early evening, judging by the low angle of the sun out the window at the end of the hall.

Nate pushed the door open. No one was at the front desk, but the strains of Rachmaninoff's "Prelude in C Sharp Minor" drifted from somewhere in the back. Nate gave himself a second to listen to the haunting melody. How many times had he played it growing up? His fingers itched to move across a piano again.

He shoved them into the pocket of his jeans.

"Hello," he called tentatively.

No response.

He called again, louder.

A few seconds later a youngish man in khakis and a casual shirt jogged to the front. "Sorry. I didn't know anyone was here."

"No problem." Nate sized the guy up. He didn't exactly look like a lawyer. "I'm Nate Benson. I'm taking over the office next door. I was told you had the key."

"Yeah. Of course. I'm Brandon." The guy stuck out a hand, and Nate shook it.

"I think Cynthia left it up here somewhere." Brandon moved a few stacks of papers on the front desk. "No offense, but you have your work cut out for you. You seen that office yet?"

Nate shook his head, careful to keep his expression neutral. "No, why?"

"Oh, man." The guy let out an exaggerated groan. "Let's just say Bernie was not what you would call organized." He looked Nate in the eye. "At all."

Nate shrugged. How bad could it be?

But five minutes later, after Brandon had finally found the key and Nate had opened the door to his office, he knew.

It was *bad* bad.

The office was small. Or at least it looked small. It was hard to tell with the dozens of boxes scattered across the space, most of them with papers

11

spilling from their interiors onto the floor. A large desk stood against the back wall of the office. Aside from a small corner that held a computer monitor, the entire surface of the desk was strewn with a carpet of paper at least three inches thick. And that wasn't to mention the two-foot-high stack of papers on the leather office chair. Two large filing cabinets stood next to the desk. Nate wasn't sure if he should hope that they held a system for organizing this mess or that they were empty.

He shoved a hand through his hair. Dad hadn't sent him here to prove himself.

He'd sent him here to fail.

Nate wove his way gingerly across the paper-strewn floor to the desk. The mess would have to wait for another day. Right now, all he wanted was to find out which building had an empty apartment, get a key for it, lie down, and figure out how his life had gotten so off track.

When he reached the desk, he shoved the chair aside, rolling his eyes at himself as half of the precarious tower of papers crashed to the floor. Ignoring it, he powered on the computer. Hopefully Bernie had kept better electronic records than he did paper records.

It took some clicking around, but he finally found a database titled Occupancy. He clicked on it, holding his breath. If this didn't give him the information he needed, he'd end up having to spend the night here. Not an appealing prospect for his first night of so-called freedom.

Nate scrolled through the master file. There must be a few hundred properties here. Most of them with addresses in towns Nate had never heard of. He vaguely recognized a couple of the names as little blips of towns they'd passed through on the bus ride here. But he had no way to get to any of them. He needed something in Hope Springs.

There. A one-bedroom apartment.

And it looked like this one was just down the road, on Hope Street.

Most of the records looked outdated, but hopefully this apartment really was vacant as Bernie had noted here.

Now he just needed a key.

Nate pulled open the desk drawers but came up empty.

He scanned the room. If the keys to the vacant properties were in one of the boxes, he was sunk. It could be weeks before he found them.

His eyes fell on the filing cabinets again. They had to be in there, didn't they?

Two giant steps over the piles of papers landed him in front of the cabinets. But when he tugged the first drawer handle, it stuck. He tried another and then another.

Nope.

Both cabinets were locked.

And he hadn't seen a key for them in the desk. Who knew where it might be in this mess—if it was here at all? Bernie could have easily taken it with him when he left.

Nate laid his forearm across the top of the closest filing cabinet and rested his head on it. It would be nice if something happened easily for once.

He was pretty sure he'd seen some paper clips scattered across the desk. Not that he had any idea how to pick a lock. But it was worth a shot.

He waded back through the papers and rummaged around the desk until he came up with one. He examined it for a second, then unbent it. It looked nothing like a key.

But he made his way back to the filing cabinet and stuck the end of the paper clip into the keyhole. He wiggled it up and down, then side to side. Nothing.

After ten minutes, he had to face the facts: he was a terrible lock pick.

He glanced around the room. Now what?

There.

In the opposite corner, next to one of the boxes, half buried in papers. It looked like a toolbox.

Nate hurried across the room, almost slipping on a loose sheet of paper. He uncovered the toolbox and surveyed its contents.

A screwdriver, four nails, and a hammer.

Not much, but he could probably work with it.

He scooped up the screwdriver and hammer and recrossed the room.

After studying the first cabinet a minute, he stuck the screwdriver in the keyhole, drew the hammer back with his other hand, and smacked the handle of the screwdriver with a solid blow.

Three more blows and the lock released. Nate yanked open the drawers.

More papers.

But no keys.

He dropped his head but moved to the next filing cabinet. They had to be in here.

He lined up the screwdriver and was about to strike it with the hammer when the door to the office burst open.

"What are you doing?"

Nate spun toward the door. Brandon stood there, looking half startled, half amused.

"I need to get into this to find the keys." Nate turned back to the cabinet.

"Does that actually work?"

"Yep." Nate lined the hammer up again and hit the screwdriver square in the middle of the head.

He didn't stop until the lock released four blows later.

"Nice."

Nate glanced over his shoulder. Brandon was still there, looking mildly impressed.

Nate grunted. The dude might as well learn sooner rather than later that he wasn't here to make friends.

He yanked the drawers open. The top two were more papers.

But the middle drawer held several panels with hooks to hang keys. About a quarter of them were full. Nate squatted alongside the cabinet and scanned the address labels above each key.

But there wasn't one for any property on Hope Street.

His shoulders dropped.

That would have been too easy.

He wrenched open the next drawer, even though it was pretty clear fate or God or whoever was not smiling on him today.

The first key he saw was labeled 612 Hope Street.

"Thank you." He grabbed it and stood, not really sure who he was thanking.

"What is it?" Brandon looked like he was about to take a step into the room but then thought better of navigating the mess and stayed put.

"The key to my new apartment." Nate crunched through the papers to get to the door. He grabbed his suitcase and flipped off the light switch.

Brandon stepped backwards into the hallway, and Nate followed, locking the door behind himself, though it might do him a favor if someone broke in and took everything.

He'd probably be better off starting from scratch. Just like with his life.

# Chapter 4

Violet straightened and massaged a kink in her lower back.

She gave the Regency style dresser she'd been polishing a final once over. The finish had been dull and scratched when she'd bought it, with a watermark right in the middle of the top, but the stain was barely visible anymore.

She pulled off the old t-shirt of Cade's she'd worn to protect her clothes and moved to the workshop's sink to wash her hands. Although it was the middle of tourist season, it'd been a slow day. She'd only had a handful of customers. And most had browsed the store without buying anything. The others had made only small purchases—some postcards, an old washboard, and a vintage camera. She needed to make a big sale soon if she was going to pay the bills this month.

She stepped through the double doors leading to the sales floor. After such a slow day, she was thankful it was time to flip the sign to closed. But on her way to the front door, she got sidetracked by the stack of mail she'd never opened. A postcard with a picture of a sunrise over the ocean sat on top of the pile. She smiled as she picked it up and flipped it over to read Sophie's neat handwriting. *I think I may be the most blessed woman in the world.*

Violet sighed as she hung the card on the bulletin board behind her desk. Sophie was definitely blessed. She'd finally found her way back to the man she'd loved for years. And now they were married and off on their honeymoon.

Images of her own honeymoon sprang to mind. Cade's expression of wonder as they swam with dolphins, his insistence that they get ice cream every day, the way he'd looked at her like he'd treasure her forever. Out of habit, Violet rubbed at her wedding ring. But her thumb only met bare skin, and her heart jumped. Her ring was upstairs in her jewelry box, where she'd placed it this morning. Her eyes traveled to the bare white patch of skin in its place.

She forced herself to move on to the rest of the mail. A second notice from the electric company. A water bill. And two credit card bills.

She dropped the stack onto the desk. It was too hard. She was never going to catch up. Sales had been slow the last couple years, but she'd managed to survive on Cade's small life insurance policy. But that was gone now.

Maybe it was time to admit she couldn't keep the store going without Cade. But this place was filled with his presence. The shelves he'd made to display the porcelain dolls. The platforms he'd built in the windows to display items that wouldn't fade in the sunlight.

The music box.

She popped onto her toes to take it down from the shelf above her desk. Settling into her chair, she wound the key under the box, then cradled it in her hands as the couple on top spun in circles. This had been the first piece she and Cade had bought together. The piece that had sparked Cade's plan to open an antique shop. Violet had been unsure, but Cade had convinced her that with his business background and her art education, they could make it work.

And they had—for a while. Violet snapped the music box shut. She refused to let her memories go to their argument that day. How she had suggested it was time to close the shop. How they had fought. How she had refused to go with him to pick up a new piece. How he'd never made it home.

It didn't matter if she had once wanted to close the store. She owed it to Cade to keep it going now, whatever it took.

"What am I going to do now, Cade?" she asked the empty shop.

She knew his answer as clearly as if he were standing right there: "Pray and leave it in God's hands."

But she wasn't sure she had the strength to do that this time.

She dragged herself toward the door, feeling a decade older than she had when she woke up this morning. All she wanted now was a cup of tea, a bath, and her bed.

As she reached for the lock, her eyes fell on a man grabbing the door handle outside.

She jumped and pressed a hand to her heart.

Couldn't the guy read the hours posted on the door? The store had closed twenty minutes ago. That's what she got for letting herself get distracted instead of locking up on time.

But she pasted on a smile and tugged the door open. Her store wasn't known for its hospitality for nothing.

"Hi there. I'm sorry, but I'm closed for the day. I reopen at ten tomorrow morning, though." She winced at the artificial cheerfulness in her voice.

The man took half a step back with a scowl. "I'm not here to shop."

"Oh." Violet closed the door a fraction. She'd had enough salesmen drop by unexpectedly to know the signs. The twitchy movements. The look like he expected her to throw him out at any moment. "I'm sorry, I don't need any—"

"I'm here to move into my new apartment."

Violet studied the man. There was an empty apartment upstairs, right across from hers. But she didn't know anything about anyone new moving in.

"I'm sorry, I think you must be mistaken. This is an antique shop."

The man craned his neck toward the second story and pointed up. "Yes, and those are apartments up there, correct?"

She nodded. There was no point in denying that.

"And one of them is empty?"

Again she had to nod. "Yes, but the building's manager didn't say anything about a new tenant."

He stared at her, and she shifted, glancing past him down the nearly empty street. What would she do if he tried to force his way in?

She moved to close the door again, but the man pressed a hand against the glass. "That's because I'm the new manager."

⌒⌒⌒

For a few seconds, it looked like the woman was going to shut the door in his face. Or call the police. With the hand that wasn't holding the door open, Nate reached into his pocket. He handed her the business card Dad had given him.

She looked from the card to him and back again. "This doesn't prove anything."

Apparently she wasn't the trusting type.

He fished for the key he'd gone to so much trouble to procure. He held it out to her. "Does this?"

She tugged on one of the dark curls framing her face. "Do you have some ID?"

Nate stared at her. Was she serious?

But he let go of the door, relieved when she didn't immediately slam and lock it, and slid his wallet out of his pocket. He turned it so she could read his ID.

"See. Nate Benson. As in Benson Property Management." He brandished the business card again.

"Why didn't I get a notice that the building was under new management?"

Nate let out a *pfft*. "You will. I just got here today. I have a few, ah— papers to sort through."

*And the award for best understatement of the year goes to Nate Benson.*

"Well, what does this mean? Is this going to affect my lease? I haven't—"

Nate held up a hand. "I'm sure it won't. But like I said, I have a lot of paperwork to go through yet. Right now, all I know is that I'm looking for apartment three at six twelve Hope Street. Is that here?"

With one last long look, the woman nodded and let her lips relax into the tiniest smile. It made her look . . . sweet.

Nate shoved the thought back. He had no business thinking anyone looked sweet. Or pretty.

"For future reference, the apartment entrance is at the back of the building. But you can come through here this time." She stepped aside and opened the door all the way.

Nice of her to let him cross through his own building.

He tried to smile as he stepped inside, although he was pretty sure his face got stuck at grimace.

The store was bigger than it looked from the outside, with space for several large dining tables set with fancy china, half a dozen or so dressers, a large desk, and more. Smaller displays held porcelain dolls, old tools, and various knickknacks. Off to the right was a doorway that looked like it led to another, smaller room. Nate supposed the store was cute, if you liked that sort of thing.

Which he most decidedly did not. He didn't understand why people didn't throw all this junk away. All these reminders of pasts they couldn't outrun.

The woman locked the front door, then led him through a set of double doors to a large workshop area filled with what appeared to be projects in various stages of completion. The sharp tang of mineral spirits hung in the air, coating Nate's tongue. He followed the woman around several large pieces to a wooden door that led to a hallway. A narrow staircase ran along the far wall.

She waved toward the steel door at the bottom of the staircase. "The residential entrance." She pointed to the strip of mailboxes. "You'll have to put a new label on this one."

He shrugged. He wasn't exactly expecting a heap of fan mail.

The woman's curls bounced as she started up the steps. He watched his feet as he followed. Halfway up, the smell of mineral spirits faded, replaced by what could only be apple pie. Nate's mouth watered. Someone in the building must bake.

The floor widened out into a large landing at the top of the staircase. There were two apartments to the right, one to the left.

"That's apartment three." The woman pointed to the apartment on the left. A mat that had probably once said welcome lay in front of the door, its letters long since faded into a black smudge.

The woman moved to apartment two, across from his, and stuck her key in the lock. She gave him one last look over her shoulder, then disappeared inside.

Well.

At least he wouldn't have to worry about putting on a friendly act with the new neighbor.

Nate faced his own door. But before he could unlock it, the sound of a door opening behind him made him turn again. Now what did she want? But the apartment door across from his was still closed. A tiny white-haired woman stood on the doorstep of the apartment at the front of the building.

"I thought I heard voices out here." She walked slowly toward him, her back stooped, and her right leg dragging slightly.

Nate wasn't really in the mood to meet anyone else. But watching her walk was painful. He stepped toward her, so she wouldn't have to come as far.

When he stopped in front of her, she held out a hand twisted by arthritis. Her sharp knuckles dug into his fingers as she squeezed his hand. "I'm Mrs. D'Angelo. Do you like pie?"

Nate blinked at her. What kind of question was that? Who didn't like pie?

"Thanks, but I should get my stuff unpacked." He gestured lamely toward the single suitcase parked outside his apartment door. "Maybe next time."

He fought not to squirm under the stare she leveled at him. "I'll hold you to that. It's been too long since we've had a young man around here." She started to shuffle toward her apartment. "I look forward to getting to know you."

Nate grunted in answer. She'd be looking for a long time. He wasn't here to get to know people. He was here to do his work, prove his worth to his father, and—well, that was about it, really. There was nothing else for him anymore.

Mrs. D'Angelo was still in the hall when Nate unlocked his own door and stepped inside, pulling his suitcase behind him.

Once he'd closed the door, it took a moment for his ears to adjust to the silence. It was almost unnerving.

He hadn't known a moment of quiet in the past seven years.

He took in the space. The door led right into a small living room with a worn plaid couch and small TV. To the left, the kitchen was complete with citron appliances and a chipped table. He left his bag at the door as he moved slowly through the apartment, observing the 1980s style bathroom, the small but functional laundry room, and a decent size master bedroom.

The apartment was nice enough, and he supposed he should be grateful Dad had arranged a job for him. But Nate didn't want any of this.

How many times had he told Dad he could make his own life, that he'd find success on his own terms? He swallowed the acid that burned his throat at the knowledge that Dad had been right all along. When it came down to it, Nate was nothing but a giant screw up.

But he was a screw up with a second chance. Even if he didn't deserve it, he had to make the most of it, if only to prove Dad wrong.

Nate strode to the door and retrieved his suitcase as if he had a purpose. He dragged it to the bedroom and lifted it onto the bed.

Should be interesting to see what Dad had thought he'd need to survive in his new life.

He opened the suitcase to find a toothbrush, toothpaste, and deodorant on top of a stack of three dress shirts, two suits, and four ties.

He picked up one of the suit coats, remembering the day Dad had taken him to pick it out for his internship in Dad's office. He'd hated how the coat made him feel—all stuffy and claustrophobic. But Dad said it would grow on him.

It never did.

Nor did the internship, which he'd quit after only a month to focus more intensely on his music.

And now here he was again: wearing a suit and working for Dad.

Nate tried to pull the coat on over his t-shirt. But he'd been a scrawny kid the last time he'd worn it. His shoulders and chest had broadened now, thanks to daily weightlifting. The coat strained at the shoulders, and he could barely lift his arms.

He moved to put the empty suitcase away, but the sound of something sliding inside stopped him. He was sure the main part had been empty.

He tipped the suitcase to the side.

The zip of something sliding against the fabric liner was quiet but unmistakable. He unzipped the small side compartment and slid his hand in, feeling around until his fingers brushed against something hard and smooth.

He pulled it out, and his breath caught.

It was one of the shells he and Kayla had collected on their trip to Florida as kids.

Had the shell been stuck in the suitcase all this time? Or had Kayla put it there as a message to him?

He opened the drawer of the small nightstand next to the bed, sliding the shell into it.

Just because he couldn't forget didn't mean he wanted to remember.

# Chapter 5

Violet traced Cade's name on the smooth gray stone, then ran her finger over his favorite Bible verse, inscribed below: "Those who hope in the Lord will renew their strength. They will soar on wings like eagles; they will run and not grow weary, they will walk and not be faint."

She sighed, settling onto the grass in front of the stone. Cade was in heaven, where he would never grow weary or faint again. But she was stuck here. About as weary and faint as a person could get.

All week she'd resisted coming to the cemetery. But one more Sunday of worshiping without Cade had done her in. Christ had always been the center of their relationship, from the time they'd attended Sunday school together as kids.

But now every time she went to church, it felt like one person was missing from the relationship. Not that she needed Cade to have faith. That came from the Holy Spirit alone. She knew that. But Cade had encouraged her and helped her grow in her faith. She missed the deep spiritual conversations they'd had, the feeling that not only their hearts but their souls were connected.

She ran her hand over the daisies she'd planted at the beginning of summer. They'd been scraggly then, but now that it was August, they'd filled in to create a cheerful blanket in front of the gravestone. She leaned forward to smell them, the guilt she'd been trying to push down all week working its way to the front of her thoughts. Guilt over packing Cade's stuff away. Guilt over her inability to keep the store going. Guilt over the way her heart rate had sped up on the few occasions she'd run into her new neighbor over the last couple days. It was only because it still surprised her to see a man living in the building again after three years of only her and Mrs. D'Angelo. She knew that perfectly well. It's not like she and Nate had said more than a muttered "hello." But it still felt like a betrayal of Cade.

She pushed to her feet and peered down to the lake. The day was hot and still, and only the tiniest ripples marred the surface. It reminded her of the day she and Cade had gone snorkeling just off the beach. The water had been flat and smooth, and Cade had been sure they'd find fish and seashells and maybe even some treasure. But the water was so murky that they'd barely been able to see their own hands in front of them. Even so, Cade hadn't been discouraged. He'd said the most disappointing adventure with her was better than any day without her.

Violet wrapped her arms around her middle as a chill wracked her body in spite of the heat. Had she ever told him she felt the same way? Because she knew for a certainty now that the worst day with him had been better than every single day without him.

She kissed her fingertips, then pressed them to the top of the gravestone. She didn't let herself look back as she crossed the cemetery to her car, parked in the church parking lot.

"Violet!"

She lifted her head and turned toward the yard to her left.

"Hey, Dan." She tried to perk up her voice so he wouldn't worry. Leah's younger brother had moved back to Hope Springs only six months or so ago to join his dad as pastor of the church. But he'd quickly become a friend to all of Leah's friends. He'd offered a shoulder for Violet on more than one occasion.

"How are you today?" Dan's creased forehead told her he knew where she'd come from.

"I'm doing okay." It didn't pay to tell him she was good. He would see right through it.

"I haven't talked to you much since Sophie and Spencer's wedding. You doing okay with that?"

She gazed toward the church next door. She couldn't describe the mix of emotions that had swirled through her as Sophie walked down the aisle. Joy for her friend, of course. Wistfulness for her own wedding day. Anger at how short her time as a wife had been. And—she hated to admit it—a shard of jealousy that had worked its way into her heart. Sophie had never wanted to get married and have a family. Whereas Violet—she and Cade had been planning to start their own family since they were fifteen. So how was it fair that Sophie was now living the life Violet had dreamed of? While Violet was stuck in a life that had gone all wrong.

"It was hard, but I'm okay," she finally answered Dan.

He laid a hand on her arm. "It's okay if you're not, you know. We all understand."

Violet nodded and pressed her lips together. Her friends had all been so careful to let her know it was okay if she couldn't be one hundred percent happy at the wedding. But the thing was, none of them could understand. Not really. They were all marrying and moving forward with their lives. Her life on the other hand—the brakes had been put on that the day she buried Cade.

"I got a postcard from them the other day." She didn't have to feign the joy that had brought her. "Looks like they're having a great time."

"I bet. When do they get back?" Dan pulled out his phone to check his calendar.

"Two more weeks. Her parents insisted on getting them this trip, and since the cherry harvest went well this year, Sophie managed to convince Spencer to agree to it." Violet pressed down the flutter of nerves over Sophie's return. Her oldest friend had only come back to Hope Springs—and back into her life—a year ago. Now that she was married, what if she cut Violet out altogether again?

*You're being ridiculous.* Sophie had been nothing but the perfect best friend in the past year, even as she was busy planning a wedding and helping Spencer open a new farm store on the orchard they owned.

"Let's plan to grill out when they get home. I'll make burgers." Dan's eyes widened as he checked his phone again. "Oh, I'm supposed to be leading Bible study. Like ten minutes ago."

Violet couldn't help the laugh. Dan was quickly becoming notorious around the church for losing track of time. But his love for his flock was so apparent that no one held it against him.

As Dan jogged toward the church, Violet strolled to her car. The guilt and sadness that had pressed so hard at Cade's graveside had eased a little, and for that she was grateful.

By the time she got home, an energy she hadn't felt in a long time pulsed through her. The shop wasn't open today, since it was Sunday, but that didn't mean she didn't have plenty of work to do. Her workshop was way too full of half-finished projects. Projects that couldn't make her money until they were out on the sales floor.

She jumped out of the car and ducked into the workshop, pulling one of Cade's old t-shirts on over her sleeveless top. Its familiar comfort wrapped around her as she set to work. She wasn't sure how long this energy would last. But she was going to make the most of it while it did.

Nate slapped another lease agreement on top of the pile he'd already gone through and pushed back from his kitchen table. It hadn't even been a week, and already he wasn't sure how he was going to survive another day—let alone a lifetime—of working for his father.

He'd spent all week sorting through the mess at the office, and he'd barely gotten through a quarter of the files. But that wasn't the worst of it. The worst was the fact that Dad called every day—always at a different time, which Nate knew was to check up on him.

That was why Nate had spent his entire Saturday in the office yesterday, waiting for Dad's call. It had finally come at six o'clock. Nate's only satisfaction was the surprise in Dad's voice when he had answered on the first ring. Dad had surely been expecting the phone to go to voice mail so he could leave a blistering message about Nate not living up to his responsibilities.

But Nate had made it clear to Dad that he wouldn't be in the office today. So what if he'd implied it was because Sunday was for church? In the eighteen years he'd lived under his parents' roof, he'd never been allowed to miss one weekend of church, so it was no shock that Dad thought he still attended. As if he wanted anything to do with a God who had failed him.

Instead of worshiping, Nate had spent the day holed up inside his apartment with the files he'd brought home.

It wasn't like he had anything better to do anyway.

But his eyes kept drifting to the window, where sunlight streamed in, casting a sharp line across the living room floor. Maybe he should get some fresh air.

Nate stood and stretched. Ten minutes and then he'd get back to work. When he'd told Dad about the mess in the office, Dad had been less than sympathetic. He'd expected Nate to get it cleaned up and get him a status on all their properties on the peninsula in two weeks.

It was an impossible task. Nate knew that. So did Dad. That's why he'd assigned it, Nate was sure.

But if the only way to see Mom and Kayla again was to kill himself working for Dad, then that's what he'd do.

He stepped out of the apartment and gave his neighbors' doors a quick glance. He'd talked to Mrs. D'Angelo a few more times during the week. She kept pressing him to come in for a piece of pie, but he kept declining. His other neighbor, though—he'd only run into her a couple times. And they'd never said more than "hi" to each other.

Which was perfectly fine with him. He wasn't here to make friends. He was here for a new start. And the only way to ensure that was to keep his life to himself.

Nate jogged down the stairs to the first floor. He paused as a high-pitched whining sound caught his ears. It took a second to place it, but he was pretty sure it was a sander. The sound was coming from behind the back door to the antique shop.

A momentary wave of curiosity swept over him. But he nudged it aside. Keeping his life to himself meant minding his own business.

He pushed the outside door open and stepped into the small parking lot. Beyond it, a grassy hill dropped gradually to the rocky beach below. The weight that had been pressing on his shoulders all week eased a little as the scent of the lake drifted up to him. He let himself take a moment to look around. He had to admit this was a pretty town. It might even be a nice place to live, if he'd been given the opportunity to choose it for himself.

Nate wandered toward the water, glad he'd thought to pick up some shorts when he'd gone shopping for new clothes the other day. The heat clung to him, dampening the skin at the base of his neck.

At the bottom of the hill, the grass gave way to small pebbles and crushed shells, leaving the beach a brilliant white. A couple hundred yards to the south, the beach looked darker, sandier. Towels dotted the ground, and a handful of people swam in the water. To the north, the pebbly beach continued a quarter mile or so, until it was taken over by large boulders, some jutting into the water.

Nate turned north.

The crunch of shells under his feet was satisfying after the stifling silence of his apartment, and he let himself walk farther than he intended. When he reached the boulders, he climbed up on one, then stepped across to another and another, until he was perched on top of one that stood several feet into the lake.

He let himself just breathe. When was the last time he'd been free to do that?

A new feeling settled over him. Not peace, exactly—he was pretty sure he'd never feel that again—but something a little softer than the despair that had hung over him for seven years.

He shouldn't allow himself even this brief reprieve. Not while Kayla had to deal with the consequences of his mistake every day. But if he didn't take just a moment, he would never survive this assignment to see her again.

It wasn't until the sun had shifted to shine directly in his eyes that he realized how low it had sunk in the sky.

He stood reluctantly. Sitting out here all evening wasn't going to win him any points with Dad.

By the time he got back to his building, the sun had dropped to the horizon. Lines of purple and red burst from it, painting the sky and the

31

water in hues Nate wasn't sure were real. He allowed himself one more look, allowed himself a second to feel the awe the sunset had once inspired in him. The awe that had led him to write an entire song about the one who made it.

But that awe was misplaced.

He knew that now.

Because a God who could paint a sunset like that but couldn't protect his sister—that wasn't a God he wanted anything to do with.

He locked the awe away and opened the door.

He was at the foot of the staircase when a loud crash reverberated through the building, followed by a muted cry.

He stopped with his foot on the first step, his heart thrusting against his chest wall, and stared at the door that led to the antique store's workshop. It was probably nothing. He should ignore it.

Even if his neighbor needed help, he wasn't the one to provide it. Hadn't he proved that when he couldn't do anything to help Kayla? He couldn't handle the thought of feeling that helplessness again.

But what if his neighbor was hurt and no one else came?

He jumped off the step and yanked the back door to the antique store open. As he scanned the space, he didn't see anyone. "Hello? Are you okay in here? I thought I heard—"

"Over here." The woman's voice was faint and shaky. "I think I need help."

# Chapter 6

Fire surged from Violet's wrist to her shoulder as she lay sprawled on the floor, her arm trapped under the armoire that had crashed on top of her. She wasn't sure how much longer she could fight down the scream.

Footsteps pounded across the floor. "What happened?" The voice sounded familiar.

A second later, a face warbled into view above her. It was her new neighbor. Nate.

She had no idea where he had come from, but this was the first time she could say she was genuinely happy to see him.

He squatted at her side. "I'm going to lift this. Do you think you can move your arm out when I do?"

Violet nodded. Or at least she thought she did.

"Ready?" Nate planted his hands close to the spot where her arm disappeared under the armoire. A second later, the pressure eased. She slid her body away from the armoire, biting her lip to keep from yelling. A small whimper managed to escape.

There was a thud as Nate set the armoire heavily on its back, then crouched at her side. "That looks pretty bad. I think it's probably broken."

She turned her head to examine her arm. Her wrist was bent up and then down at an odd angle, and a huge lump had formed below her elbow.

The room whirled around her, and she slammed her eyes closed again.

"Take a deep breath." Nate was moving next to her, but she didn't open her eyes.

She focused on inhaling and exhaling in a slow rhythm.

"Do you think you can stand?"

"I—" She licked her lips. "I think so."

But the moment she sat up, the room spun, and fireworks exploded behind her lids and through her skull.

The whole world tilted to the side, and she felt strong hands lowering her to the floor.

"Did you hit your head?"

"I'm not—" She swallowed against the nausea. "I might have."

"Okay. It's okay. I'll, uh—" Nate slid his arm under her shoulder blades and lifted. "I'll carry you. Is there someone who can drive you to the hospital?"

Violet tried to think. She was sure there was, but she couldn't for the life of her come up with anyone's name right now aside from Cade's. She wanted him to be here. To take care of her.

"Okay. Don't worry. It's fine. I'll take you." Nate sounded on the edge of panic, and she felt like she should reassure him. But her voice seemed to have disappeared.

"How am I going to take her?" Nate muttered, and Violet wondered vaguely who he was talking to. "I don't have a car."

"My keys." Why did it take so much effort to say two words? "Upstairs. My door's unlocked."

Nate maneuvered them through the door and into the hallway, then lowered her to the steps. She leaned against the wall. Its coolness felt good.

"Will you be okay here for a second?"

She nodded. The dizziness was starting to wane. She opened her eyes in time to see his legs disappear up the staircase.

A few seconds later he thundered down the steps.

He squatted next to her, passing her a bag of frozen corn. "I couldn't find an ice pack."

He reached a hand behind her again, but she waved him off. "I think I can walk now."

He stood, taking half a step back but not moving too far away, as if afraid she might keel over any second.

The poor guy's face was whiter than the paint on the wall.

He hovered next to her as she walked toward the door, then reached in front of her to push it open. She caught a scent of lemon and mint as she passed in front of him. For some reason, it calmed her.

Ten seconds later, he was unlocking the passenger door of her car and holding it open for her.

She sucked in a sharp breath as she lowered herself into the seat. Every tiny movement of her arm felt like someone was taking a hammer directly to her bones.

"Okay." Nate was muttering to himself again. "Good. Okay. We're good."

If she weren't in so much pain, his pep talk to himself might be amusing.

He jogged around the car and dropped into the driver's seat, glancing at her as he lifted the key to the ignition. His hands were shaking so much it took him two tries to start the car.

"You okay?" His brow creased into worry lines as he looked at her.

"Yeah." She felt stronger now, and her voice came out sure. "I could use a little help with the seatbelt, though."

"Oh." He looked over her shoulder to where the seatbelt hung untouched next to the door.

She used her right arm to press her left arm tighter to her body, trying to keep it as still as possible. "I don't think I can grab—"

He leaned across her and tugged on the seatbelt.

There was that lemony-mint scent again. She tried not to notice when his hand accidentally brushed her shoulder as he pulled the seatbelt across her lap. Once it clicked into place, he sat back in his seat, hands clamped on the steering wheel.

She was overcome by a ridiculous need to comfort him. "Relax. I'm fine. It's just a broken arm."

Jaw hard, he nodded, then reached a stiff arm to shift the car into reverse. "I'll need directions to the hospital."

If Nate gripped the steering wheel any tighter, he'd probably rip it off the console. But he couldn't make himself relax.

Not when he hadn't driven in more than seven years. When he wasn't supposed to be driving at all. He wouldn't get his license back for another year.

That was, if he didn't break the law by driving with it revoked.

But this was an emergency. What was he supposed to do? Make her drive herself to the hospital when she couldn't even fasten her own seatbelt? When she could have a concussion?

He allowed himself a split second to glance at her. She clutched her arm to her torso, and her face was drawn in pain. But she didn't look like she was about to pass out anymore. So that was something.

Her eyes slid to his, and he snapped his attention back to the road.

"What happened anyway?" The question was out before he could re-mind himself that he was driving her to the hospital, not striking up a friendship.

"I was trying to move the armoire—"

"By yourself?" The thing had to weigh at least three times as much as her and was a good two feet taller. What had she been thinking?

"Well, I had to get it out on the sales floor. My friend Spencer usually helps with that kind of thing. But he's on his honeymoon, so—"

"You could have asked me." He didn't know where the offer came from. He most definitely didn't want her asking him for help with anything. But it was better than finding her crushed by some giant piece of furniture.

She gave him a sideways glance.

Okay, fine, he hadn't exactly given off the neighborly vibe. But then again, neither had she.

"Take a left here." She groaned, and when he looked over, her forehead was wrinkled in pain.

That familiar feeling of helplessness rolled over him. "You okay?"

"Yeah." Her features smoothed slightly. "Just tried to point." She gave a half laugh and Nate's jaw relaxed.

Five minutes later, he pulled into the hospital parking lot. His grip on the wheel didn't loosen until he'd shut down the engine. They'd made it. He checked the rearview mirror just to be sure, then let out a long breath.

"You don't have to come in if you don't want to." But the look in her eyes said the opposite. She didn't want to go in there alone.

"Come on." He unclicked her seatbelt, then got out and jogged to open her door. He held out a hand to steady her as she stood, careful not to bump her arm. The wrist and elbow had turned a mottled black and green.

He let his hand hover behind her back as he shepherded her toward the emergency room door, careful not to actually make contact.

There were only a few other people in the waiting room, and Nate dropped into a seat as she went to the desk to register. He didn't want to intrude on her privacy.

But a second later she settled into the chair next to him, passing him a clipboard. "Could you help me with this?"

He eyed the form. "You hurt your left arm."

She shifted so that she was closer to him and peered at the form over his shoulder. "I'm a lefty."

"Oh." He unclipped the pen and picked it up. "Me, too."

He turned his focus to the form, arm poised to write. "Okay. Name?"

She didn't say anything for a second, and he glanced at her to make sure she was okay.

"You know my name."

He shook his head. He really didn't. "Nope."

Her mouth fell open. "That's kind of rude. I told you that first day. When you came barging in the door of my antique store."

"First of all—" Nate tapped the pen on the clipboard. "I did not *barge* into your store. And second of all, you never told me your name."

She opened her mouth, then clamped it shut as realization dawned in her eyes. "Oh. I guess I didn't." She dropped her gaze. "It's Violet. Violet Somers."

"Violet. That's a pretty—" He cut himself off. What was he doing? "That's a good name." He cleared his throat. "Uh, address?"

"Well, that you know."

*Duh.* He wrote it down, ignoring the flustered swirling in his gut.

After they'd worked through the rest of the form, he brought it to the counter for her.

The few minutes of separation were good. They gave him a chance to push aside the thoughts he'd been having sitting next to her. Thoughts about how pretty her dark eyes were. And how she smelled like a spring day.

Those weren't thoughts he had any business thinking.

When he returned to the seating area, he contemplated taking a seat across from Violet instead of next to her, but fortunately the nurse came out and called Violet's name.

She gave him that half smile again as she passed him to follow the nurse. "I'll be back soon."

Nate nodded. "I'll be here."

# Chapter 7

Violet turned off the TV. She was trying to follow the doctor's orders to take it easy, but if she had to watch one more game show, she might go crazy. Fortunately, the store was always closed on Mondays, so she wasn't losing any money right now. But Mondays were usually her days to catch up on paperwork and projects. Which was going to be a lot harder now.

Thankfully, the doctor had been able to set her arm relatively quickly last night. And he was pretty sure she wouldn't need surgery.

For the hundredth time, Violet wondered what would have happened if Nate hadn't heard the crash last night. Would she still be lying on the floor of her workshop right now?

She offered a silent prayer of thanksgiving to God for sending her help right at the moment she needed it.

Even after she'd been so unfriendly and unneighborly with Nate all week. It wasn't like her. She'd been voted friendliest senior in her high school class, for goodness' sake. But that was a long time ago. Back when life was easy and everything was going according to her plans.

*So you can only be kind when your life is going well?*

Violet shook her head at herself. Hadn't Dan's sermon yesterday been about loving your neighbor? Not that he'd been referring to literal neighbors.

But still . . .

Violet got up. "Fine, Lord, you win. I'll be a good neighbor."

She moved to the kitchen and surveyed her pantry. Cookies seemed like the right way to welcome a new neighbor. But how was she supposed to make them one-handed?

She lifted her left arm the little she could to study the cast. It wrapped from between her thumb and forefinger all the way to the middle of her upper arm.

Well, if she couldn't make him cookies, she could do the next best thing: buy them. Actually, he'd probably appreciate that more anyway. Peyton's chocolate chip cookies were a taste of heaven.

She slipped her sandals on and made the short walk to the bakery at the other end of Hope Street. If possible, it was more humid out here than it had been yesterday. A few people strolled listlessly from shop to shop, but not many people were out today. Mondays were always slow in the tourist town.

By the time she reached the bakery, sweat trickled from her hairline down her forehead. She stepped gratefully into the air-conditioned shop, savoring the mixture of bread dough and fresh-baked cookies that hung in the air.

"Be with you in a second." Peyton's voice carried from the back.

"It's just me. Take your time." Violet moved through the small bistro-style seating area to the display case, her mouth watering at all the treats spread out inside.

"Hey, Violet. What brings— Oh, my goodness, what happened to you?" Peyton rushed out from behind the counter. She wrapped Violet into a one-armed hug on her good side.

"Lost a fight with an armoire last night. It's broken in three spots. My arm, I mean. Not the armoire." At least she prayed the armoire wasn't broken. She hadn't had the courage to check yet. It was one of the most expensive pieces she'd ever purchased. And if she'd busted it . . .

41

"Jared was on call last night. But he didn't say anything about—"

"It's just a broken arm. I didn't call an ambulance."

"You drove with a broken arm?" Peyton looked ready to scold her, but Violet jumped in.

"My new neighbor drove me. He heard the crash and came to see what happened." A fresh wave of gratitude washed over her.

"Oh, thank goodness." Peyton pressed a hand to her heart. "How long do you have to wear the cast?"

Violet wrinkled her nose. That was the worst part. "Six weeks."

Peyton slipped behind the displays and grabbed one of the red and white striped bags she packed cookies in. "So, this new neighbor. When did he move in?"

Violet shrugged. "Last Tuesday, I think. Maybe it was Wednesday. Anyway, I thought maybe I should get him some cookies. As a thank you."

"Ah." Peyton busied herself selecting cookies and dropping them into the bag. "How old is he?" She kept her voice casual, but Violet heard the suggestion in it. Peyton was thinking what all their friends would think. Maybe this guy would help her finally move on from Cade. They didn't understand that she didn't want to move on. The only man she wanted was Cade. And since she couldn't have him, she was content being alone. Or at least as content as she could be.

"Around our age, I'd guess." Though she'd never been good at figuring out that sort of thing.

Peyton raised her eyebrows but didn't say anything more. She rolled the top of the bag down and grabbed a sticker to close it. "So is he good looking?" Peyton kept her head down, concentrating harder than necessary on ringing up the sale.

But still, Violet's face warmed. "I don't know. I guess he's okay." Unbidden, Nate's blue eyes popped into her head. They were nearly the same shade as Cade's. And yet where Cade's had been open and inviting, like the lake on a summer day, Nate's were steely and guarded, all churned up like the water during a storm.

"He keeps to himself mostly," she added, as if that had anything to do with his appearance.

"Well, I'm glad he was there when you needed help. And who knows . . ." Peyton passed her the bag of cookies.

Violet started to tell Peyton it wasn't like that. But acknowledging she understood Peyton's insinuation would only add fuel to the fire. So she simply thanked her friend and stepped out into the sticky air.

As she walked home, she worked to direct her thoughts anywhere but to her conversation with Peyton. But she couldn't help rolling Peyton's question about Nate's appearance over in her mind.

Fine, she could admit it. Nate was attractive, with his slightly shaggy brown hair, square jaw, and strong build. But just because he was good looking didn't mean she was interested in a relationship with him. There were plenty of attractive men around Hope Springs, and she'd never felt any desire to date a single one of them.

*But your stomach doesn't turn upside down when you see any of them.*

Violet silenced the voice in her head. That was neither here nor there.

By the time she got home, she had almost changed her mind about giving Nate the cookies. She didn't want to risk giving him the impression that she was interested in him as anything more than a neighbor.

But then she pictured the concern on his face when he'd found her on the floor, the way he'd carried her, the relief he'd shown when she'd walked out of the ER with only a broken arm and no concussion. The least she could do was give him a few cookies and a heartfelt thank you.

Nate's heart lightened as he reached the back door to the apartment building. He had to admit, he wouldn't mind running into Violet. Just to check how her arm was doing. But the lights in the antique store were off, and her apartment door was closed. He considered knocking, but what would he say?

Throwing her door one last glance, he stepped into his own apartment and immediately fell onto the couch. The springs stabbed into his back as he rubbed his eyes. He hadn't made much more progress on the mess in the office today. At this rate, it'd be next year before he got through everything. Of course, it didn't help that his thoughts had kept drifting to Violet all day.

Where they did not belong.

But he couldn't stop himself from picturing the deep brown of her eyes, a shade darker than black coffee. Or the gratitude in them when he'd brought her home from the hospital last night. He couldn't remember the last time anyone had looked at him with anything approaching gratitude.

He sat abruptly. He had to stop this. He had no business thinking about her—or anyone for that matter—that way. Anyway, the case manager for his extended supervision would be here in twenty minutes. He should probably clean up.

Not that there was much to clean. His eyes swept over his sparse furnishings. The dishes from the microwave dinner he'd had last night and his cold cereal this morning sat on the counter next to the sink.

He dragged himself toward the kitchen. His life felt so small right now. So insignificant compared to the big plans he'd had for his future.

Halfway to the sink, he paused. He thought he'd heard a knock on the door, but it was so quiet he could almost convince himself he'd imagined it.

But as he turned on the water, it sounded again, louder.

His eyes flicked to the clock on the microwave. His supervisor was early.

Well, she'd have to deal with the mess in his sink then.

He smoothed the bottom of his rumpled dress shirt and strode to the door. Might as well get this over with.

The moment he opened the door, he beheld the most beautiful sight he'd ever seen.

A plate of chocolate chip cookies.

He lifted his eyes to Violet's face.

A shy smile played with her lips. "Um. Hi." Her voice had a musical quality to it.

"Hi." Nate's eyes went to her unwieldy cast. "How's the arm?"

She held it at a slight angle away from her body, and Nate wondered how uncomfortable the big cast was. Especially in this heat.

"Oh. It's okay." She dropped her head to stare at the plate, and a long curl fell onto her cheek. His gaze got caught on the shaft of light that spilled from the front window onto the side of her face.

"I just wanted to— Here." She thrust the plate of cookies at him.

He resisted the urge to snatch them from her and eat the entire plate in one bite. "Why?"

Her eyebrows pulled down into a sharp V. "What do you mean why?"

"Why are you giving me cookies?"

The sound that escaped her was a combination of exasperation and something else—amusement maybe. "To thank you for getting me to the hospital last night. And to welcome you to the building. To Hope Springs."

Nate could only look at her. He hadn't done anything to deserve cookies. Even if they did smell divine.

Her cheeks flushed a light shade of pink. "You don't have to take them if you don't want. It's kind of cliché, isn't it? How much more small-town America can you get, right?" She pulled the plate back, and it was all he could do not to lunge for it.

"No." His voice was louder than he intended, and he forced himself to lower the volume. "I mean, thank you. They look delicious." He took the plate. Then he lifted it to his face and inhaled. He didn't care that she was giving him a strange look.

"Sorry." He lowered the plate. "I haven't had anything homemade in a long time."

A soft smile lifted her lips. "Okay, well, enjoy." She took a step back.

Nate moved to close the door, but something stopped him. "Wait. Want to have one with me?"

She hesitated so long he was sure she was going to say no, but she finally gave a slow nod.

He stepped aside and held the door for her to enter the apartment.

They settled at the kitchen table, and he grabbed a jug of milk and two glasses.

As soon as he sat down, he sank his teeth into a cookie. The dough was soft and sweet, the chocolate melting on his tongue. He closed his eyes and savored it. It was the best thing he'd ever tasted.

His eyes snapped open. "Wait. How did you make cookies with a broken arm?"

Violet choked a little on her cookie. "Busted." She took a long drink of milk. "I didn't exactly make them. I mean, I was going to. But then I couldn't figure out how to do it one-handed." When she smiled, her eyes crinkled just the tiniest bit at the corners. "My friend Peyton owns a bakery.

She made them." She gave a sheepish grin. "But I did walk there to pick them up."

Nate laughed to cover up how much her admission touched him. She had a broken arm and was supposed to be resting, but she'd taken the time to go out and buy him cookies?

He wasn't worth that kind of effort. And yet it warmed him to know someone had thought of him.

"Well, tell your friend Peyton these are the best cookies I've ever eaten. Seriously." He shoved the rest of the cookie in his mouth and reached for another.

"I will." She popped the last dainty bite of her cookie into her mouth and slid her chair back.

But he didn't want her to go yet.

"You'll have to tell me where else to go in town. Seems I've been missing out."

Her face lit up. "Did you see the fudge shop right next door? My friend Ariana owns it, and she gets orders from people all over the world."

"Do you know everyone in Hope Springs?"

"It's a small town. If you need groceries, Trig's is the best. It's—" She turned as if orienting herself. "About four blocks that way." She pointed to the west. "And then three blocks that way." She pointed south as she rotated her whole body.

Nate couldn't hide his amusement over her method of giving directions. Her cheeks flushed even deeper, but she laughed. "Sorry, my husband always said I give the worst directions. But it's the way that makes sense to me."

Ah, so there was a husband. Nate wondered where he'd been. His eyes went to her hand. No ring. And Mrs. D'Angelo had said there hadn't been a man in the building for a while. Maybe Violet was divorced.

Not that it mattered. He had no business wondering about her marital status.

"Let's see. What else should you know?" She tapped an unpainted nail against her lips, then lowered it and pointed at him. "The Hidden Cafe has the best burgers in town. Oh, and if you're looking for a church—"

"I'm not." The smile inspired by her enthusiasm fell right off his face. Time to shut this conversation down.

She stopped talking, eyes widening. "Not what?"

"Not looking for a church." He checked the time on the microwave. His supervisor would be here any minute. "Thanks again for the cookies, but I actually have an appointment in a few minutes."

"Oh, of course." Hurt and confusion warred in Violet's eyes, and she looked away.

He felt bad about that, but it was for the best. She wouldn't want to get too friendly with someone like him anyway.

She crossed the room as if it were on fire and yanked the door open with her good arm.

"Oh, excuse me." Another woman's surprised voice came from the hall-way. "I'm looking for Nate Benson's apartment."

Nate groaned inwardly. His appointment was here. He moved closer to the door, where a tall, light-haired woman he'd guess to be in her early thirties stood blocking Violet's exit.

"You found it." Violet's response rang with false cheerfulness as she neatly stepped around the woman.

"Thanks again for the cookies," Nate called to her back, but she disappeared into her own apartment.

The blond woman glanced over her shoulder at Violet's door, then at him. "Mr. Benson?"

He nodded and shook the hand she held out.

"I'm parole officer Linda Jensen. It's nice to meet you."

Nate supposed he should return the sentiment, but he wasn't terribly excited about meeting the person who was going to be keeping tabs on him for the next two years.

"Come in." He stood aside and let her pass into the apartment.

She marched straight into the kitchen and deposited her briefcase on the table, then started opening his cupboards.

It's not like he'd had any privacy for the past seven years, but it still felt like an invasion. This was supposed to be his new home. His new life.

The woman pulled out a pad of paper and made some notes. "Not a lot of food here."

"Yeah, my neighbor was just telling me where the store is. I've been living off gas station food for the last week." He gave a meager laugh. "Actually, she brought these cookies. If you want one."

The parole officer kept writing. "Not right now, thanks. What happened to her arm?"

Nate regarded her coolly. What was she getting at? Did she think he would hurt his neighbor? That he would hurt anyone?

He took a deep breath. He was overreacting. She was just curious.

"She was working in her antique shop and a big piece of furniture fell on her."

He swallowed. What if she asked how Violet had gotten to the hospital? He didn't want to lie. But if he told her—

Officer Jensen nodded vaguely. "I have a series of standard questions I'll need to ask you each time we meet. You are expected to answer honestly." She didn't give him time to respond before launching into the first question. "Have you had any alcohol since your release?"

Nate stared at her. Was she serious? He'd never touch another drop. One time had been enough to ruin his life forever. "No."

She made a notation on the sheet, then rattled off a slew of questions about his actions over the past week. He wanted to tell her he'd done nothing—had no intention of doing anything aside from getting through the days—but he answered her questions with yes or no. Finally she put the sheet aside.

"And the job?"

"It's fine."

"You're working for your father, correct?"

"Yes, ma'am." The words barely made it past his gritted teeth.

"You're lucky." Officer Jensen rummaged through her briefcase. "A lot of people's parents do nothing for them when they get out."

Nate clamped his mouth tight. She thought what his dad was doing to him was out of kindness? It was simply another form of imprisonment.

"I know mine wrote me off. That's part of why I became a parole officer. Everyone deserves a second chance." She grabbed something out of her bag and held it out to him.

Nate took the small plastic cup.

He knew what it was for, and it didn't exactly scream second chances.

He fought down the shame that tried to swamp him and went to fill it.

# Chapter 8

Violet circled the armoire, trying to determine how much damage it had sustained in the fall. It looked okay from the front and sides, but it was still lying on its back, so it was impossible to tell if it had suffered any structural damage. She'd have to wait until Spencer got home to find out. She'd learned her lesson about moving big pieces herself.

She eyed her cast again. She'd spent the whole morning going through bills, pecking numbers on the keyboard with one hand. But as the numbers on the bills had added up, that had quickly become too depressing. So she'd decided to get some projects done back here.

Except she couldn't figure out anything she could do one-handed. She scanned the shelves. She could probably wash the Spode blue Italian china set she'd picked up at an auction a few weeks ago.

The only problem was she'd placed it on a fairly high shelf for storage.

She moved toward the ladder perched next to the back door of the workshop. If she could get up high enough, she could probably hold the box in her right hand and use her left to balance it.

As she approached the door, she glanced out the small window in it. She hadn't seen Nate since he'd disappeared into his apartment with that pretty blond last night.

She didn't know why the sight of the woman had made her stomach sink. It's not like she cared what Nate did one way or another.

She grabbed the ladder and dragged it across the floor, cringing as its foot squealed against the polished concrete.

She wrestled it into place next to the shelf, then looked up to examine the box's position.

This was a bad idea. But she didn't have any other options right now.

She gripped the ladder with her right hand and took a tentative step onto the first rung, holding her left arm as close to her body as she could with the bulky cast.

She slid her grip up a couple inches, then brought her other foot up to the step.

There.

One rung done. Only four more to go.

She pressed her lips together in concentration and worked her way up another step.

On the way to the third rung, the ladder wobbled, and she almost lost her balance, but she grabbed the shelf until she was steady.

Her breath came in short gasps.

She reached for the next rung.

The door behind her banged open and footsteps pounded across the floor. "What are you doing?"

She jumped, almost losing her balance again.

But this time a hand landed on her leg to steady her.

She worked to slow her breathing. It was a second before she could look down. But she already knew who it was.

Nate.

Her heart shouldn't have skipped at his voice.

Which didn't change the fact that it did.

"I need to get this box down." She tried to move her leg to the next rung, but his hand tightened.

"Get down. You're not going up there." Nate's voice was stern, and indignation rose hot in Violet's belly.

"I was under the impression this was my store."

"Yeah. And it's my building." Nate grabbed her right arm and tugged. She had no choice but to step down or fall.

The moment her feet were on the floor, she rounded on him. "I can't sit around here doing nothing for the next six weeks. My store will fall apart."

Nate studied her for a minute. "You don't have to do nothing. But no ladder climbing with a broken arm, okay? Or moving furniture. If you need something, come knock on my door. I have to be at my office from eight to five. But I'm around any time after that."

She flicked a glance at the clock behind him. "It's only three now."

The slow smile he gave her softened his whole face. "I decided to skip out early today. I wanted to—" He broke off and looked away. "I wanted to check on you. Make sure you weren't doing anything else that could get you killed. Good thing, too."

He moved to scale the ladder, and she used her right hand to steady it.

She kept her eyes on the floor. But that didn't stop the warmth climbing up from her toes. He had wanted to make sure she was okay?

"Which box is it?"

She looked up to point to the box, but he was gazing down at her, and their eyes locked for a second. The storm she'd seen swirling in his the other day was still there, but it seemed calmer today.

Her throat was suddenly too dry, and she shifted to look past him. She pointed to the box. "That one. Labeled Spode blue Italian."

He reached to grab it, then backed down the ladder, his movements sure. "Where do you want it?"

"By the sink. I need to wash them before I put them out." She followed him as he crossed the room to the oversize sink.

He set it on the long countertop Cade had installed for her.

"So what is Spode blue Italian, if you don't mind my asking?"

She grinned. If she didn't mind him asking? She loved finding new people who wanted to know more about antiques. "It's a kind of china made by Spode, one of the great ceramic manufacturers in England." She opened the box and pulled out a bowl. "See the blue and white designs? They were incredibly popular on ceramics imported from China in the 1700s. But imports couldn't keep up with demand, so Spode started making its own blue and white designs. They're called blue Italian because they show scenes from the Italian countryside." She passed him the bowl. "See? Can't you just picture yourself there?"

Nate wrinkled his nose. "What's wrong with new dishes?"

Violet stared at him. Was he kidding? "Well, they do still make blue Italian, but the new ones have no story yet. No history. Imagine all the people these dishes have seen. All the eras of history they've been through. It's just—" She broke off at the look he was giving her. "What?"

"Nothing." He shook his head and moved away.

"You don't like antiques."

"I have no strong feelings about antiques one way or another." He came to a stop next to the armoire. "It's just—sometimes history is better left buried. For all you know, these plates belonged to a mass murderer."

"Yeah." Violet couldn't hold back the sarcasm. "I hear Ted Bundy ate off blue Italian."

Nate shrugged. "I'm just saying. Not everything about history is good. Sometimes it's better to get rid of everything and start fresh."

Violet considered him. She thought she sensed something deeper under the surface. "Is that what you're doing in Hope Springs? Starting fresh? Is that why you moved in with only a suitcase?"

Nate watched her, and she held completely still. For a second, she thought the storm in his eyes might break.

"I just don't think it's healthy to hold onto the past is all," he finally said. "It can keep you from moving forward."

Violet swallowed hard. The past was all she had to hold onto. Without it, she would come unmoored.

Remembering the past didn't keep her from moving forward. It gave her a reason to get up every day.

Nate turned to the armoire. "I think I can pick this up for you. If it's not too damaged?"

She wanted to ask more about why he'd come to Hope Springs. But he didn't owe her any explanations.

She pushed her curiosity aside and crossed the room to stand next to him. "I've checked it out as much as I could. I think it's okay."

Nate moved to the spot where the top of the armoire rested on the ground. His biceps strained against his sleeves as he lifted. He grunted as he got the wardrobe to waist level and repositioned his hands. Then he maneuvered it the rest of the way upright.

Violet hurried behind the armoire as Nate bent and braced his hands on his knees. "That's heavier than it looks."

"Oh, thank goodness." She set a hand on his shoulder without thinking but yanked it away the moment she felt the warmth of his skin on her fingers. "It's okay."

"That's good." Nate straightened and moved to grab the cart she'd been trying to load the armoire onto the other day.

"What are you doing?"

"If you can hold the cart still, I should be able to get it on there." He spun the cart so that the handle was facing her, and she gripped it with her right hand, bracing it with her hip. Nate moved to the far side of the armoire.

Maybe she'd been too quick to judge him. The first day she'd met him, she'd decided he was rude and standoffish, and so she'd been rude and standoffish in return.

But now she could see he had a generous heart, even if he tried to hide it.

Nate loaded one end of the armoire onto the cart, then braced it with his hand as he moved to the other side.

"Careful." She bit her lip. If that thing fell again . . .

Nate shot her an exasperated look, and she ducked her head. He probably didn't exactly consider her the world's foremost expert on safety at the moment.

With a few more grunts, he managed to maneuver the armoire onto the cart. She stepped aside as he grabbed the handle.

"Where do you want this?"

"I have a spot ready for it in the front corner." She opened the double doors and moved aside so he could steer the cart through.

For someone who didn't like antiques, Nate sure was moving the piece carefully. He stopped every few seconds to check the clearance at the top of the doorframe. The armoire squeaked through with only a centimeter or so to spare.

Violet led the way to the bedroom setup she'd been working on the other day, with a Louis XV style headboard and dresser. The armoire would create the perfect effect of a luxurious eighteenth-century bed chamber.

Nate considered the space, as if mentally sizing it up.

"It will fit." She rolled her eyes. "I measured it."

He gave her a doubtful look.

"You don't think I know how to use a tape measure?" She only used one on a daily basis.

"I'm sure you know how to use a tape measure." Nate's voice held the first trace of amusement she'd ever heard from him. It softened his whole demeanor. "But I think you may have done it wrong this time."

"Okay." She placed her good hand on her hip. "Tell you what. If it doesn't fit there, I'll buy you another plate of cookies. But if it does—" She cocked her head to the side and squinted at him, trying to come up with a good wager. "You have to let me give you a tour of the store and tell you about the antiques." She relished the opportunity. She'd make him come to see their worth.

"You're on." He bent to lift the armoire, and Violet held the cart handle again.

Once it was off the cart, Nate alternated moving each side until it was only inches from the spot she'd cleared for it.

"You sure you want to go through with this bet?" He rested with his arm on the door pull. "I can tell you right now it's not going to fit."

She had to admit the space she'd left looked too small now that the armoire was right next to it. But she was confident in her measurements. "I'm sure."

She chewed her lip as Nate angled the armoire back and forth. "Push it a little to the left."

"No cheating." But he moved it to the left, then wiggled it some more until it slid right into place, a small gap between it and the dresser on one side and the wall on the other.

"Ha."

Nate gave an exaggerated sigh. "Fine. You were right. Happy now?"

She grinned. "Yep. And I'll be even happier once I show you the joys of all the antiques here."

Nate pivoted to look around the large space. "*All* the antiques?" She heard the wariness in his voice.

"Yep. Hope you have some time."

"This clock is one of my favorites."

Nate had to chuckle. She'd said that about nearly every antique she'd shown him so far. And she'd shown him a lot. If the clock she held now was correct, they'd been at this tour for over an hour already.

"See how this window gives you a peek at the gears inside? I love how it gives you a feel for how the clock works without losing that sense of mystery and wonder."

Violet's face was animated, her eyes bright. With every object she showed him, she spoke faster, as if she was afraid he would take off any second.

She shouldn't have worried. He may not share her love of antiques, but her passion for them had completely captivated him.

"How old is it?" He mainly asked to keep her talking.

"This one would be late 1700s, early 1800s."

He let out a low whistle.

"I know. Isn't that amazing? This thing was around when our country was being founded. Just think what it's seen. Sometimes I—" She broke off and set the clock down, turning to grab an old iron from the table next to it. "So this—"

"Wait. Sometimes you what?"

The way her cheeks had turned pink made him curious.

She gave an embarrassed laugh. "Fine. Sometimes I make up stories for the items in here. You know, like this clock." She set down the iron and rested her hand on the clock. "I like to think it sat in the parlor. And when a young lady was waiting for her suitor, she would pace to it to check the time and then go sit down. And then a couple minutes later she'd do the same thing. And then when he came, she'd forget to look at the clock the whole time he was there. But when it was time for him to leave, she'd look at the clock in surprise and wonder how the time had gone by so quickly."

Nate tried to take his eyes off her, but he couldn't. He wished he could see the past like that. Like this place of endless hope and joy. Instead of a string of mistakes and regrets.

She turned her back to him and rearranged a few trinkets. "It's silly, I know. Just something to keep myself amused."

"It's not silly." He cleared his throat. "Well, it's a little silly. But that's what's so—"

A loud chime sounded from the other end of the store, and Violet spun toward the door. A group of older women with cameras around their necks filed into the building.

"Excuse me for a second." Violet hurried toward the women.

"Sure. I should get going anyway." Before he let himself get any more caught up in the feelings that had been tugging at him as she spoke.

He allowed himself one last glimpse of her as he crossed the store. She was talking with the women, who were all laughing at something she had said. She seemed to have a unique gift for bringing joy.

Probably because she'd never known sorrow. At least not the way he had. Some people had charmed lives that way.

Nate looked away. One more reason to leave her alone. He didn't want her to get caught in the trap of his tainted past.

He was nearly to the doors that led into the workshop when he spotted the smaller room to the right. He almost kept walking. But he caught a glimpse of the edge of a piece of furniture. Something about it felt familiar.

He moved closer to take a look.

The moment he reached the entry to the room, he stopped and caught his breath. A Bosendorfer grand piano. He took a few steps forward, until he was standing close enough to touch it. His fingers itched to feel the keys, but he held them back.

The piano pressed on an empty spot deep in his soul. A spot that had once been filled by music. Snatches of the songs he'd written filled his head, and it took all his willpower not to sit down and let the melodies out. He'd promised himself he'd never play again. If it weren't for music, his life would be on track right now.

"It's beautiful isn't it?"

He jumped and took a step back. How long had Violet been standing next to him?

"Yeah." His throat was too dry.

"It's a shame. It's been here forever, and I just can't sell it. It'd be nice if I played, so I could enjoy it for myself at least." She pressed her fingers to the C and D keys, and he winced at the dissonance.

She lifted her hand off the piano. "Yeah. I could use some lessons. You don't happen to play, do you?"

Nate stuffed his hands in his pockets to keep from touching the keys. "I used to. A long time ago."

"Well, it has to be like riding a bike, right?" She nudged him with her cast. "Maybe you can teach me."

He shook his head. "That's not part of my life anymore."

"So this is the perfect chance to make it part of your life again." Her smile was genuine, open.

He had to leave before this went any further. "It will never be part of my life again. Look, I have to go."

He walked away, ignoring the almost overpowering desire to look back.

# Chapter 9

The waves rolled over his feet and then retreated. Nate let the cold zip up his legs as he watched the sun rise. Not many people were out at dawn on a Sunday morning. Just the way he preferred it.

So why had the sliver of loneliness worked its way into his heart?

He should be happy. After skipping out of work early Tuesday, he'd put in extra hours at the office the rest of the week and had finally managed to finish sorting through all the scattered paperwork. Now he could start to reconcile it with the electronic records and figure out which properties had expired leases or were in default on their payments. If he kept up the long hours, he might be able to meet Dad's unreasonable deadline for the report.

Plus, he'd be able to avoid seeing Violet.

He'd run into her in the hallway only once since she'd given him the tour of the antique shop, and they'd had some ridiculously mundane conversation about the weather. It was painful.

He could tell she was hurt from the way he'd run out of the antique shop the other day. But he'd had to. Being with her had started to make him want something he couldn't have.

He needed to stay focused on what he was here for. To do his penance. To prove to Dad he wasn't the world's biggest mistake—even if the mistake he'd made had been a colossal one that would define him for the rest of his life. And to earn the chance to see Mom and Kayla again.

Nate took another step but jerked his foot up quickly as something sharp poked into his heel. He bent to pick up the shell fragment that had stabbed him. But it reminded him of the shell sitting in the drawer of his bedside table.

The sliver of loneliness widened into a plank.

He chucked the shell into the water, watching as it floated for a second before being swallowed by the waves. Is that what would happen to him too?

"Duke, come." A guy's angry yell traveled down the beach.

Nate lifted his head in time to spot a big dog barreling at him, water spraying up from his legs. There was no time to get out of the way. The dog sped past, and a wall of water hit Nate square in the face.

"Sorry about that," the guy called as he chased the dog.

But Nate laughed and wiped at the water.

He'd just figured out how to ease his loneliness.

Violet hummed one of the songs from worship this morning as she pulled into the parking spot behind her building. The service today had been lovely. Somehow Dan always knew what she needed to hear. His sermon had been about the loneliness that could only be filled by God.

She had to admit her loneliness had been deeper than usual this week, with Sophie still gone and Nate—whom she'd just started to consider a potential friend—avoiding her as if he feared her love for antiques might rub off on him. But between Dan's reminder that God was the only one who could meet all her needs and a wonderful lunch at the cafe with her friends, her heart was lighter than it had been in days.

Violet gathered up her purse and Bible and was halfway out of the car when something big and powerful slammed into her, knocking her back into her seat.

A slobbery tongue slapped kisses onto her cheek, and she raised her good arm to fend it off. Water dripped from the dog's fur onto her skirt. Violet felt at the dog's neck in search of a collar she could use to get it under control, but it didn't have one.

"Maverick, down."

The dog's ears perked at the distant male voice, but its kisses were relentless.

Violet gave in and held her hand out to the dog, letting it sniff her for a minute. Then she moved her hand to scratch behind its ear. The dog laid its front paws across her lap and leaned into her.

"There we go, buddy. You're not so big and bad, are you?"

The dog responded with a contented groan.

"I'm so sorry." Nate raced up to the car. "I thought a swim would calm him down, but it seems to have riled him up more." Nate's hair was windblown, and a thin sheen of sweat shone on his forehead.

"You got a dog?" Violet hadn't pegged him as a dog lover.

Nate grabbed the dog by the scruff of the neck, pulling him off Violet. "Are you hurt? Is your arm okay?" He groaned. "Oh no, look at your skirt."

Violet straightened her drenched skirt as well as she could, ignoring the muddy paw print in the middle, and stepped out of the car. "I'm fine. I thought this was a strictly no pets building, though."

Nate shrugged. "I changed it. Although I'm kind of regretting that now. They didn't tell me this dog was the devil's child."

Violet considered the animal. He wasn't a beautiful creature, with his splotchy gray and black coat, cropped tail, and ears that hung past his muzzle. But Violet could see the appeal in him. She moved around Nate to the other side of the dog and squatted next to the animal, rubbing his ear again. The dog lowered himself to the ground and rolled over.

"Okay. How'd you do that?" Nate sounded both amused and mystified, and Violet risked a look up at him. His mouth lifted into a smile.

She didn't like the way her heart sped up when he did that. She directed her attention to the dog, busying herself with scratching its belly.

"I always had dogs growing up. I haven't had one in years, though. My husband was allergic. Anyway, this sweet guy just wants some attention."

Nate huffed. "I've given him attention all morning. He repaid me by using my bedroom floor as a bathroom."

Violet couldn't stop the laugh that snorted out. "Sorry. That's not funny." But she couldn't have sounded too sincere around her giggles.

"No, it's not." Nate's voice held a laugh around the edge of the exasperation, and the sound drew her eyes to him again.

"So, do you have any experience with dogs?" She vaguely remembered her mom's frustration with puppy training the first dog she and Jade had convinced her to buy.

She locked the memory away before the ache she always felt when she thought of Mom could rear up again. One constant heartache was enough.

Nate gave a short laugh. "I figured they couldn't be that hard to figure out. Turns out I may have been wrong."

Violet patted the dog one more time and stood, glancing down at the wet skirt plastered to her knees. She must look ridiculous.

The dog sidled from Nate's side to stand in front of Violet, and she bent over to pet him again.

Nate snorted. "Thanks for the loyalty there, Maverick." The dog didn't move.

"Is that really his name? Maverick?"

Nate's forehead creased. "Yeah. Why?"

Violet wrinkled her nose. "It's such a clichéd name. You're a big boy dog so you need to have some big macho name. When clearly he's a sweetheart."

"Well, what would you name him then?" Nate's ocean eyes landed on hers, and hard as she tried to look away, she couldn't.

"Obviously he's a Tony."

Nate laughed out loud this time. "Tony. That's the most ridiculous name I've ever heard for a dog." Nate bent down and patted the dog's head. "Come on, Maverick. I still have to figure out what to do with you while I go spend all my money on the supplies you need."

Nate's hand was perilously close to Violet's on the dog's head, and she straightened, letting her arm drop to her side.

"You mean you got a dog before you had any dog supplies?"

Nate straightened, too. "Um, yeah." He ducked his head. "Not my smartest move ever."

Violet studied the dog, who perked his ears at her. Her plan had been to come home from church and spend the afternoon cleaning, then curl up with a book.

"I could watch him while you go out."

Nate's eyes met Violet's again. Something warred in his, but it passed in a moment. "I couldn't ask you to do that." He patted his leg for the dog to come.

"You didn't ask. I offered."

Nate studied her, as if not sure she was serious. "You're sure you wouldn't mind?"

"Absolutely sure. That's what neighbors are for, right? Anyway, I've missed having a dog around." She squatted and wrapped her arm around the dog. "We'll have fun, won't we, Tony?"

Nate gave her one last appraising look. Then he walked toward the alley, calling over his shoulder, "His name is Maverick."

Violet grinned at his retreating form. "Not if I have anything to do with it."

The sound of Nate's laugh drifting back to her only made her grin wider.

# Chapter 10

Violet pulled the back door of the antique shop closed behind her and locked it. She should be happy. It had been a good day for a Friday. She'd managed to sell a couple of big pieces, along with several smaller items. If things kept up like this, she might be able to make her rent payment on time. Not that it meant she'd be caught up on what she owed in back rent, but at least she wouldn't fall further behind.

But for some reason she couldn't put her finger on, her heart felt heavier than it should. She glanced up the staircase, her thoughts tracking to Nate's apartment. Were he and the dog in there? She'd bonded with the dog when she'd watched him last Sunday—she'd even managed to train him to answer only to Tony. Nate had pretended to disapprove, but she'd seen right past his tough act to the laughter hiding in his eyes.

Over the past few days, she'd gotten used to running into them as Nate took the dog out before work. Yesterday, she'd waited with him on the hill as he let Tony out. And after work, he'd stopped by the antique shop to ask if she needed anything else moved. She'd ended up deciding on the spur of the moment that she needed a whole dining setup rearranged, and he'd spent a good hour helping her. But she hadn't seen him at all yet today.

Not that it mattered.

Violet grabbed her mail from the box at the foot of the stairs, then trudged up to her apartment. But once she was in the cozy space, she couldn't figure out what to do. It was such a beautiful evening that it was almost a shame to spend it indoors. She moved to the window in the small dining area and slid the curtain aside. Although it was after five, the sun was still high in the sky, and groups of children splashed in the water. A few couples strolled along the shoreline. Violet's heart tightened. She and Cade used to do that—long walks where they talked about everything or nothing at all.

She hadn't been able to bring herself to walk on the beach since his death.

She let the curtain fall and moved to the couch. Maybe she'd read. But the moment she picked up her book, she set it down. For the first time in a long time, she didn't feel like reading about someone else's life.

She felt like *doing* something with hers.

Maybe she could go for a walk. Not on the beach. She didn't think she could handle that. But the Sugarbush trail was only half a mile away.

She changed into a pair of running shorts and maneuvered her arm into a t-shirt. The tennis shoes were harder to put on one-handed, but she finally managed.

The moment she opened her door, a shaggy creature crashed into her legs. She couldn't help the smile. "Hey there, Tony. I missed you this morning."

She looked up as Nate closed his apartment door. He was dressed in khakis and a gray dress shirt that made his eyes look steelier than usual. But the steel softened as he met her gaze. "I had to get to work early this morning, so we were out before the sun was up."

She wrinkled her nose. Early mornings were not her favorite time. "Too early for me then. Where are you two off to now?"

"I just got home, actually, so I thought I better let him out for a few minutes. Poor guy has been cooped up all day."

"Well, I didn't hear a peep from him, if it makes you feel better." She gave Tony a pat and moved toward the steps. "I thought I'd go for a walk on the Sugarbush. You two want to come?"

The surprise on Nate's face was probably echoed on hers. She hadn't been planning to invite them along. The words had just come out. But now that they had, she was glad. She wouldn't mind some company. It'd keep her thoughts from drifting to Cade the whole time.

"Sure." Nate's answer was quick. "Just one thing—what's the Sugarbush?"

Violet laughed. "It's a hiking trail. The trailhead is down the road. It's really pretty and—"

She stopped. This wasn't a tourism video.

Nate took stock of his dress clothes. "Give me a second to change." He passed her Tony's leash. "I'll meet you two outside."

⁓

Nate let his eyes drift to Violet. She'd set a quick pace for their walk, and her face was bright. She pointed to the little restaurant they were passing. "Have you eaten at the Hidden Cafe yet?"

He shook his head. The scent of home cooking wafting from the cafe had almost lured him in more than once, but so far, he'd stuck with frozen dinners. They were good enough for him.

After another five minutes, Tony's tongue was lolling to the side, and Nate was beginning to wonder if a walk was a good idea on such a hot day.

But Violet steered them toward a wooded area to the right. "The Sugarbush."

Nate picked out a narrow packed dirt path that wound between thick stands of trees. About a hundred yards in, he lost sight of the trail as it jogged to the left. It didn't look like much, but he was willing to give it a shot.

As soon as they stepped into the shade of the trees, the temperature felt ten degrees cooler, even though the humidity still clung to him. They walked single file until the trail widened after a few yards. Violet fell into step beside him.

They strolled in comfortable silence, watching Tony, who kept his nose to the ground and made constant snuffling sounds. Every few feet, he stopped for a longer sniff. Nate tried to tug him along, but it quickly became clear Tony was going to be the one to set the pace.

"This is nice," Nate said after a while, then felt his face warm. He hadn't meant to say the words out loud. "I mean, I had no idea this was here."

Violet pointed at a patch of red berries. "Hope Springs has lots of surprises like this."

She plucked a berry and passed it to him. He held it up and examined it. He hadn't been hiking a lot in his life, but he was pretty sure you weren't supposed to eat random berries in the woods.

"Relax, it's a raspberry." Violet popped one in her mouth. It stained her lips a darker red.

Nate forced his eyes off them and stuck his own berry in his mouth. He made a face at the tartness.

Violet picked another. "Yeah, they're not quite ripe yet. That's how my husband always liked them, but I prefer to wait until they're a little darker."

Nate hesitated with a second berry halfway to his mouth. He shouldn't pry, but that was the third or fourth time she'd mentioned a husband since he'd met her. "If you don't mind my asking, where is your husband? I haven't met him."

The flush drained from Violet's cheeks, and he wished he could take the question back. It's not like it was any of his business.

Violet resumed walking. Nate hesitated a second, then took his spot beside her.

"He died. Three years ago." Her voice was quiet, and Nate wanted to kick himself. He'd never considered the possibility. Not when she seemed so joyful all the time.

"I'm so sorry." It wasn't enough, but what else could he say?

He wanted to know more. What had happened? How had he died? How had she picked up the pieces to remain this cheerful person?

But he sensed she didn't want to talk about it.

After a while, she glanced at him. "So what brings you to Hope Springs, anyway? Your girlfriend?"

He nearly choked. "My what?"

"Sorry, fiancée maybe?"

Who on earth was she talking about? "I don't have a girlfriend or a fiancée."

"Oh." She turned to look at a small pond off the right side of the trail. "Sorry. I just assumed that woman the other day—"

Nate ran the last few days through his mind. He couldn't think of a single woman he'd had contact with besides Violet and Mrs. D'Angelo. Unless she meant—

"Oh, that was my—" He hesitated. If he said parole officer, she'd turn around and sprint back the way they'd come. "That was just a business associate."

"Oh." She tucked a wayward curl behind her ear. He had no idea what she was thinking right now. What surprised him was how badly he wanted to know. Did it change anything, her knowing he didn't have a girlfriend?

"So what did bring you to Hope Springs?"

Nate licked his lips. That question opened up way too many land mines. He decided to go with the most immediate reason. "I came to work for my dad."

She tipped her head to the side. "You don't like it, though?"

His head swiveled to her. "How—"

"It's not that hard to tell. Your hands are clenched into fists. Your jaw is clamped tighter than a lockbox. And you always seem kind of down when you have to go to work in the morning."

Nate gaped. He'd have to be more guarded with her. If she'd figured all that out just from looking at him, who knew what else she might discern.

"So why are you working for your dad if you hate it? Why not quit?" She swatted at a mosquito on her neck.

If only he could. "It's not that simple."

She watched him, as if waiting for more of an answer. But he couldn't give one. Not without making her hate him. And right now she was the only friend he had. Besides Tony.

"So, let's say it was simple." Her voice was easy, and he relaxed a little. "What would you do if you could do anything?"

Nate knew the answer to that without thinking about it. But he wasn't about to share it. That part of his life was dead.

"I don't—" But he broke off as Tony's leash jerked out of his hand.

"Tony!" He lunged for the leash, but it was too late. Tony dashed into the trees, a deer sprinting a couple yards ahead of him.

"Tony!" Nate yelled in his strictest voice. But the dog kept running. He was already at least fifty yards into the woods. "Come!"

"Tony!" Violet's yell wasn't as hard as Nate's, but it was nearly as loud.

Within seconds, the dog had disappeared. Nate squinted in the direction he had run, his heart banging against his ribs. Tony was supposed to be the one friend who would never leave him.

"Tony!" Nate called again.

"He went that way." Violet pointed to the east, where a thick clump of trees hid anything else from sight. "Come on."

Nate followed as she set out at a fast clip in the direction Tony had disappeared.

It was starting to get dark in the woods, and Nate fought down the panic. The trees stretched as far as he could see in every direction. "How large is this forest?"

He was half afraid the forest would be so large Tony could be lost forever and half afraid it was so small that Tony would come out at a road on the other side and be hit by a car.

Violet stopped, turning in a slow circle as she squinted into the distance. "It's pretty big. He'll get tired out and rest soon, and then we'll catch up with him." She gave his arm a reassuring pat.

"Over there." Violet pointed into the trees and set off at a jog, her casted arm swinging at her side.

"Tony!" This time, Violet's voice sounded different—a cry of recognition instead of a call into the unknown.

Nate's head popped up in time to see Violet running full-out toward the dog, who was straining to get to her but was held back by something. The dog let out a sharp cry that went straight to Nate's heart. He'd let his dog get away and now he was hurt. Wasn't there anyone in the world he could take care of?

Violet dropped to her knees next to the dog just as Nate reached them.

"His leg's caught in some old barbed wire." Her voice was calm, and Nate concentrated on it to steady himself. Panicking wasn't going to help Tony.

He leaned over Violet, who had her arm wrapped around the dog, and examined the wire. It was wound tight, trickles of blood darkening the fur where the barbs pierced the leg. Nate inhaled sharply.

"Can you untangle it?" Violet asked, in between cooing to the whimpering dog.

Nate tried to find a loose spot in the wire. "I think so. Can you hold him still?"

Violet nodded, whispering "It's okay, boy," over and over as she stroked the dog's ears. Tony leaned against her, and his whimpers slowed.

Nate moved around Violet to kneel at the dog's other side. The barbed wire bit into his hand as he lifted it away from Tony's leg. The dog yelped and tried to pull away, but Violet continued to pat him, and Nate strained at the wire again.

After several minutes, he managed to work the barbs free. Blood stained the dog's gray legs, but the wounds didn't seem too deep.

Nate fell back, rubbing a hand against his forehead to wipe away the sweat that had collected there from their dash through the woods.

"Nice work." Violet looked up, and her eyes widened. "You're bleeding."

Nate waved off her concern. "It's not too bad."

Violet eyed him dubiously, then gave the dog a pat and slid closer to Nate.

He hissed in a breath as she took his bloodied hand in hers.

"Sorry."

He didn't bother to tell her that the breath hadn't been one of pain.

She opened her water bottle and poured it over his hand, washing away the worst of the blood. "These don't look too deep, but that fence is pretty rusty. Are you up to date on your tetanus shot?"

Nate swallowed and nodded. He knew the exact date of his last tetanus shot.

"Good." Violet moved to Tony and poured the remaining water over his leg. Tony whimpered but licked her. "I think he's going to be okay, too. Right, boy?"

The dog gave her a mournful look, and she patted his head. "Come on."

She stood, then held out a hand to help Nate up. He took it, forcing himself to ignore the sparks in his fingertips.

"You too, boy." She patted her leg, and Tony stood. He took a few limping steps, then started to jog ahead of them.

"I don't think so, boy. Come." Nate hooked the leash onto the dog's collar. Tony looked up at him with his big dark eyes. "Don't give me that look. You were very naughty."

"Oh, don't be so hard on him." Violet touched his arm for a fraction of second. "He's sorry." As if to prove her right, Tony let out a deep sigh.

"Sorry isn't always enough. Some things don't deserve to be forgiven." He kept his voice light to hide the truth behind his words. He knew only too well that some things were beyond forgiveness.

Violet stopped walking, as if his words had shocked her. As if she wanted to talk about them.

Nate kept going.

After a few seconds, her footsteps jogged up beside him. "You aren't really going to hold this against him forever are you? I think he learned his lesson, poor guy."

He sighed. "I suppose I'll forgive him eventually. Once he makes it up to me."

"And how's he going to do that?"

Nate shrugged. "A week of dishes duty, maybe."

Violet burst out laughing, the sound rich and bright, filling the woods. "Remind me not to eat at your house for the next week."

VALERIE M. BODDEN

Nate laughed, too. He wanted so badly for his heart to feel as light as hers.

But a heavy lump settled in his stomach. Perhaps Tony could be forgiven someday.

After all, his mistake had hurt only himself.

Nate's, on the other hand, had cost his sister everything.

# Chapter 11

Nate checked the time again. How was it only two o'clock?

He'd had Officer Jensen meet him here this morning to avoid any more awkward conversations with Violet about her. But their meeting had been done for a few hours now, and still the clock refused to budge.

He contemplated the remaining stack of leases. He should skip out and enjoy his Saturday. He could finish them next week. But Dad hadn't called yet today. And if Nate wasn't here when he called, it'd be one more strike against him.

He turned back to the computer. He'd asked Violet to stop in and check on Tony if she got a second during the day, and she'd assured him that she would.

He trusted her. But maybe he should give her a quick call. Just to ask how Tony was.

Not because he wanted to hear her musical voice.

He did a quick search for the antique store online and dialed the number before he could change his mind.

"Hidden Treasures. How are you today?"

Just hearing her voice should not make him smile like this. He tried to keep his tone casual. "Hey, it's me. Just wanted to see if you've had a chance to check on Tony or if I should—"

"Nate." Her greeting was warm, and he had to remind himself that was how she always sounded. It had nothing to do with him. "I checked on him this morning and once about an hour ago. He almost convinced me to close the store and take him for a walk, but I stayed strong."

Nate relaxed into his seat. "And how'd Tony take the disappointment?"

"Oh, you know—" He could picture her waving a hand through the air. "He didn't. So I brought him down here with me."

Nate sniggered. "And that's staying strong?"

Violet laughed, too. "I know, I know. But he was so insistent, and he gave me that look. You know the one where he tilts his head way to the side and looks at you out of the corner of his eyes?"

Nate did know. It was how Tony had gotten two treats out of him last night when he'd deserved none for the way he'd behaved in the woods.

"Well, if he gives you any trouble, put him back upstairs. I'll be home in a couple hours." He was getting used to the way the word *home* felt on his tongue.

"Sounds great. And Nate?"

"Yeah?"

"I hope you have a good afternoon." The sincerity in her voice touched something in Nate's core. This wasn't the casual "have a good day" that a store clerk threw out a hundred times a day. This was heartfelt, meant just for him.

"Thanks." He swallowed. "You, too."

The moment he hung up, he was readier than ever to go home. But he couldn't pretend it was only Tony he wanted to see anymore.

He turned to the stack of leases, the smile refusing to let go of its hold on his lips. He entered the information for a property in Grace Falls, wherever that was, and moved on to the next.

By the time he'd entered half a dozen leases, his spirits had dampened only a little. They all seemed to be up to date on their leases and payments, which made his job that much easier.

The office phone blared, and his mood instantly soured. He'd hoped he might be able to go at least one day without Dad checking up on him.

He snatched the phone off the cradle. "Benson Properties."

"Nathan."

Nate could practically feel his blood pressure go up, just like it did every time Dad called.

"Do you have the report I requested?"

Nate scrutinized the dozen or so leases stacked on the desk. "I will in about an hour. I'll email it to you then."

"Good. I have an investor waiting to see a list of potential properties in Hope Springs. So make sure you include expired or almost expired leases or any that are in default on their payments."

"Okay." Nate made a note, then rushed on before Dad could hang up. "Do you think I could come visit Mom and Kayla this weekend? After I get you the report, I mean."

Nate let his hope build at the hesitation on the other end. Was Dad really considering it?

"Two and a half weeks is hardly long enough to prove you're a different man, Nathan. Send that report right away."

Nate pulled the phone away as the dial tone blared in his ear.

He slammed the phone down and grabbed the next lease. But his hand froze as his eyes fell on the names at the top of the paper. Violet and Cade Somers.

He flipped the page and skipped over the legalese to find the needed information. The lease expired in two and a half months.

Nate wondered if Violet knew that. After all she'd been through in the past few years, it probably hadn't occurred to her to check into renewing her lease. Technically, according to the terms of the lease, it was already too late for a guaranteed renewal. Meaning Nate could kick her out and get someone else in there if he wanted to. Which he didn't.

He brought up her account on the computer to review her payment records. His heart sank. According to this, she was three months behind.

Nate set the lease aside and finished up the rest. He used the database to compile a list of properties with expired leases or in default, then scanned the list quickly for Violet's name.

When he came to it, he highlighted the row and hit delete.

One less property wasn't going to hurt Dad.

He saved the file and sent it off. Then he locked up and headed for the one place he wanted to be right now.

Home.

Violet threw the tennis ball down the hill and watched Tony chase after it, his ears flopping as he ran.

"Fetch it here, Tony." She used her most commanding voice.

But Tony apparently wasn't buying it. He carried the ball a few feet up the hill, then dropped it and watched as it rolled back down.

"Tony!" Violet bent in half and shook her head, then stood and ran after the ball herself. He'd done the same thing twelve times already, but she had been so sure that this time he would finally get it.

Tony sniffed her as she bent to pick up the ball, and she gave him a quick rub behind the ears. "It's okay, boy. You'll figure it out next time."

She checked the time on her phone again. Hopefully Nate would be home soon. She was supposed to be at Dan's in half an hour for dinner with her friends. She was dying to see Sophie and Spencer, who had finally gotten home late last night.

Tony gave her a lick, and Violet wiped her cheek. "Come on, let's try again." She started to climb the hill.

"Looks like he has you trained well."

She lifted her head, a smile already tugging her lips up at the sound of Nate's voice. He stood at the top of the hill, hands in the pockets of his khakis, grinning down at them.

"What are you talking about?" She grinned right back at him. "This is exactly what I taught him to do." She covered the last few steps up the hill and stood in front of Nate. A light five o'clock shadow dusted his cheeks and chin, making him look rugged.

His stance was relaxed, but she couldn't help noticing the tension in his shoulders.

"Rough day?"

He looked away. "It was fine."

He seemed ready to say more. She waited, but then he seemed to change his mind. "Thanks for watching Tony."

"Of course. I think I enjoyed having him around as much as he enjoyed being around."

Nate squatted to give Tony a scratch behind the ears. "As long as you don't teach him to like you more than he likes me."

"Oh, don't worry." She lowered herself to scratch Tony's neck, and the dog stepped closer to her. "He already likes me better."

Nate gave her shoulder a playful shove. "Yeah. I can't deny that. But then, you're definitely the more likable of the two of us."

Violet's eyes snapped to his, but he was gazing out toward the lake.

She straightened. "I'd love to stay and play, but I have to get going. What're you boys up to tonight?"

"Oh, you know—" Nate stood, too. "We have big plans with a frozen dinner and some mindless TV."

"Sounds fun." Violet had spent her share of nights the same way. "See you later."

With a last scratch of Tony's ears, she headed for her apartment. She needed to grab her keys and the pasta salad she'd managed to wrangle together with one hand last night.

But when she reached the door to the building, she couldn't help looking over her shoulder.

Nate had settled onto the grass, his knees up in front of him, his gaze directed toward the lake. She let herself wonder for a second what he was thinking about. Something almost haunted hovered behind his eyes most of the time, and she couldn't help wanting to ease it. Whatever it was.

But that wasn't her place.

She was his neighbor and maybe almost a friend.

But nothing more.

She slipped through the door and jogged up the steps. If she stood here wondering about her new neighbor any longer, she'd be late for dinner. And she was starving. The store had been so slammed today she hadn't had time for lunch.

Which had been a good problem to have for once.

She opened the door to her apartment, her mouth already watering at the thought of Dan's burgers. But she stopped inside the doorway as a strange sound hit her ears. It was like the constant rush of a waterfall.

But there were no waterfalls in her apartment the last time she'd checked.

Had she left a faucet on this morning? She'd done that once in the weeks right after Cade died. Fortunately, it had only been for a few minutes while she went downstairs to get the mail, and the overflow drain had kept up with the water flow.

She moved into the kitchen. The sink was off, and the dishwasher wasn't running.

So then where . . .

Water sloshed over her sandals as she stepped into the hallway, and she yanked her foot back in alarm.

The hallway had turned into a stream, flowing from the laundry room toward the bedroom. She followed it toward the source.

When she got to the laundry room, she stopped dead, her good hand over her mouth. The utility sink was on the floor, and water was spraying from a broken-off pipe jutting out of the wall.

"What did— How?" She dropped to her knees alongside the sink, ignoring the spray of water against her right arm as she groped behind the washer for a shut-off valve. There had to be one, didn't there?

Finally, her hand landed on what felt like the spigot of an outdoor faucet. But when she tried to turn it, nothing happened.

"Come on." She twisted harder. But her fingers simply slipped against the metal.

Now what? She couldn't sit here letting her apartment become a lake.

But by the time a plumber got here, that's exactly what would happen.

She didn't stop to think about it. Just jumped up and ran as quickly as she could without falling through the wet hallway, down the stairs, and out the door.

"Nate!"

He wasn't in his spot at the top of the hill anymore, and she jogged across the parking lot, scanning the hillside.

There.

On the beach, watching Tony splash in the waves.

She hesitated. She'd worked so hard not to go down there. But if she didn't now, she might as well bring the lake indoors.

She set off at a run down the hill, calling Nate's name every few seconds. She was halfway to the bottom when he turned around. Even from here, she could make out the smile that took over his face the moment he noticed her.

But she didn't have time to dwell on it.

She drew to a stop and waved him toward her. "I need your help!"

In under three seconds, he'd called Tony out of the water and was running up the beach toward her.

She waited, trying to catch her breath.

"What's going on? What's wrong?" Concern tightened his voice as he reached her.

"A pipe broke. There's water everywhere."

"Where?" Nate started up the hill at a jog, and Violet ran to match the pace of his longer legs.

"Everywhere," she repeated.

"I mean, where in the building?"

Oh, that made more sense. "My apartment. The laundry room. The sink fell off the wall. I tried to turn the shutoff valve, but it was stuck."

He nodded and opened the door, waiting for her to pass through.

She ran up the stairs. Tony's claws clicked on the steps behind her.

"I just put a load of laundry in maybe twenty minutes ago. Right before I took Tony outside—" She looked over her shoulder, but Nate wasn't there anymore.

She swiveled. How had he disappeared?

The door to her store was closed and locked, and he hadn't passed her on the stairs.

"Nate?"

There was no answer. On the step below her, Tony cocked his head, ears perked.

"Nate?" She called louder this time.

A clanging resounded through the entryway. She looked down. She was pretty sure it had come from under the stairs.

She retraced her steps, more than a little baffled. A narrow hallway ran alongside the stairs, separating them from her store, but as far as she knew, there was nothing there but an old storage closet.

But the door to the closet was open, and a light was on inside. She jumped as the banging began again.

"There we go." Nate's voice carried from the closet, and she moved closer.

She was just outside the door when he emerged, almost plowing into her. "Whoa. Sorry about that." He took a quick step back, and so did she.

She peered over his shoulder. Apparently it wasn't a storage closet after all. A large furnace took up most of the room.

"What'd you do?"

"I turned off the building's main water supply. Just until we can get the shutoff valve upstairs working or replaced." He set down the wrench he'd been holding and flipped off the light. "Let's go check it out."

Violet wanted to tell him he didn't have to do that. That she could take it from here. But the truth was, she appreciated the offer too much to turn it down.

She led the way up the stairs.

Nate stopped at the landing. "Let me put Tony in my apartment. Don't want him to get your place all wet."

She gave him an incredulous look, and he burst out laughing. The sound was so unexpected, she couldn't help joining him. It was the first time she'd heard him really laugh. It sounded good on him.

But as she opened the door to her apartment, their laughter cut off.

A trickle of water had worked its way from the hallway into the living room.

"Well that's not good." Nate stepped past her and followed the water to the laundry room. She walked slowly behind him, thinking about how long this was going to take to clean up. She ducked into the bathroom to grab every last towel out of the linen closet.

"Uh, do you need this stuff in the boxes?" Nate called.

"Oh no." She dropped the towels. In her panic to get the water turned off, she hadn't thought about the boxes of Cade's stuff still sitting on the laundry room floor.

She dashed into the room and squeezed past Nate in the small space. The bottoms of the boxes had transformed into an ugly dark brown as water seeped into them.

"Let's get them out of here." Nate held out his arms, and she passed him a box. Then she grabbed one of her own, grateful he didn't ask what was in them. She choked down the sobs threatening to escape. For some reason, the thought of Cade's things being destroyed hurt more than the thought of giving them away.

They deposited the boxes on the kitchen counter, then went back for more.

When they'd moved them all, Violet started pulling items out as Nate disappeared from the room. She was grateful for the moment of privacy as she spread Cade's stuff across the dining table and chairs, the couch, anywhere there was a dry space.

Fortunately, the only thing that seemed to be damaged was the corsage Cade had worn to their senior prom. She laughed as she rubbed its flaking petals.

"At least you still have your sense of humor." Nate stopped at the entrance to the kitchen, glancing around the room.

Violet gestured toward the corsage. "Cade hated wearing that thing. Kept saying it was poking him all night. It's why none of the guys in our wedding wore a corsage."

Nate gave her a gentle smile. "I got the shutoff valve turned off. I'll go turn the main water supply on, then I'll help you clean up this flood."

"Oh, you don't have to—"

But Nate cut her off. "I know I don't have to. I want to. That's what neighbors are for, remember?"

⌘

Thirty minutes later, the floor was finally dry. Violet pushed onto her heels and shoved her hair out of her eyes.

"I think that's good."

Nate looked up from where he was crouched by the washer. "Yeah, I think we got it all." He rocked his head from side to side. She knew the feeling. They'd been on their hands and knees way too long sopping up the water. She couldn't imagine how much longer it would have taken without his help.

"Thank you. I really had no idea who to ask for help."

"Well, I'm always right next door." Nate stood, reaching to massage his back. Violet had a sudden flash of rubbing Cade's back after he'd installed the washer years ago. Did Nate have the same firm muscles? Violet shoved the thought aside and pushed past Nate toward the kitchen.

She started sorting through Cade's stuff.

After a minute, Nate's footsteps shuffled behind her, but they stopped at the doorway.

"Thanks for helping me save all this. I should have taken it to the thrift store a long time ago, but—" She didn't trust herself to continue.

"You're welcome." Nate's voice was soft, and she risked a look over her shoulder, letting their eyes meet. Neither looked away for a heartbeat.

"Anyway." Nate cleared his throat. "It shouldn't be too big of a deal to replace that pipe and get you a new sink. I could do it tomorrow if you'd like."

Violet couldn't seem to get a read on this guy. How could the same person be so aloof and yet so open at the same time? She followed him to the laundry room to examine the broken pipe. Not that she had any idea what to look for.

Nate stepped out of her way and bent to scoop up the pile of wet towels.

"Oh, don't, you're going to get all—"

But it was too late. Nate had already hugged the mass to his body.

"Wet," she finished anyway, around a laugh.

"I don't think either of us can really get any wetter at this point." Nate gestured at her own sopping shorts.

"Yeah. Guess I'd better change before I head out for dinner at my friend's house." She passed him a laundry basket, and he dropped the towels into it.

A sudden thought struck her, but the words stuck in her throat. She knew her friends wouldn't mind. But she also knew they'd read way too much into it.

Still, Nate had saved her home. She owed him dinner at least. "Actually, why don't you come with me? As a thank you." She carefully avoided his eyes.

"That's okay. I was going to—"

"Eat a frozen dinner and watch TV with Tony," she finished for him. "Come on. My friend Dan makes these amazing burgers."

His eyes brightened, and she could tell he was wavering.

"Plus, Peyton usually brings something from the bakery."

He raised his arms in surrender. "When you put it that way, how can I resist?"

"That's what I thought." Violet grinned in triumph. "Change into something dry and meet me here in twenty minutes."

She led him to the door and leaned on it for a second after he left. Thank goodness he'd moved in. Eighty-year-old Mrs. D'Angelo would have been absolutely no help in a situation like this, bless her.

Violet pushed off the door and grabbed her phone on her way to change.

Dan answered on the first ring. "The burgers are almost ready. Where are you?"

Violet pulled a flower print skirt and a white sleeveless blouse out of her closet as she talked. "Sorry. Plumbing emergency."

"Oh no. Do you need help?"

Violet laughed. "Like you know anything about plumbing."

"I knew I never should have used my plumbing failure as a sermon illustration." Dan groaned. "I'm never going to hear the end of that, am I?"

"Not likely. But don't worry, your willingness to make a fool of yourself is what people love about you."

"Great." But Dan was laughing, too. "Anyway, I could have provided moral support."

"Thanks. I'm sure moral support would have stopped the water gushing all over my laundry room floor." Violet opened her makeup bag and started putting on a light layer. Normally, she wouldn't care about wearing makeup when she was just having dinner with her friends, but tonight felt different. "Don't worry about it. My new neighbor saved the day."

"The same new neighbor who rescued you when you fell? The guy's turning out to be a real hero." Dan's voice was half teasing.

"Yeah. I know." Violet tried to ignore the implication. "Anyway, I invited him to come tonight. You know, as a thank you. I get the feeling he doesn't get many home-cooked meals."

She broke off. What was she thinking, bringing a man who wasn't Cade to meet her friends? Even though she wasn't bringing him as a man. It was just as a thank you. But that wasn't how her friends would see it.

"Actually, you know what, forget it. I don't want to inconvenience you or—" She dropped her makeup brush into the bag.

"Violet, relax." Dan's gentle voice calmed her frayed nerves. "Of course he's welcome."

Violet let out a long exhale. "Okay." She wasn't sure that was what she wanted anymore. But there was really no way to uninvite him now.

# Chapter 12

Nate dug through the half dozen t-shirts he'd bought at the discount store the day after he'd moved in. None of them seemed right for meeting Violet's friends. He wasn't usually a polo shirt type of guy, but he'd bought one for the office. Maybe that would work.

He dragged a hand through his hair.

Why was he standing here wondering what to wear? It was just dinner with a bunch of strangers.

"Ah, Tony, what have I gotten myself into?" He grabbed the polo shirt off the hanger and pulled it over his head.

He wasn't sure why he'd agreed to go in the first place. He hadn't made new friends in years, and the thought of being around others was daunting.

But the thought of staying home with the dog to eat yet another frozen dinner was worse.

"Alright, boy, wish me luck." Nate put Tony in his kennel and passed him a treat. At the dog's mournful look, he passed him another. "I won't be gone long."

He ducked out of his apartment and knocked on Violet's door.

"Come in."

He had to take a calming breath before he opened the door, and he scolded himself. He was acting like a teenager on his first date, not a grown man going to have dinner with his neighbor and her friends.

He glanced around the apartment. Aside from her late husband's things scattered around the open surfaces, you'd never know the place had been a disaster twenty minutes ago.

In the kitchen, Violet had her head buried in her refrigerator. She seemed to be wrestling with something.

"You need some help?"

"Nope." Her voice was muffled. "Just grabbing this." She emerged with one arm wrapped around a large bowl that looked like it was about to plunge to the floor. "Well, maybe a little help."

He dashed across the room and scooped it out of her hand right as she lost her grip.

It smelled divine. "What is it?"

"Pasta salad. I made it last night."

He ogled her. "You made it? With one hand?"

She shrugged. "Once you learn to maneuver a knife right-handed, it's not so hard."

He shook his head. "Have you always been so—"

She watched him expectantly as he broke off. "So . . . ?"

He searched for a word. "Uh, determined?"

She laughed and pointed a finger at him. "That's not what you were going to say."

He let himself be pulled in. "No, but it was the safer thing to say."

She smacked his arm as she walked past him out the door. "Well, to answer your question, yes, I've always been so stubborn."

"Good to know."

He followed her to her car, trying not to notice how her white shirt highlighted her creamy skin and dark hair. Or how her floral scent drifted over him, fitting right into the summery evening.

He shook his head. What was the matter with him?

As she got into the driver's seat, he stowed the pasta salad in the back, then slipped into the passenger side.

"You can relax." Violet raised an eyebrow as she backed out of the parking spot. "Most of my friends don't eat people."

He let himself smile and eased his fisted hands open. "So, this friend of yours makes good hamburgers, huh?"

They kept the banter light as Violet navigated the city streets. Ten minutes later, she drove into the parking lot of a large church. There were three other cars in the lot, although the building itself was dark.

Nate's stomach tightened. What kind of bait and switch was this? "Your friend lives at a church?"

Violet pointed to a two-story brick house next door. "It's easier to park here."

"Ah." The tension in Nate's shoulders eased a little, but he still felt like a shock wave had gone through him. He hadn't been in a church since the night of the accident. And he didn't ever plan to step foot in one again.

Violet twisted to maneuver her arm awkwardly toward the bowl in the backseat, but he grabbed her wrist to stop her. "You really are stubborn, aren't you? I'll get it."

Her eyes moved to the spot where his fingers rested against her skin, and he lifted his hand. He took an extra second to grab the bowl as she stepped out of the car.

But finally he couldn't draw it out any longer, and he had to get out, too.

His stomach lurched as he stood. This was ridiculous. He'd spent the past seven years living with felons, for heaven's sake. How hard could it be to have dinner with a group of normal people, none of whom had probably been convicted of so much as a parking ticket.

And anyway, these people were strangers. To them, he was a blank slate, a person with no history.

Nate avoided looking toward the church as he followed Violet along the side of the house toward the backyard.

An amazing whiff of hamburgers rolled over Nate. He only hoped Violet couldn't hear his stomach rumbling.

As they neared the corner of the house, the sound of music reached his ears.

He recognized the song immediately as "Resurrection Power."

He'd rehearsed it a thousand times. And played it probably a hundred times on stage.

He did his best to tune it out.

The minute he rounded the corner into the backyard, he almost stopped short in his tracks. He'd expected a small group, maybe three or four people. But there had to be at least a dozen people seated around the patio, plates on their laps. A light-haired woman noticed them first, and before Nate knew what was happening, she'd run across the yard and thrown her arms around Violet.

Violet hugged her back, laughing and—was she crying, too? Nate watched in alarm. He had no idea what to do in this situation.

A dark-haired man walked up. "Don't worry about these two. They haven't seen each other in three weeks. There were bound to be some tears." He extended his hand to Nate. "I'm Spencer."

Nate shook the man's outstretched hand. "Nate."

The woman pulled out of Violet's arms and held out a hand to him, too, swiping at a tear under her lash line with her other hand. "I'm Sophie. I hear we have you to thank for keeping our Violet in one piece. And saving her from a flood."

Nate shook her hand but ducked his head.

Violet seemed to sense his discomfort. "Come on, I'll introduce you to everyone. Then we need some food. I don't know about you, but I'm starving."

They walked closer to the patio, where everyone was talking and laughing and eating. It was such a normal scene. Like the family get-togethers his parents used to host for his birthday every year. A quiet longing took up residence behind his eyes, and he looked toward the table to clear it. A spread of food covered every surface.

"Hey, everyone." Violet's back was to him, but Nate could hear the smile in her voice, and it made him smile, too. "This is Nate. My neighbor."

The conversation stopped abruptly as Violet's friends swiveled toward him.

He tried to hold onto the smile, but his mouth had gone dry.

"Hi," he managed to croak, lifting his hand a few inches in a lame imitation of a wave.

The man at the grill set his spatula down and approached Nate, holding out a hand. "I'm Dan. It's nice to meet you." Nate shook his hand, grateful for the ease with which the man accepted a stranger to his house.

"And this is the group." Violet lifted an arm to gesture at the rest of the people there. "Ethan and Ariana." She pointed to a couple seated together on a stone bench, then to another couple seated at a small bistro table. "And Jared and Peyton."

"The cookie maker?"

They all laughed, and Nate relaxed a tad.

"The one and only." Peyton offered a warm smile. "Hope you liked them. It was the least we could do after you rescued Violet like that."

Nate dug his sandal into a crack between two patio stones. "It was no big deal." These people had to stop treating him like some kind of hero.

"And—" Violet turned toward a small group on scattered lounge chairs. "Emma, Tyler, and Leah."

He stared at the last woman. For some reason, she seemed familiar.

"We've met." The woman jumped up from her chair and came to stand next to him as if they were old friends. "Nate was my seatmate on the bus ride back from visiting my friend in Sibley."

Nate winced. Would they make the connection to the state penitentiary in Sibley?

"Actually, I was showing him pictures of your wedding." She turned to Sophie. "I think he said you looked enchanting."

Nate did a double take. He didn't particularly remember saying anything about the wedding one way or another. And if he'd said Sophie looked enchanting, he was probably being sarcastic, since he'd had no interest in hearing about some stranger's wedding. But Leah seemed completely sincere.

"It looked like a lovely wedding," he finally managed to get out. He shuffled awkwardly from foot to foot.

"Well, eat up, you guys." Dan passed him a plate, and Nate spent the next few minutes concentrating on loading it with two hamburgers, Violet's pasta salad, homemade fries, and a pile of fruits and veggies.

Violet surveyed his heaping plate. "I guess it *has* been a while since you've had a decent meal." Her laugh sparkled across the backyard.

Nate grinned back. It didn't matter how awkward this night got. It had been worth coming just for the food. "I'd take more if my plate weren't already overflowing."

He followed Violet to two empty chairs right in the middle of the others. As soon as they were seated, Violet set her plate down and folded her hands in her lap, eyes closed. Nate watched her for a second, then pretended not to notice what she was doing. If she wanted to thank a God who didn't listen, that was her business.

He took a giant bite of hamburger. The flavor popped on his tongue, and he couldn't help the "Mmm" that came out.

Next to him, Violet opened her eyes and laughed, then took her own giant bite. "Thank goodness. I was bragging up your burgers, Dan, and you lived up to the hype. Didn't he?" Her elbow bumped at Nate's side. He just nodded. His mouth was too full of his next bite. He couldn't remember the last time he'd had an actual meal like this.

Nate listened to the conversation jumping around him, simply enjoying the sounds of their interaction. He appreciated that no one was giving him the third degree. They simply let him eat, occasionally including him in their conversation as they told stories about their week but not demanding anything from him.

When his plate was finally empty, Peyton passed him a cookie and offered to take his plate. As she reached for it, she whispered to Violet, "You were right," and winked.

Violet swatted at her, but a light blush crept up her neck to her cheeks, and Nate got the impression that whatever she had been right about had to do with him. It warmed him in a way he hadn't expected.

"So, Nate." Dan settled onto a chair across from him. "You're from Sibley?"

The food in his stomach congealed at the question. He was going to have to step carefully here. "Not originally. I grew up in Wescott, which is about an hour west of Sibley."

"I love the western part of the state. All those bluffs and valleys along the river."

"Yeah." Nate didn't know what else to say. He longed to go home to see his mom and sister, but other than that, the area had no appeal for him anymore. He shoved the last of his cookie into his mouth, hoping Dan didn't have any more questions for him.

"So what brought you to Hope Springs?" Dan's voice was entirely friendly, without a hit of suspicion.

"My father owns a large investment firm. They bought out a property management place here, and he wanted me to get things up and running."

"I work with my dad, too. Just started recently. It's nice, isn't it?" Dan looked thoughtful. "Though it is a bit of an adjustment."

Nate almost snorted, but he managed to force a short nod instead. Adjustment was an understatement.

"How long have you worked with your dad? Got any advice on how to make it easier?"

This time he did snort. "I'm the last person who could give you advice. I've only been working for my dad a couple weeks, and I'm not sure how I'll survive much longer."

Dan nodded, his expression thoughtful. "Well, I'll let you know if I figure anything out."

Nate thought Dan would get up then, but he settled farther into his chair. "So what'd you do before you worked for your dad?"

Nate grabbed his water bottle and took a long swig to buy time. He scrambled to come up with a lie. Any lie. This was why he didn't go out, didn't talk to people. Eventually, people weren't content to let you be a stranger without a history anymore. They wanted to know about your past—and they didn't care if you didn't want to tell about it.

When he couldn't come up with a convincing lie, he settled on a half-truth. "A little bit of everything." He'd taken his rotation in the laundry room, kitchen, and other duties. Not that he'd had a choice.

"Okay, everyone." Sophie stood, and everyone's attention swung to her. "I have honeymoon pictures. Let's go inside, and I'll show them on Dan's TV."

Nate let out a relieved breath. He may not have any desire to see honeymoon pictures from two people he'd just met, but if it got him out of talking about his own past, he was all for it.

They all stood and grabbed platters and dishes off the table. Nate shooed Violet away from the table, taking the bowl of pasta salad out of her hands. Didn't the woman know how to take a break?

The smile she gave him was almost enough to make him wish she'd pick up something else, so he could take that for her, too.

He followed the others inside and set the food on the counter.

Then they all moved into the living room. Nate took a place next to Violet on the worn plaid sofa, careful not to look at her. He couldn't allow himself the luxury of basking in her smiles.

A few seconds later, images of Rome and Venice and Florence were flashing across the TV screen. Sophie and Spencer took turns telling them about the sights and the food and the gondola captain who had misunderstood Sophie's name and called her Soapy the whole ride.

Nate joined the others' laughter. They seemed like a fun group. A kind and welcoming group, when he deserved anything but.

Next to him, Violet shifted. Her face, which had been carefree and animated outside, was now strained and pale. Her cheeks were drawn in, as if she was biting them, and she stared at her hands in her lap as she rubbed at her bare ring finger. Nate wanted to reach over and squeeze her arm, ask her what was wrong. He sat on his hands instead.

"Excuse me." Violet stood and rushed past him, raising a hand to her eyes as she bolted for the hallway.

# Chapter 13

Water blasted from the bathroom sink, and Violet cupped her shaking hands under the flow, splashing the water onto her face. The cold felt like a million scalpels slicing at her, but she didn't care.

She splashed herself with another handful.

What was wrong with her? She should be happy for her friends. She *was* happy for them.

They'd had a lovely wedding and a lovely honeymoon, and now they were starting on their lovely life together.

A life that Violet would never know.

She forced herself to take a few deep breaths, to get herself under control.

She repeated the verse that had sustained her through the past three years: "The Lord is my rock, my fortress and my deliverer; my God is my rock, in whom I take refuge." God was her refuge. Her strength was in him, no matter what she lost in this life. She let the reminder wash over her, willed it to seep into her heart.

After a few minutes, she examined the damage she had done to her makeup. Most of it was gone, though she had to wipe away a small smudge of mascara. Then, steeling her shoulders and painting a smile on her lips, she strode to the living room.

Nate half stood as she reappeared, remaining like that until she had taken her place next to him on the couch again. He slid closer to her as he sat, so that his arm brushed against hers. His nearness was nice. She felt like he was offering her some of his strength.

"You okay?" He said it so close to her ear that she could feel the whisper of his breath on her hair. At her nod, the tension in his shoulders eased.

When Spencer and Sophie had reached the end of their photos, Dan stood. "Okay, well, guys' turn to do dishes tonight." The other guys groaned.

Spencer threw a pillow at Dan. "You know they wouldn't have remembered if you didn't say anything."

"You wanted me to lie?" Dan blinked innocently at Spencer.

"Not lie. Conceal the truth." But Spencer was already heading for the kitchen.

"That's the same thing, just for future reference," Sophie called after him.

Oh, that banter. How she missed that with Cade.

Nate pushed to his feet as the other men stood.

Violet grabbed his arm. "You don't have to help them."

Nate smiled down at her. "Well, technically, I'm a guy, so I think I do." He winked and was gone, leaving her suddenly breathless.

Sophie leaned toward her the moment Nate was in the kitchen. "So, he's cute."

"Shh." Violet smacked her friend's arm.

"You should ask him out." Sophie had never been one to mince words.

"What?" Violet waved a hand as if the thought had never occurred to her. "I'm not interested in him like that. He's just my neighbor."

"Okay. Then you ask him out, Leah." She kept her eyes on Violet as she said it.

Violet's chest tightened, but she knew what Sophie was doing. She turned to Leah. "You should." Actually, now that she thought about it, she realized how stupid she'd been not to realize it earlier. Of course her beautiful friend would be a perfect fit for Nate.

Leah shook her head. "Not interested."

The tightness in Violet's chest eased, which made no sense. She didn't want to go out with Nate. So why did the thought of Leah going out with him bother her?

She glanced over her shoulder to see how he was doing with the other guys in the kitchen. Jared was regaling Nate with a story of some crazy incident or another, and Nate looked more relaxed than she had seen him since they'd met. As she stared, he looked up and caught her eye. Before she could think how to respond, she realized her face had been overtaken by a goofy grin. She raised a hand to wave at him, ignoring the way her friends nudged each other.

"So anyway—" It was long past time for a subject change. She turned to Peyton. "Are you and Jared getting excited for your big day?" Next Valentine's Day, she'd watch two more of her friends move on with their lives while hers stayed still.

They talked wedding plans for the next twenty minutes, until a resounding "Done!" echoed from the kitchen. The men stood in a circle, their arms above their heads as if they'd just had a team huddle.

"If dish washing were a sport," Sophie called, "you guys would get the medal for world's slowest washers."

Spencer plopped onto the couch next to his wife. "And here I was going to offer to do the dishes at home for the rest of our life. But if you think I'm too slow . . ." He rubbed a hand absently up and down her back.

Sophie leaned into him. "I don't care how long it takes you. If you actually do that, you will be the best husband the world has ever known."

Spencer raised an eyebrow. "*If* I do it? You know I'd do anything for you."

Violet looked away as he leaned over to drop a kiss on the top of his wife's head. The ache to have that again was growing in monstrous proportions right now.

Dan looked around at the group, then clapped his hands once. "You a Star Wars fan, Nate?"

Everyone else groaned.

Violet better warn Nate before it was too late. "Don't say yes—"

"Of course." Nate shot her a questioning look.

"Oh no, now you're doomed," Leah called from across the room. They'd all been obliged to listen to the minute details of every piece of Dan's Star Wars memorabilia more than once.

"Trust me, man, you don't want to get sucked into that," Spencer called to Nate. "Dan is the epitome of a Star Wars geek."

Nate laughed. "That's okay. I'm a closet Star Wars geek, too." He smiled at Violet. "Unless you wanted to get going?"

Violet shook her head. "Take your time. I'm exactly where I want to be." She settled back on the couch and raised her feet to rest them on the coffee table, watching out of the corner of her eye as Nate disappeared up the stairs behind Dan.

"I like him." Like his wife, Spencer was nothing if not straightforward.

Violet refused to look at either of them. She knew they were both staring at her, waiting for her to say that this was the guy she'd been waiting for and now her heart was healed, and she'd live happily ever after. But that wasn't how it worked.

Nate passed the scale model of the Star Destroyer back to Dan. He had to hand it to the guy, he sure had an extensive collection of Star Wars memorabilia. He was like a walking encyclopedia of the entire Star Wars empire. Not that Nate minded. Dan had a laid-back manner that made him easy to listen to. And he didn't demand that Nate reveal anything about himself.

It wasn't until Dan yawned that Nate realized it must be getting late. The Death Star clock over the door confirmed it was already midnight.

"Oh man, I'm sorry. I've way overstayed my welcome."

Dan gave him an easy smile. "Not at all. Just got up early today for a meeting." He set the TIE Fighter on his shelf, next to a bobble head of Boba Fett. "Violet is probably worried that I've bored you to death by now, though."

Nate followed Dan toward the door of the extra bedroom that served as his Star Wars room.

At the door, Dan stopped, looking thoughtful. "It's probably not my place to say, but Violet's been through a lot the last couple years."

"Yeah, I've gathered that." Nate waited for Dan to step through the doorway, but Dan remained planted, as if he had more to say.

"It's just— She's still fragile." Dan rubbed a hand down his face. "Just be careful with her."

Nate stared at him. Be careful with her? What did Dan think he was going to do, throw her off a roof?

And then he realized.

"Oh—um—no." Heat rose to his cheeks. "It's not like that. We're just neighbors. I think she invited me tonight because she felt sorry for me, to be honest."

Dan bobbed his head up and down slowly and gave him a searching look.

Nate adjusted his stance, trying to find somewhere else to direct his eyes. "Anyway, thanks for dinner and for showing me your collection." He sounded oddly formal, but he had no idea how else to react.

"Yeah, of course. I hope you'll join us again in the future."

Nate followed Dan down the hallway. He'd have to be careful if he'd given Violet's friends the impression he saw her as anything more than a neighbor. He didn't want to give her the idea that he wanted more.

The only problem was, he wasn't sure how to keep from giving himself that impression. Especially when his heart lightened three pounds when he walked into the living room and his eyes fell on her. She was leaning her head back on the couch, eyes closed.

Spencer and Sophie were the only others still there.

Sophie waved at him.

"Is she asleep?" he whispered.

"No, she's not," Violet fake whispered from the couch, a smile tickling her lips.

Nate felt the smile lift his own lips. "Sorry it's so late. Dan's collection is pretty—"

"Extensive?"

"Boring?"

"Lame?"

The other three all chimed in at once.

Dan stuck his tongue out at them.

"I was going to say impressive," Nate said.

"Oh, don't encourage him." Violet groaned and stretched. "Ready to go?"

He held out a hand to help her up, telling himself it was only the neighborly thing to do. Judging by the look on Sophie's face, she wouldn't have bought his excuse.

But, then, neither did he.

He pulled his hand back and shoved it in his pocket before Violet could reach for it.

Dan was right. He had to be careful. Violet was fragile, and he was the last person who deserved a woman like her.

Dan and Spencer held out their hands, and Nate shook them. He was about to move toward the door when Sophie reached out with open arms. Nate hesitated, then leaned in for her hug. He couldn't remember the last time anyone had hugged him, and he blinked away sudden moisture.

Even without really knowing him, these people were offering him their food, their conversation, their friendship.

If they did know him—if they knew what he'd done—would they take it all back? Would they abandon him just like everyone else in his life had?

Nate wasn't sure. He sensed something different about these people and the friendship they offered. But he wasn't about to take any chances by letting himself get close to them.

Violet's eyes slid to Nate for the umpteenth time. They were only a few blocks from home, and he'd barely said three words since they'd gotten in the car, except to say that her friends were nice and she'd been right about Dan's burgers.

He'd seemed so open and relaxed at Dan's, but now his shoulders were stiff, his jaw set. Had she done something to upset him?

But that was ridiculous. They were just neighbors. He didn't know her well enough to be upset with her.

He was probably tired. Goodness knew he wasn't the only one.

She let out an involuntary sigh. She had enjoyed the night with her friends, even if seeing pictures of Sophie and Spencer's honeymoon had dragged her back to memories of her own honeymoon. A honeymoon she had to remember alone.

She felt Nate's gaze slip to her. She swallowed but kept her eyes forward. If he was ready to talk, she didn't want to scare him off.

After a second, he looked away again.

Violet's shoulders sagged. He wasn't going to talk after all.

But his voice reached for her, quiet. "Everything okay?"

Violet turned her head toward him in surprise. His eyes were right on her. She turned back to the road, but not before a surge of something unidentifiable swept through her.

"Of course. Why wouldn't it be?"

"I don't know." Nate drummed his fingers on the car door. "You seem sort of . . ."

"Sort of?" Violet prodded. "Are you going to call me stubborn again?"

Nate laughed—a gentle laugh his heart wasn't really in. "No. I was thinking you seemed wistful, I guess."

"Huh." Now that he put a label to it, Violet realized that wistful was exactly how she felt. But she wasn't sure what she was wistful for. Cade, of course, but she thought it was more than that this time. The life they had—the life she had lost. She hadn't only lost a husband when Cade died; she'd lost their life together. She'd lost a piece of herself.

But a familiar stirring deep in her soul told her it was still there, buried. Even if she wasn't sure how to get to it.

"Sorry. It's none of my business." Nate clasped his hands in his lap and resumed staring out his window.

"No. It's not that." Violet lifted a hand toward him but pulled it back before making contact. In the confines of the car she was suddenly aware of how close they were to each other. "It's just, I couldn't really put a word to it, and I think you nailed it."

Nate gave her a slow smile. But there was a layer of sadness behind it, too. Violet wanted to know what had caused it, but she was afraid to ask.

He turned away as she pulled into the driveway. They walked up the stairs in silence, then stood on the landing, an unspoken energy pulsing between them.

"You were a hit tonight." She set a hand lightly on his arm. "You're welcome to join us again anytime."

"Thanks."

Violet couldn't take her focus off the way his lip quirked up on one side when he spoke. She resisted the urge to step closer to him.

Wild barking broke out from behind Nate's door, and that weird energy dissipated. They both laughed.

"I guess Tony knows you're home."

"I guess so." Nate took a step backward. "I had a nice time tonight."

He turned and disappeared into his apartment.

"Me, too," she whispered.

# Chapter 14

Violet hummed along to the radio, her window open to soak up the warm breeze on her way home from church. The humidity had finally broken, and the day was actually comfortable. It'd be the perfect day to spend outdoors.

On days like this, she and Cade used to explore the various tourist attractions on the peninsula that locals so often took for granted. Her favorite was always the Old Lighthouse. The combination of the aged logbook, the smell of weathered wood, and the view across the lake to the spot where it disappeared into nothingness had always stirred her soul.

An odd restlessness wrapped around her. She wanted to go to the lighthouse. She wanted to break out of this odd half existence she'd been living in for the past three years.

But she wasn't sure she was completely ready to do that. At least not on her own.

Her mouth pulled into a frown.

Maybe she'd stay home and curl up with a book.

As she turned onto Hope Street, she slowed, trying to figure out what she was seeing.

A man was walking down the sidewalk, holding what appeared to be a large sink.

An incredulous laugh escaped as she realized who it was and what he was doing.

She was still chuckling as she pulled up alongside him and rolled down the passenger side window. "Nate!"

He looked over in surprise, but his face broke into a smile the moment he saw her.

Her heart jumped, and she told herself it was only because he'd surprised her. So what if she'd begun to suspect there was more to it than that? She wasn't brave enough to examine what it might be.

"Why are you carrying that sink down the street?" She tried to stop the laughter, but she couldn't get it under control. He made the most ridiculous sight she had seen in she didn't know how long.

"Well, I tried to get it to walk itself, but it's not quite as obedient as Tony. Which is saying something." His laugh made her heart do another flip.

"Where did you get it?"

He gave her an odd look. "There's more than one place to get a utility sink in Hope Springs?"

He had a point. But the hardware store was almost a mile away. Had he really carried the huge sink that far just for her?

"Get in. I'll give you a ride the rest of the way."

"Oh, sure. The last three blocks are the hardest."

"Have it your way." She eased down on the gas pedal, watching with satisfaction as he jogged to keep up.

"I'm kidding. I'd love a ride the rest of the way."

She pulled over and waited for him to stash the sink in the trunk and jump into the car.

A slight sheen of sweat shone on his arm as it came to rest on the console between them.

He glanced over at her. "You look nice."

She focused on the road, telling herself it was the warm day that made her suddenly hot. "Thanks. I'm just on my way home from church." She bit her lip. She'd only said it to explain why she was more dressed up than usual, but he'd made it perfectly clear how he felt about church.

He brushed over the comment. "I can install this right away. Unless you have other plans?"

"No, that's fine. I was thinking about going to the Old Lighthouse today, but . . ." The thought of going alone still hung heavy on her heart. "Anyway, I'll just stay home."

"I don't want to change your plans. You go. I can do this while you're gone. You won't be much help with a broken arm, anyway."

She faked a huff at that. "That settles it, I'm staying to prove you're wrong."

But he wasn't wrong, she quickly discovered. There wasn't much she could do with one hand, aside from pass him tools every once in a while. And even then, he only asked her to pass them to give her something to do.

Eventually, she wandered into the living room, where Cade's stuff was still scattered. For some reason, the thought of re-boxing it didn't hurt as much this time. She ran downstairs to grab some new boxes, then started repacking everything.

She'd take it all to the thrift store tomorrow, when her store was closed. She wasn't sure she was completely ready yet. But ready or not, it was time.

After she'd finished packing the boxes, she pulled out her phone. She might as well get her weekly call to her sister out of the way. With a sigh, she tapped Jade's number.

She counted the rings. After eight, Jade's voice mail kicked in, just as Violet had known it would. Just as it had every week for the past six years. Ever since Mom had died and Jade had taken off for L.A.

A beep sounded from the other end of the line, and Violet began to leave the same message as always. "Hey, Jade, it's your sister." But then, instead of the usual "give me a call sometime," she let out what she really wanted to tell Jade. "I just called to say that I miss you, and you're the last family I have, and I really don't think it's fair the way you've pushed me out of your life. I know we both said some things after Mom died, but it's been six years. I think it might be time to talk again."

She yanked the phone away from her ear and dropped it on the coffee table. Her hands were shaking, and she sank to the couch. Had she really done that?

What if something happened and those were the last words she ever said to her sister? Angry words. Just like the last words she'd said to Cade.

Violet reached for her phone. She had to call Jade back and apologize.

"I think that should do it." Nate was drying his hands on his shorts as he stepped into the living room, but the moment he saw her, he stopped. "You okay?"

"Yeah. No." She set the phone down. "I don't know."

He moved closer and perched on the arm of the couch. Only a few inches separated the top of his leg and her shoulder. She stared at the scar on his knee. How had she never noticed that before? It was white and cut a jagged line from the outside to the inside of his leg.

"Want to talk about it?"

She shook her head. "It's just my sister. She's been ignoring my phone calls for six years. I'm not sure why I thought today would be any different."

His hand squeezed her shoulder, and she lifted her head. His eyes, normally so guarded, reflected an understanding that shook her. She looked away.

"Anyway, I didn't mean to get angry and leave a message like that."

Nate snorted, and she glared at him. He thought it was funny?

"Sorry. It's just—" He gestured to the phone. "You call that angry? That was about the sweetest message I've ever heard."

Violet chewed her cheek, considering. It's not like she'd yelled at her sister. But still— "I told her I didn't think she was being fair."

"Well, *do* you think she's being unfair?"

Violet nodded. So unfair. She could admit she should have been more supportive when Jade had said she wanted to pursue a career in acting. But they had literally just buried their mother, and Jade's desire to act had come out of nowhere. Violet had wanted her to slow down and deal with what had happened before she made any major life decisions. And, fine, maybe she had been a little selfish, too. She hadn't wanted Jade to leave her.

But Jade hadn't cared about any of that. She'd packed a suitcase, taken her share of Mom's inheritance, and skipped town on the first flight out.

And she hadn't looked back once.

Nate stood, and she tried not to regret the separation. "Telling people the truth isn't the same as lashing out in anger. Your sister will recognize that. Maybe it's what she needed to hear. You never know, she might be getting ready to call you right this second."

Yeah, Violet wouldn't hold her breath.

But she set the phone down. She could always leave another message later.

She blew a stray piece of hair off her face. "Anyway, how's the sink coming?"

"Come see."

But her eyes were locked on the hand he held out to her. Did he really want her to take it? Did she want to?

As if he'd just realized what he was doing, he jerked it back and shoved it into his pocket.

She followed him down the hallway, leaving plenty of space between them. But she couldn't shake the question: what would it have felt like to hold his hand? Was his rough and calloused like Cade's or smooth and unblemished? Would her hand disappear into his, or would it be just the right size?

There was no way to keep her distance in the cramped laundry room, and she caught a whiff of that mint and lemon scent she was beginning to recognize him by.

"Voilà. Good as new." Nate held out his hands to the sink as if he'd performed a magic trick.

Which he may have. You would never know that just yesterday this place was a disaster. And the new sink was nicer than the crusty old one that had been in here before.

"It looks great. Just let me know how much I owe you."

Nate blinked at her. "Owe me?"

She gestured at his handiwork. "You know, for the sink. And for your time."

"You don't owe me anything. I'm the landlord. This is my job."

"Oh." Violet didn't know why that should disappoint her. She should have realized that he would have done the same thing for any of his tenants. It's not like he'd singled her out for special treatment.

"I also noticed a crack in the wall over here, so I patched it up with some joint compound." He slipped past her to move to the spot where a crack used to run from the top corner of the hallway almost to the floor. It had been there when they moved in, and Violet had long since stopped noticing it.

She stepped closer to examine the spot. The wall was smooth now, although slightly discolored from the wet compound.

Violet squinted at it, trying to detect any hint of the crack that had marred it only this morning. Surely no wound could be covered up so completely. But the wall was totally smooth.

If only it were that easy to patch the cracks in her heart. There wasn't enough joint compound in the world. And yet, she had to admit that since Nate had moved in next door, the cracks were getting a little duller around the edges.

"Thank you. That was very kind of you."

He held up a hand. "Oh, I didn't do it for free."

She raised an eyebrow. "I thought you were my landlord and that was your job."

"Well, this was extra."

"And how much will it cost me?" She couldn't fight down the smile that kept creeping to her lips. The glint in his eyes was too inviting.

"It will cost you one trip to the Old Lighthouse."

"Oh." Violet let out a long breath. She hadn't wanted to go to the lighthouse alone. But did she want to go with Nate?

Something in her gut jumped, and she realized—she did.

"It's a deal." She held out her hand and shook his, trying not to notice that hers fit perfectly into it after all.

# Chapter 15

The narrow spiraling stairway creaked under his weight, and Nate winced. Violet had told him the lighthouse was more than one hundred and fifty years old, and if he had to guess, the stairs were original to the place.

"You're sure people are supposed to go up here?" Seemed like a lawsuit waiting to happen to him.

But Violet grinned down at him from four steps above. "You're not afraid of heights, are you?"

"No, but—" He kept climbing, until he was on the step below her. They were eye to eye now, and the openness in her dark eyes made him completely forget what he was going to say.

"Come on." She turned to keep climbing. "We're almost to the top."

He made himself keep moving. He had to snap out of it. Obviously she didn't feel whatever it was that jolted him every time he looked at her. He shouldn't have invited himself along in the first place. He'd sensed her hesitation when she'd agreed to bring him. She'd only gone along with it because she thought she owed it to him after he'd worked on her apartment.

"This is it," Violet called over her shoulder as she disappeared on a platform at the top of the steep stairway. A couple seconds later, Nate emerged onto a wide landing. The floor was bare wood, and the walls were aged-looking concrete.

Violet stood in the middle of the space, looking straight up. Nate had to stop a moment to take in the expression of sheer awe on her face.

"Come here." She kept her head tilted back, the gentle curve of her neck bobbing with her words. "Check out this light."

Nate sidled closer, forcing his eyes off her and onto the light fixture. He had to admit it was impressive. Especially when he considered how long it had stood the test of time.

After a few seconds, Violet grabbed his arm and tugged him toward a narrow open door. "You have to see the best part yet."

She let go of him as she stepped through the doorway and moved immediately to the edge of the observation platform, letting her good hand rest lightly on the railing there.

Nate gave the platform a hard stare. If you asked him, it looked ready to collapse any second.

Violet turned toward him. It was windier up here than it had been on the ground, and her hair blew in wild tendrils around her face. But it was her smile that caught him off guard. It was warm and open but also sort of private, as if it were just for him.

"Come on." She held a hand out toward him. "It's beautiful out here."

*Yes, it is.*

Nate shook himself. He had to stop thinking like that. So what if Violet was beautiful? So what if his heart felt a strange contentment every time he was near her? That didn't mean he had a right to act on his feelings.

He would have to close off his heart. He'd gotten good at doing that over the past seven years anyway. It had been the only way he could survive.

Ignoring her hand, he stepped onto the observation deck. He followed it all the way around the circumference of the lighthouse, as much to get his heart under control as to take in the view.

And the view was spectacular.

The lighthouse was perched on a bluff above the lake, amplifying the building's height. On the inland side, the view stretched out across the surrounding countryside, over the tops of acres and acres of trees.

But it was the lake side that drew his attention. Half a dozen sailboats bobbed on the waves at varying distances from the shore. Farther out, larger ships stacked with cargo containers worked their way toward the port to the south.

Nate squinted toward the horizon, trying to make out the far shore. But the water disappeared into the sky.

Something about the lake pulled at Nate, and he moved closer to the railing, until he was standing next to Violet.

"Pretty amazing, isn't it?" She was staring straight down to the spot where the surf crashed against the rocks that jutted into the water. The boulders had been worn smooth over time. She had that wistful expression again.

"Do you come here often?"

She gripped the railing, lifting her head to peer toward the horizon. "I used to. With Cade. I actually haven't been here since he died."

"Oh, I'm sorry, I shouldn't have presumed . . . If I had known—" What an idiot. He'd invited himself along on a trip to a place that was sacred to her and her husband. No wonder she'd hesitated. "I didn't mean to—"

But she laid a hand on his arm. "I'm glad you did. I don't think I would have had the strength to come alone. And I've missed this place."

She swiveled toward the lake again but kept her hand on his arm. He should move, but he couldn't make himself do it. If being here with him was any comfort to her, then he wasn't going to take that away.

*She probably wouldn't be as comforted if she knew the monster you really are.*

Nate shoved the thought deep under everything else. Now was not the time to tell her.

"So what's that island?" He pointed to the north, where he could faintly make out an island about a mile off shore.

"That's Strawberry Island. It has a great beach and some shops and stuff. It's a sweet little place. We should go sometime."

Nate froze. Had she said *we*?

But he knew she had. It was why his heart rate had tripled and his mouth had gone dry.

He allowed himself a glance at her out of the corner of his eye. Her head was turned toward him, as if she were studying him. He wondered what she saw when she looked at him.

Whatever it was, it wasn't the real him. Or at least not all of him.

He should put this to a stop before it started.

*It's already started.*

Well, then, before it went any further.

Getting into a relationship with her would mean having to let her see the real him eventually. And he couldn't handle that.

Neither could she.

He turned toward her. "Violet, I—"

But the look in her eyes stopped him. For the first time since he'd met her, he didn't see that hint of sadness that always lingered there. Instead, her eyes were filled with a new brightness that he couldn't bear to destroy. Not today.

"Yes?"

He swallowed. "I just wanted to say—" His eyes darted to the water and back to hers. "Thanks for bringing me here."

"You're welcome." Her words were a whisper, barely louder than the wind, and she took half a step closer.

Nate couldn't take his eyes off hers.

A bang from behind made them both jump. A young boy emerged onto the lighthouse deck, followed by an even younger boy, an older girl, and two harried looking adults.

"Talon, do not climb the railing," the woman yelled, darting across the deck to pluck the smallest boy off the bottom rung of the railing.

Violet laughed lightly. "I think that might be our cue to leave."

Nate nodded, swallowing his disappointment, and followed her to the door.

# Chapter 16

Nate laughed at himself. Was he really whistling on the way to work?

His heart was lighter than it had been in years. And it was all thanks to a certain dark-haired neighbor. In the nearly two weeks since he'd gone with her to the lighthouse, they'd talked almost every day. Sometimes just a word or two on the landing, but more and more often, he stopped by her store after work or they walked Tony together.

Instead of dreading the days now, he woke up looking forward to them because they meant he might get at least a few moments with her.

Nate hated to admit how much he had come to cherish those moments. He wasn't supposed to be allowing himself that pleasure. But he couldn't seem to resist. Every time he told himself it would be the last time, he found himself craving her company again. It wasn't only that she was attractive—though she certainly was.

But it was the way she listened to him, like what he said really mattered, even when they were only talking about the weather.

The way she always took the time to pet Tony.

The way she asked him to help her with things around the store.

For the first time in a long time, his life didn't feel meaningless. Talking to her, helping her, even in these small ways, had given him something he'd been missing for a long time—purpose.

"What's up with you?" Brandon was unlocking the door to the office building when Nate walked up.

"What do you mean what's up with me?"

"I mean you have the most bizarre look on your face."

Nate frowned. He and Brandon had talked a few times, and he liked the guy well enough. But that didn't mean he was about to spill his feelings to him. "Bizarre how?"

Brandon fell into step next to Nate as they climbed the staircase. "I don't know. You actually look . . . happy, I guess. For a change." He led the way up the stairs. "I mean, don't get me wrong. It's good to see. Just different."

"Of course I'm happy. It's Friday." Nate opened the door to his small office.

But Brandon didn't retreat to his own office. "No, it's not that." He slugged Nate's shoulder. "It's a girl, isn't it?"

"It's not—"

"Has to be." Brandon pointed both index fingers at Nate. "It's that blond who's stopped by a couple times, isn't it?"

Nate's mouth opened and then closed. He'd thought having Officer Jensen meet him here instead of at the apartment would lead to fewer awkward questions. Apparently he'd been wrong.

"She's a business associate." Nate stepped through his office door and closed it firmly.

"Ah, a business associate." Brandon's chuckle carried through the closed door.

Nate sighed. It wouldn't hurt anything to let Brandon think Officer Jensen was his girlfriend. It was better than him knowing who she really was.

Nate took a seat at the desk he'd moved in front of the office's small window. He'd just turned his computer on when his phone rang. He groaned. So much for his good mood.

"Benson Properties."

"My investor wants to take a look at one of our properties." Dad didn't bother with saying hello anymore. Apparently, Nate wasn't worth the effort.

"Which one?" Nate had learned that it was best to be just as abrupt as Dad. It hurt less that way.

"Six twelve Hope Street. Which I'm not seeing on this report you sent me. But he assures me it's one of ours."

Nate could have sworn he heard his heart hit the floor. Of course it wasn't on the list. He'd left it off on purpose. His throat went dry. "I'll have to look into that and get back to you. When does he want to see it?"

"Today." Dad's voice was flat, unapologetic about the last-minute assignment.

"Oh, I don't know if I'll be able—"

"This is your job, Nathan. When I tell you to make something happen, you make it happen."

"Well, I don't know if that property is available or—" The small lie would be worth it if it helped Violet.

"For the right price, any property is available. Look it up right now. What's its status?"

Nate turned to the computer, scrambling for a way to buy more time. He needed to talk to Violet. Give her a chance to catch up on her payments and renew her lease before Dad could pull it out from under her.

He pecked in the address, even though he already knew the status.

"I don't have all day, Nathan."

"Yeah. It's here. The lease expires in two months."

"Excellent. And they didn't exercise their option to renew?"

"No, but—"

"What about payments?"

Nate closed his eyes and pinched the top of his nose. "They're a little behind, but I think there might be extenuating circumstances—"

"Does the lease agreement make any allowance for extenuating circumstances?"

Nate wanted to punch the wall. Dad knew it didn't. "No."

"Good. Then we have no problems. My guy will meet you there in an hour. Don't drop the ball on this."

"I really think—"

"Look, Nate—" Dad's voice softened the slightest bit. "I've been happy with the work you've done so far. If you can make this investor happy, I'll think about arranging a time for you to see Mom and Kayla."

Nate opened his mouth. He should respond. But before he could, Dad hung up.

Nate stared at the phone a second, then slammed it down. Dad had no idea what he was asking Nate to do. Didn't Dad know it wasn't just buildings they were dealing with—it was people's lives? And this particular building involved the life of someone very special.

Nate shoved his chair back.

He'd already ruined the life of one person he loved. Why not another?

Not that he loved Violet. At least, he didn't think he did. But he did care about her, much as he'd tried not to. And if he wasn't mistaken, she'd started to care about him, too.

But that would come to an end the moment he told her what he had to do.

But he had to do it. There was no question about that.

He owed his first loyalty to Mom and Kayla.

And if that meant cutting off any future chance of happiness for himself, then he'd have to accept that.

He only wished Violet didn't have to get hurt in the process.

Violet jumped as the chime on the store's front door gave a violent jangle. What on earth? Customers didn't usually barrel into an antique shop so much as mosey in, sometimes lowering their voices as if they were in a library.

She set down the paint brush she'd been using to apply a new coat of varnish to a bookshelf and hurried to the sales floor.

A spontaneous smile lifted her lips the moment her eyes fell on Nate. She couldn't deny that the moments she'd spent with him lately had been some of the best she'd had in the past few weeks—the past few years, if she was being honest.

Violet moved toward him. "Hey, I was just thinking of you." Her face warmed. She shouldn't have said that. Even if it was true.

But at the look on his face, her smile wilted. "Nate? What is it? What's wrong?"

She wove through the Victorian living room setting she'd rearranged yesterday. He looked agitated and angry. She reached for his hand, but he pulled away.

She swallowed, trying not to take the movement personally.

"Do you have a minute?" The question was brusque and businesslike. Somehow between yesterday and today they'd gone from being friends to being just neighbors again.

She nodded stiffly and gestured to the curved-back Victorian loveseat. But Nate shook his head and took a seat on the stiff chair across from it. Violet lowered herself to the loveseat alone.

"My dad just called to tell me he has an investor interested in renting this property." He stared at the coffee table between them as he talked.

"But I'm renting this property." Obviously, he knew that, so why hadn't he just told that to his dad?

"I know. But your lease expires in two months."

Violet rubbed at her forehead. Was that right? Had five years really gone by since she and Cade had signed the lease on this place? "Okay, then I'll renew it."

Nate shook his head. "The guaranteed renewal option is expired. You would have had to sign that four months ago."

"What?" Violet jumped to her feet. What was he telling her? That he was going to kick her out of her own store? "I didn't know that. Isn't there something you can do?"

Nate raised his hands as if he were completely helpless. "I'm sorry. Maybe if you were current on your rent, I could make a case, but . . ."

A wave of shame swept over Violet. She'd never meant to let things get so far behind. But it had been so hard to keep things going these last few months. And her broken arm wasn't helping any.

The betrayal that rolled through her made her shudder. How could Nate have pretended to befriend her, to care about her, and then turn on her like this? Had that been his plan all along?

Tears built behind her eyes, and she turned away so Nate wouldn't see how he'd affected her.

"Hey." His voice was too close, and she took a step away, but his hands landed softly on her shoulders. Gently, he spun her toward him.

She blinked hard, but a traitor of a tear crept out and slipped down her cheek.

"This isn't what I want. You have to understand that." He bent his knees until his face was in her line of sight. She wanted to look away, but she couldn't make her head turn. He looked sincere.

She nodded once and pressed her lips together. It may not be what he wanted, but that didn't change anything.

"I'm going to do what I can to help, okay? But I can't make any promises."

She sniffed and nodded again. He watched her for a second, then took a step closer, sliding his arms around her. She stiffened as he pulled her in to him. But then her good arm lifted to wrap around him. She let herself lean into him, resting her head on his chest.

She'd almost forgotten what it felt like to be held like this.

His arms didn't feel the same as Cade's. They were slightly shorter. Slightly broader.

It should feel wrong to stand here in his embrace. But to her surprise, she didn't want him to let go.

"There's one more thing—" His voice was muffled as he spoke into her hair.

"What's that?" She was afraid to ask, and yet, with his arms around her, she was pretty sure she could handle anything.

"Apparently, the investor—"

But he broke off as the chime above the door clanged.

"Is here," he muttered as he let her go.

# Chapter 17

This was the investor Dad had found? The guy was dressed like a used car salesman and wore a smarmy grin Nate wanted to punch off his face. But he put on a neutral expression and held out his hand. If he played this right, he might be able to convince the guy to open his new venture—whatever it was—in another location.

"John Talmadge." The guy's hand was moist as it landed in Nate's.

Nate resisted the urge to wipe his palm on his pants. "I understand you're looking to lease a property from us."

"Not a property." Talmadge's voice was well-oiled. "This property."

Behind him, Nate heard Violet's sniffle, followed by her retreating footsteps. He didn't allow himself to look at her. "With all due respect, I always advise clients to consider all possible properties before settling on one." Not that he'd ever advised any other clients, but Talmadge didn't need to know that. "If I may ask, what kind of business are you planning to open?"

"A bar."

Nate opened his mouth, then slammed it shut. Dad really wanted to support a bar after a bar had taken so much from them?

Then again, it wasn't the bar's fault Nate hadn't stopped that night.

That was on him and only him.

"So can you?" That Talmadge guy was talking, and Nate realized he must have asked him a question.

He had to stop thinking about what he'd done in the past. The mistakes he'd made.

He had to focus on what he could do now. Before he made another mistake. There must be a way he could steer the guy toward a different property. "I think we have a couple other properties that might be a better fit. Let me put some things together for you, and I'll take you to see them next week."

Talmadge's smile hardened into an expression that said he was used to getting what he wanted. "You can show me some other properties. But I'm telling you right here and now that this is the one I want. And your father told me you would get it for me. I understand you have a lot riding on this."

Nate was sure his smile was just as hard and unyielding as Talmadge's. "Just keep an open mind. I'll get you exactly what you need."

"You won't mind if I take a look around as long as I'm here? In the interest of keeping an open mind." Talmadge smirked at him and pushed his way through the shop, shoving an old tricycle to the side.

Nate snatched at the handlebars to stop the tricycle before it crashed into a table of figurines.

He followed Talmadge into the workshop, where Violet had retreated. She was at the far end of the room, facing the shelves, though Nate doubted she was actually looking for anything. She kept her back to them as Talmadge pulled out a tape measure and ordered Nate to hold the end against the wall.

Nate stared at it a second, then grabbed it. No sense antagonizing the man. He had to keep on his good side if he was going to convince him to choose another location.

Talmadge paced to the other side of the room and leered as he read the measurement. "Perfect size for a kitchen."

Nate's eyes darted to Violet. Her good hand gripped the shelf above her head, the knuckles white.

"Let's see the upstairs." Talmadge reeled in the tape measure and started for the door into the hallway.

Nate couldn't help the gasp that escaped, but he quickly covered it with a cough. Talmadge wanted to take over the upstairs as well? That would leave Violet homeless.

Violet's head dropped to her arm. Nate longed to go to her and promise to make all this right. To make this go away.

But he wasn't sure that was a promise he could keep.

Instead, he followed Talmadge out the door and up the steps.

Ten minutes later, he finally ushered Talmadge out of the shop, less sure than ever that he'd be able to convince the guy to consider another location.

As soon as Talmadge was gone, Nate peered warily into the workshop. He couldn't blame Violet if he was the last person she wanted to see right now.

She was sanding a coffee table, her movements jerky and sharp. Her hair fell over her face, but he caught a glimpse of the tight lines around her mouth. He let himself indulge in watching her a moment longer, then cleared his throat.

She looked up. But instead of her usual room-brightening smile or even the hardened anger he expected, her face was completely blank.

He moved cautiously toward her. "I'm sorry about all of this. I really am. I'm going to try to steer him to another property."

Violet set down her sandpaper and marched toward the sink, swerving to make a wide arc around him.

His stomach dropped, but he slid around an old sewing machine table to meet her at the sink.

He touched the top of her hand, but she yanked it back as if he'd shocked her.

"Just don't." Her voice was as carefully flat as her expression. "I heard what that man said. You have a lot riding on this deal. So just do it and get it over with."

"Violet, I'm not—"

"I have work to do. You should go." She watched the floor as she slid past him toward the front of the store.

Nate stood there, torn between following her and doing as she'd asked. The chime above the front door jingled, and a second later, he heard Violet greeting her new customers cheerfully, in the same voice she'd greeted him with when he'd come in.

Maybe he'd been wrong to imagine she'd been glad to see him when he got here, that they'd started to develop a connection over the past couple of weeks. Obviously she showed that same warmth to everyone.

A soft chorus of laughter carried to him.

Nate nodded to himself.

Then he ducked out the back door.

# Chapter 18

Violet slammed her laptop screen shut.

What was the point anyway?

Nate was going to pull the store right out from under her, and there was nothing she could do about it.

The worst part was, she had let herself start to feel something for him, when she'd promised Cade that would never happen.

But it had been so nice not to be lonely for a change. She'd let herself get pulled in by Nate, with his brooding eyes and his smile that came easier and easier the more time they spent together.

But that had all been an act. She'd found out yesterday that the real Nate was a ruthless businessman who was willing to sell her out for whatever it was his dad was offering.

The door chimed, and she spun in her chair, pasting on a smile. Who knew when she might be helping the last person to ever walk through the doors of the store?

But her smile cracked the moment she saw him. "What do you want?" She congratulated herself on keeping her voice firm even as her heart pulsed against the restraints she'd put around it.

He crossed the store, not saying anything until he stood right in front of the counter. She kept her eyes on the wind chime that hung from the ceiling behind him.

"Look, I know you're upset—"

She clamped her mouth shut. Much as she wanted to yell and scream at him, ask him how he could betray her like this, she knew she never would.

"You have to believe me, Violet, I'm doing everything I can to make sure you can keep your store. But you're going to have to help me out."

She let her eyes skip to his for a second. The sincerity there shook her. It was just an act, too. It had to be. So she wouldn't fight back.

Well, he needn't have worried. After three years of fighting to keep this store going, she didn't have much fight left. The weariness that had lightened over the last couple weeks had cloaked her soul again, darker than ever.

She stood. "Do what you have to do Nate. I'm done." She wasn't sure if she meant with the store or with him.

It would have to be both.

"You can't give up." He came around the counter, holding a hand out in front of him as if she were a wild animal and he was afraid he'd spook her.

He stopped a few feet in front of her. "I went through your lease with a lawyer buddy of mine. We both think that if you caught up on your back rent by the time your lease expires, you'd have a case for renewal."

"You said I would have had to renew four months ago." She crossed her arms in front of her.

"I know." He scrubbed his hands over the scruff on his cheeks. "But we spent all night going through the lease line by line, and he found some unclear wording in the guaranteed renewal clause that he thinks a judge would find in your favor."

"You want me to hang the future of my store on 'unclear wording'?" She couldn't keep the sneer out of her voice. That was thin at best. So what if he said he'd spent all night going over her lease? It was just another ruse.

"It's not much to go on, I know. And it's not the only angle I'm working on. But it's something at least."

"And you want me to take your dad to court over this or what?"

"It won't come to that. My dad is a hard man, but he's fair. If we show him what the lease says, he'll uphold it." Nate's voice was stony. He didn't sound at all like an adoring son who wanted to please or impress his father.

"Do you think there's any way you could catch up on your back rent?" He said it gently, without accusation. "It looks like it's two months' worth."

"Plus this month's in a couple days." She knew it wasn't fair to be angry with him for asking. He was the landlord, after all, and she did owe the money. But it was so much. If the only way to keep the store was to pay it off within the next two months, she wasn't sure there was any hope.

He waited, watching her as if he really cared what she answered. Of course he did. He wanted his money before he shoved her out of here.

"Maybe—" He started pacing the small walkway between the counter and the Queen Anne dining set. "What about a loan from the bank?"

She shook her head. "I'm already maxed out on loans."

"Okay." He was still pacing, picking up speed. "What about family? Do you have anyone who might be willing to lend you some money?"

"I don't have any family anymore." She said it flatly. She couldn't afford to let emotion into this right now.

But he stopped pacing and gave her that soft look that usually melted her. "I'm sorry. I didn't know."

"You couldn't have." She worked to keep her hand from shaking as she waved off his sympathy. She couldn't let him touch her heart right now.

He looked hurt for a second, but then his usual shuttered expression fell into place. More pacing.

She wished he'd stop. He was making her dizzy.

After a few minutes, he snapped his fingers. "What if I found a buyer for the piano?"

Right. And why didn't she just start growing money on trees? Didn't he think she'd already scoured every nook and cranny in search of a buyer for that thing? If it ever actually sold, it would bring in enough money to pay her back rent and then some.

"Mint condition Bosendorfers aren't exactly in high demand in the Hope Springs area." She hoped her sarcasm would be enough to make him give up, but he shoved a hand through his hair, apparently thinking.

"I used to have some contacts in the music world. Let me call around and see if anyone knows someone who might be interested."

Violet opened her mouth. She should tell him she didn't need his help. Didn't want his help.

But he seemed sincere. And she didn't really have any other options. Not if she wanted to keep the store going for Cade.

"Okay." She finally managed to drag out an answer.

By the smile he gave her, you'd think she'd said he could buy a pony.

"Thank you for trusting me." He took a tentative step closer, and when she didn't move away, took another. "I can't promise I'll find a buyer, though. Do you have any other big-ticket items we might be able to sell more quickly?"

"We?"

"Yes, we. I'm going to help you through this, just like I said I would."

She watched him for another second, but she couldn't pick out anything besides sincerity in his expression. "Okay, then." She opened her laptop and clicked to the email she'd been looking at before he came in. The pictures of the huge mahogany and glass hutch were beautiful, and she knew she could sell it for a tidy profit if she purchased it, since the gentleman who had emailed her was asking for a more than reasonable price. With a little loving care, she could double her investment. But the seller was located more than two hundred miles away, on the other side of the state.

Since Cade's accident, she hadn't been able to convince herself to drive much farther than Sophie's house, a few miles outside the city.

Nate gave a low whistle. "That's a beauty."

Violet threw him a look over her shoulder. Now was not really the time for sarcasm.

But Nate leaned closer to the computer. "Look at those lines." He held up a finger to point to the curved edges of the piece. "And that whatever it's called." He pointed to the elaborate scrollwork at the top. "That takes some skill. Is that a good price?"

"Yeah." Violet scanned the email. "Really good, actually. I could probably sell it for double."

"Wow. Your problems are solved then. That's not nearly as specialized an item as the piano. There have to be plenty of people around here who would be interested."

Off the top of her head, Violet could think of three regular customers who would kill to get their hands on a piece like this. But it didn't matter. There was no way she could go pick it up. And if she arranged for a truck to deliver it, she might as well give it away for free, since shipping costs would eat any profit.

"How soon can you get it?" Nate's voice was lighter than before, as if he thought all her problems were solved.

Violet rubbed her temples. It wouldn't be that tough, would it? Just get in the car and drive. She'd done it a thousand times before Cade died. Why should now be any different?

But she shook her head. "I'm not."

"Why not?" Nate bent closer, his lemony clean scent overtaking her senses. "Is there something wrong with it?"

Again, she shook her head.

Behind her, Nate's scent weakened as she felt him move back and straighten.

Without warning, her chair spun to face him.

"Why not?" His hand was on the back of her chair, next to her shoulder.

"I can't." The words were almost a whisper.

Nate's brow creased. "This guy obviously wants to sell it to you. Look—" He leaned across her to scroll down to the bottom of the email. "See? He says he knows you'll be fair and find a good home for the piece. Your reputation must precede you."

To her chagrin, tears flooded her eyes. She tried to blink them back, but she was too slow.

"Whoa, hey." Nate crouched in front of her, resting his hands on the armrests of her chair.

Instead of feeling caged in, she felt protected, enclosed.

"What's wrong? You don't have to get the piece if you don't want to. I didn't mean to stick my nose in where it doesn't belong."

Violet attempted a laugh and quickly wiped her eyes. "You didn't do anything wrong." A shuddering breath wracked her frame. "Cade died in a car accident on his way back from picking up a piece. I haven't been able to drive more than a few miles out of town since then." To her own surprise, Violet didn't experience the wave of embarrassment that usually accompanied the admission. Even Sophie thought it was odd that she never left the city. But Nate simply nodded, his eyes registering a sort of kinship.

He let out a breath and stood slowly, giving her space. Instead of relief, Violet was overwhelmed by a sudden emptiness. She was all alone.

"What if I went with you?" Nate's eyes remained steady on hers.

"What?" Violet tried to make sense of his offer.

"I'll go with you." He said it with more certainty this time, not demanding, more like reassuring.

Violet shook her head. "I'd have to go tomorrow afternoon. You don't want to waste your Sunday like that."

"A day with you wouldn't be a waste."

A warmth spread through Violet's insides. She chewed her lip. If she had someone with her, could she handle leaving the city? Could she put the demons behind her and move forward?

She studied the piece on her computer screen again. She did want it. But this decision seemed bigger than whether or not to go pick up an antique. It seemed like a chance to decide whether to move forward with her life.

"Okay." She turned toward Nate and nodded. "Okay." She said it again, with more certainty. "Let's do it."

A slow grin spread across Nate's face, traveling from his lips to his eyes. Seeing it reassured Violet she'd made the right decision.

After so many years stuck in her grief and fear, traveling out of the city would be the first step on her journey forward.

Who knew what would come next.

# Chapter 19

There was a light tapping on the door, and Nate gave Tony a last pat on the head and closed his crate.

"Sorry, buddy, not this time." The dog gave Nate his sad puppy look and sighed. Nate passed him a treat. It amazed him how quickly the dog had managed to work his way into Nate's heart.

Another tap on the door. Nate glanced toward it with a smile, even though he couldn't see her yet.

Tony wasn't the only one who had worked their way into his heart.

He grabbed the bag of snacks he'd put together and headed for the door. The moment he opened it, he caught his breath.

She was wearing a pair of denim shorts and a blue tank top, but she managed to make the ordinary clothes look stunning.

He was grateful she finally seemed to believe that he would do whatever he could to make sure she could keep her store.

He only hoped he didn't disappoint her.

"You ready to go? I packed snacks." She held up a canvas bag.

He held up his own plastic bag. "Me, too."

"Ooh. Let me see." She grabbed his bag and peered into it. After a second, she tossed it back at him. "Those aren't road trip foods."

He peeked into his bag. "What's wrong with apples and bananas?"

"Nothing, for everyday food. But road trips are special. You need special food." She opened her own bag and held it out to him.

He burst into laughter. "Exactly how long do you think this drive will take?" She'd packed two packages of chocolate bars and a party size bag of M & Ms.

Violet echoed his laugh. "I guess I went a little overboard, huh? But I'm an M & M fiend. I might even share some if you're nice." She led the way out the door and to the parking lot.

Nate stared at her car. "Um, I don't want to alarm you, but I don't think that hutch is going to fit in here."

She rolled her eyes. "We're going to pick up a trailer when we get there. And then I'm going to figure out how to drive with a trailer hitched to my car." She pulled a set of keys out of her pocket and fidgeted with them, shifting from one foot to the other as she fingered the key chain. "Unless you want to drive?"

Nate kept his head down. "I can't." He only hoped Violet wouldn't ask why. He tried to convince himself he wouldn't lie if she did.

"It's okay, I trust you with my car." Violet held out the keys to him.

If only that were his concern. "No. It's not that."

Violet tilted her head to the side. "I thought guys liked to drive."

Nate forced a laugh. "It's not that either. It's just—" He watched an ant scurrying on the sidewalk. "I don't have my license."

Violet's mouth went slack for a second as if she thought he might be joking. "You drove me to the hospital when I broke my arm."

"That was an emergency."

She studied him, as if she wasn't sure he was serious. "So you really never got your license?"

Nate stood stock still, unable to decide how to answer her question. He hadn't said he'd never gotten his license. Just that he didn't have one now. He wouldn't have one again for another year.

Before he could say anything, Violet was talking again. "Well, I guess that settles it. I'm driving." Her voice shook.

Nate wished he could do more. That he could be the hero she needed him to be.

He took a step closer and cupped her hands between his own. "I'll be right next to you."

She took a shaky breath, looking at their interlocked hands. Nate pulled his away gently and walked around to open the driver's door for her. Just because he couldn't drive her didn't mean he couldn't be a gentleman.

Violet's arm brushed against his as she climbed into the car, and Nate fought off the wave of longing. He had to stop thinking of this as a day to be alone with Violet and remember he was just doing his part to help save her store. End of story.

But the way his heart forgot to beat for a second when she smiled at him told him he was kidding himself.

Hopefully he was doing a better job of kidding her.

✿

Violet tried to keep her hands relaxed on the wheel, but the closer she came to the edge of the city, the tighter her shoulders tensed.

She couldn't do this. Not even with Nate here next to her.

It was too hard.

She opened her mouth to tell him they had to turn around, that she didn't need the piece that badly, but he spoke first.

"So, how did you and Cade end up with an antique store?" He was looking out the window, but Violet suspected he'd noticed her tension and was trying to ease it.

She focused on answering, ignoring the landmarks going by that said she was almost to the edge of town.

"Completely his idea," she said, letting herself remember his excitement as he'd shared his plans with her. He had been so sure this was what they were meant to do—to save other people's history and pass it on to new owners who could add to that history. "I was an art major working at a dead-end office job I hated, and he was a business major waiting tables in a supper club."

"Sounds glamorous."

"Yeah. Not exactly what we thought our future would be when we graduated from college. But we didn't want to wait until we had established careers before we got married, so we settled for the first jobs we found."

"Makes sense."

She nodded. "Anyway, we hadn't even been married a year yet, and we took this trip up north. We stopped at a rinky-dink garage sale, and we were standing there looking at all this stuff. Cade said what a shame it was that most of it would end up in a landfill. And I could see that it broke his heart, but I thought, 'Well, what are you going to do about it?' But that's the thing: instead of wondering what to do about it, Cade solved the problem. He said we should open an antique shop to rescue—that's the word he used, rescue—all these memories. He had some pretty romantic notions for a businessman."

She glanced at Nate, who nodded, encouraging her to continue.

"Anyway, it took him a while to convince me, which was odd, since I was always the more whimsical, impractical one. But I couldn't see how we were going to make it work." She'd been terrified they'd end up homeless, with nothing to show for their efforts.

"But he wrote up a business plan, got approval for a loan, found a storefront." She swallowed past the memory. "He blindfolded me and brought me there. The place was a mess—the last renter had been a pottery studio—but he had a picnic spread out on a blanket and he'd written Hidden Treasures in big, messy letters on a piece of poster board and hung it on the door. He had the worst handwriting, but—" She shook her head. Her husband had been so full of charisma. "How could I say no?"

Violet pulled herself out of her memories, glancing at Nate to see if he was still listening to her ramble. Not that she would blame him if he wasn't.

But he was staring at her as if he'd never heard anything more interesting. "Sounds like he was very persuasive."

"You could say that. He was—" She didn't know what word to fill in next. Cade was so many things. "He was my everything." The words came out as a whisper, but in place of the usual tightness she felt whenever she thought about Cade, the pressure that had constricted her chest for the past three years eased a bit. She never talked about him with her friends—they had all known and loved him, too, which meant they already knew all there was to tell about him.

By instinct, Violet switched on her signal light to turn onto the highway that would carry them across the state. She hadn't noticed when they'd crossed out of the city, which must have been at least twenty miles ago. To her surprise, her hands were loose on the wheel, her shoulders relaxed. Apparently, she could do this after all.

Nate continued to ask her questions about the shop, and she told him about how they had grown, collected new pieces, made their first sale—an antique trash can of all things—speaking into the welcome of his silence.

By the time she needed a break to stretch, she had gotten to the part a few months before Cade's death when they had started to experience financial trouble.

"I thought it was time to close the shop," she confessed as she pulled into a gas station. She'd never told any of her other friends that. It wasn't that she was afraid they'd judge her; more that she feared they'd tell her maybe she'd been right and she should give it up. But she knew she couldn't do that—not now. Not when it'd be a worse betrayal than refusing to go with Cade that day.

"What did Cade think?" Nate hadn't made a move to get out of the car but instead was studying her in that uncanny and yet somehow inviting way of his.

Violet waved a hand in the air. "Cade was the most optimistic guy you could meet. He said everything would be fine. We just had to trust God." The words seared against Violet's heart. She hadn't exactly been doing a good job of trusting God lately. She took a deep breath.

Maybe this trip was the first step on that road.

Nate washed his hands, then ran them through his hair, taking a deep breath. Listening to Violet talk about Cade was both easier and harder than he'd thought it'd be. Easier because the guy sounded so likable. Harder because it was obvious Violet still loved him, and the raw pain in her voice tore at his insides.

He ripped a sheet of paper towel from the dispenser. He was grateful she'd shared so much with him. He could tell she needed the release. He'd almost been able to see the weight lifting from her shoulders as she talked. If that meant the weight on his own shoulders grew heavier, so be it.

Violet was already behind the wheel when he ducked back into the car. She gave him a sheepish grin as he eyed the handful of M & Ms in her casted hand. "Needed a chocolate break." She offered him the bag, and he grabbed a handful, popping them all into his mouth at once.

"Hey, that's not how you do it."

Nate tilted his head at her, unable to open his candy-stuffed mouth.

"Like this." With her good hand, she picked one piece of candy out of her other hand, lifted it to her mouth, and chewed before taking another.

Nate swallowed his own mouthful and grabbed another handful. "But I get more this way." He stuffed the candy into his mouth, letting her laughter wash over him.

"Well, don't come crying to me when you have a tummy ache."

The words sent a jolt through Nate. That was exactly what his mom would have said. Once upon a time anyway. Now she probably didn't care whether he had a tummy ache or even if he was alive.

Nate caught himself. That wasn't fair.

And besides, now was not the time to dwell on his family.

Violet popped another M & M into her mouth with a dainty flourish, then pulled out of the parking space.

Nate waited, wondering whether Violet wanted to talk about Cade again. He was more than willing to listen. But he didn't want to press her if she didn't want to.

She looked over at him and smiled, and he settled into the comfortable silence.

After a few minutes, Violet turned up the radio, which had been only a low, nearly indistinguishable drone in the background. Static blared through the speakers.

She scanned through the stations. "What kind of music do you like?"

He lifted a hand to rub at the back of his neck. "Whatever you like is fine." Seven years ago, he could have talked about the topic of music for hours. But now he did his best to avoid it.

"How about this?" She stopped on an oldies station, grinning at him. She obviously thought he'd protest, but he just shrugged.

145

Her lips lowered in a frown that was kind of cute on her. "You don't like music?"

"I'm indifferent about music." He hated to lie to her, but he didn't want to get into this discussion right now. The discussion about how music had been his life—until it had ruined everything.

"No one's indifferent to music." She scanned the stations again, stopping at a country song. "How about this one?"

"This is fine." Country had never been his favorite genre, but at least he wouldn't be tempted to sing along.

"Fine isn't good enough." She pressed the button again, bypassing a classical station, three talk stations, and something rather polka-like.

When she finally stopped, she gave him a hesitant look. "Is this okay?"

His chest tightened, but he nodded. If he'd been indifferent about the other radio stations, he'd have to be indifferent about the Christian station, too. He clamped his mouth shut, so he wouldn't start singing out of pure instinct. Even if the tunes still called to the musician in him, he didn't believe the lyrics anymore.

He settled back in his seat and watched the cornfields zipping by out the window. He tried not to picture the last time he was on a stage. Not to recall how he'd thought his whole life was made that night. Not to remember how it had splintered into a thousand irreparable pieces instead.

"Uh, Nate."

"Yeah?" He kept his gaze directed out the window. The corn stalks were taller than him, but every few seconds they bent almost in half in the hot breeze that had kicked up. Nate wondered if they ever bent so far, they broke.

When Violet didn't answer, he turned to look at her.

She flicked her eyes toward his lap, and he glanced down. His fingers were lifting and lowering in time to the music. He had been playing the piano chords along to the song on the radio without thinking about it.

On the one hand, he was fascinated that his muscle memory was still so strong after seven years.

On the other hand, he'd promised never to play music again. And this came a little too close.

He shoved his hands under his legs and turned to the window, but he could feel Violet looking at him.

"Were you playing lap piano?" Her teasing note caught him off guard.

"I guess I was." He let himself laugh a little.

"How do you know this song?"

"My band used to play it." The words were out before he could consider them. He immediately wanted to reel them back in. Talk of his band was leading to dangerous territory.

"You had a band?"

He couldn't help but look over at the incredulity in Violet's voice. It wasn't that far-fetched was it? "Yeah, a long time ago."

"Well, were you any good?"

He gave a stiff nod. "We were almost signed by a record label. But like I said, it was a long time ago." Hopefully she'd get the hint that he didn't want to talk about it anymore.

"Wow. What happened?"

Nate's throat constricted. "It fell through at the last minute."

"Oh." When she didn't say anything else, he started to relax.

But after a second, she broke the silence again. "Was your family supportive of your band?"

He grunted. "Hardly. My dad insisted I study business. For when my music failed." It didn't matter that Dad had ultimately been right. It still stung that he'd never thrown Nate a crumb of support. Not even when they'd been on the cusp of signing with the label.

"I'm sure your dad is glad to have you in business with him now, though."

An ironic snort erupted from him. "Sure. He loves working with the biggest mistake of his life."

Violet's head snapped to him. "I'm sure he doesn't think that."

Nate looked away from the compassion in her eyes. "His words, not mine."

Violet's gasp was only half stifled. "He couldn't mean that." Her voice was firm, as if she didn't believe any parent could ever think that of their child. But then, she didn't know that his dad had plenty of reason to say that about him.

He stared out the window, hoping the conversation was finally over.

"Do you want to talk about it?"

Nate's stomach clenched. Talking about his family was the last thing he wanted to do. "No thanks."

She nodded and looked away. He hated that he had disappointed her, but she'd be even more disappointed if she knew he deserved everything his father had said about him.

"You know, sometimes when I don't want to talk to people about something, I talk to God." Violet didn't look at him as she said it.

Nate tensed. He didn't want to have this conversation, either. "I gave up talking to God a long time ago."

Violet met his eyes for a second. If he wasn't careful, he would let those eyes capture him.

"Why?"

Nate looked away. "Because God gave up on answering."

"Maybe—"

But the GPS on Violet's phone blared out instructions to exit the highway.

Nate allowed himself a relieved breath as she turned her attention to getting them to the trailer rental place. He had a feeling that he'd narrowly avoided a conversation that would have blown their relationship—whatever it was—to bits.

It was a conversation he couldn't avoid forever.

But he was safe for now at least.

# Chapter 20

The car whined as Violet pressed the accelerator, nudging it up the steep hill. Driving with the trailer behind her wasn't as nerve-wracking as she had anticipated, not after conquering her fear to drive all the way across the state.

She couldn't have done it without Nate.

She turned to look at him. He was peering past the lush trees that lined the road to examine the house numbers. But his jaw was tight, and his hands were clenched in his lap.

"Hey." Her voice was soft.

When he met her eyes, his were stormier than ever.

"I'm sorry I asked about your family. I shouldn't have pried."

His lips tipped up the smallest fraction. "It's okay."

How could he say it was okay? How could anyone be okay after their father had said the things Nate's father had? No wonder Nate seemed so haunted most of the time.

"There." He pointed to a stately brick house at the top of the hill. Ivy climbed up one wall, and there were gaps in the mortar between the bricks. But the house had obviously been the jewel of the area in its time.

Violet pulled into the driveway and turned off the car. Then she just sat for a second.

She was stiff and tired, but an overwhelming sense of accomplishment washed over her.

"You okay?" Nate touched a hand to her arm.

"I can't believe I just did that." She felt like she'd been freed from a cage she'd stuck herself in three years ago.

"I can," Nate said simply, opening his door.

Violet stared after him a second before opening her own door. Did he really have that kind of faith in her?

"Come on," Nate called from the foot of the porch staircase.

She hurried to join him. The paint on the porch steps was chipped, and its railing tilted precariously, but the boards underneath were solid.

She knocked on the door, and the two of them waited side-by-side, standing close enough that their arms brushed every time one of them moved. She should step away, but she couldn't make herself do it. After everything they'd shared in the car, she felt closer to him. And she was afraid they'd lose that if she moved too far away.

She reached to squeeze his hand. "Thanks for coming with me. It means a lot."

He squeezed back, offering her a smile that went straight to her heart. "You're welcome."

They pulled their hands apart as the door in front of them opened. A stooped, older gentleman stood on the other side, his dark glasses a sharp contrast to his white hair and pale eyes. When he smiled at them, his face disappeared in a mass of wrinkles.

He held out a hand to Violet, then to Nate. "I'm Barney. I'm so glad you decided to come." He stepped to the side, ushering them through the door. Nate let Violet pass ahead of him, giving her another smile that brightened the dim interior.

Barney led them to the dining room, where a petite woman with white curls was packing china from the hutch into a box.

"They're here, Gladys," Barney said loudly. He leaned toward them and muttered, "She doesn't hear so well anymore. But she's eighty-eight, so what do you expect?"

The woman turned. "I heard that." She tossed a ball of crumpled newspaper at him. "And I'm only eighty-seven. You're the one who's eighty-eight."

Gladys crossed the room and held her hand out to them. Her grip was firm yet kind. "I'm so glad to know you'll find a good home for this hutch. It's been through a lot with us."

Barney wrapped his arm around Gladys's shoulders, tucking her against him.

"The stories this old piece could tell." He whistled, long and low.

Bending over to open the hutch's lower cabinets, Violet gave Nate a significant look.

"See?" she mouthed. He stuck his tongue out at her.

To Barney and Gladys, she said, "Won't you tell us some of them? Where did this beauty come from?"

Barney's eyes lit up, and Violet was in heaven as he spent the next hour telling them about how his great-grandmother had the piece shipped to her from Germany when she immigrated to America in the late 1800s.

"She also brought over all her family's china," Gladys chimed in. "But they had to sell it during the Depression." She gestured at the plate she was wrapping. "When Barney's grandmother inherited the hutch, she bought a new set, and it's been in the family ever since."

"My mother got the hutch after my grandmother," Barney said. "But I didn't have any sisters—just us four boys—so I got the hutch and the china. Not sure it was the best deal since my brothers all got cash, but it's what Gladys wanted."

Gladys swatted at him with a box. "And a good thing, too, since your brothers blew all their money gambling before they could spend a penny of it."

"That's a lovely history," Violet said, shooting Nate another pointed look. To her surprise, he seemed equally fascinated with the story they'd heard. Maybe she'd convert him into an antique lover yet. "What made you decide to sell it now?"

Barney rubbed a hand across his nearly hairless scalp. "Well, in case you haven't noticed, we're no spring chickens."

"Speak for yourself," Gladys interrupted, placing the final piece of china in the box.

Barney ducked his head "I stand corrected. I'm no spring chicken. We've decided to move into a retirement community, and we won't have room for it there."

"And you have no children to pass it on to?" Violet asked gently. She was plenty familiar with that ache. She and Cade had decided to start a family only a few months before he died. For the first few weeks after he was gone, she'd prayed she might at least be carrying his child. But God had chosen to answer that prayer with a no. She still struggled with the grief of that answer sometimes.

"We did. A daughter." Gladys offered a gentle smile. "She went to be with the Lord more than fifty years ago."

"I'm so sorry." Violet laid a hand on the old woman's arm.

"Thank you, but she knew her Savior. She's in heaven now. And one of these days, we'll be there with her."

Barney wrapped an arm protectively around his wife, who fixed him with a sweet smile. They were so cute. Is this what she and Cade would have been like when they were older?

But she had to stop thinking like that. There was no point. She and Cade would never look like this. Because Cade would never grow old with her.

She glanced at Nate. What would he be like as an old man?

She pushed the thought away. She had no intention of growing old with anyone who wasn't Cade.

Nate cleared his throat. "I don't mean to rush things along, but we have quite a long drive yet."

"Goodness, yes. If you let us, we'll go on all day." Gladys shook her head, elbowing her husband. She turned to Nate. "Now, what do you think? Do you want the hutch? Or maybe you need a minute to discuss it?"

Nate shook his head. "This is completely her decision." He pointed at Violet, and she stepped forward, ready to say she'd take it.

But Barney jumped in. "Smart man. A good husband knows when to step aside." He gave Nate an exaggerated wink, but Nate stared back blankly.

It took Violet a second to get what Barney was saying. Nate seemed to catch on at the same time.

"Oh, no, we're not—"

"I'm not her—"

They both laughed. Violet's face warmed, and even Nate's cheeks took on a hint of red.

"We're just neighbors," Violet finally said.

Barney and Gladys glanced back and forth between Violet and Nate, then looked at each other and smiled.

"They're just neighbors," Barney said to Gladys.

"So I hear," Gladys replied. Neither could contain their grins, and Violet bit her lip. Did these two strangers sense the energy she'd started to feel every time she was near Nate?

And what was that half smile on Nate's face? Did he feel it, too?

She shook herself. This was supposed to be a business trip. "We'll take it."

~

Nate shook out his arms, rolled his neck, and squatted at the corner of the hutch one more time. They'd been trying for an hour to get it loaded, but no matter how many different angles they attempted, it was too heavy for him and Violet to move on their own, especially with Violet's arm still in a cast.

"Let me give it a try." Barney stepped forward, and Nate scrutinized him. He didn't appear frail by any stretch, but the man was nearly ninety years old. Nate didn't want to be responsible for breaking him.

"Barnabas Riley, step away from that hutch right this minute." Gladys bustled into the room, pointing a spatula at her husband.

Barney stepped back. "Busted." But he nudged Nate and whispered, "I wasn't really going to do it. Just had to show her I'm still willing."

Nate laughed with him, but Violet gave the hutch a regretful pat. "Looks like it wasn't meant to be."

"Hold on a minute, dear. You're the one we want to have this." Gladys disappeared again.

Nate and Violet both looked at Barney, but he threw his hands into the air. "Even after sixty-five years of marriage, I don't understand everything about that woman." He winked at them again. "Keeps me on my toes."

Three minutes later, Gladys reappeared. "I called Sylvia, and she said her grandson can come over to help us."

"That's great." Violet pulled out a chair to sit down and stifled a yawn. She looked exhausted.

"In the morning," Gladys finished.

Violet dropped the hand that had been covering her yawn. "I'm sorry. I don't think we can come back tomorrow."

"Of course not." Gladys waved her objection away. "You can stay with us. It's getting late anyway. You don't want to drive back yet tonight."

Nate stole a subtle peek at the time. It was already eight o'clock. And Violet looked ready to drop.

She gave him a questioning look, and he shrugged, hoping she would understand that meant it was up to her.

"I guess that would work. The store is always closed on Mondays anyway." Her eyes traveled to Nate. "Unless you need to be in the office."

He should be. He really should be. If Dad called and he didn't answer, he would never hear the end of it. But right now, he cared more about what Violet needed. And she needed this hutch to save her store.

"I don't need to be in the office."

"Oh, but Tony—" Violet clasped his arm.

She had a point there. He couldn't leave his dog uncared for.

"Unless." Violet pulled out her phone. "Just a second." She wandered toward the kitchen with the phone pressed to her ear.

"Looks like I'm not the only one with a mysterious woman." Barney chuckled so hard he broke into a coughing fit.

"Oh, we're—"

"Neighbors." Gladys rested a hand on her husband's back. "We know."

Barney stopped coughing and straightened, shooting Nate a wink.

Nate was about to argue more, but Violet stepped back into the room. Her smile was enough to steal his protest.

"Sophie's going to stop by to take care of Tony tonight and tomorrow morning. I hope you don't mind, but I told her about your super-secret hiding spot for the spare key."

Nate pretended to be shocked. "How do you know about that?"

"I saw you putting it under the mat the other day when you forgot your keys, remember?"

He did remember. He had been especially enchanted by her laugh that day. It was amazing how many of his recent memories involved her.

Including this one.

"That settles it then." Gladys clapped her hands, looking more like an eight-year-old than an eighty-seven-year-old. "I'll get the extra beds made up. Then we'll all have a nice dinner together. The roast I put in earlier is way too big for Barney and me anyway."

Gladys passed close to Nate as she headed for the stairs. "Don't worry, dear. She may just be a neighbor now. But she'll be more soon." She winked, then was gone.

Nate looked from her retreating form to the other side of the room, where Violet was laughing at something Barney had said. His heart leaped, trying to break free of the tight hold he was keeping on it. But it was getting harder every moment.

Then Violet looked at him, and he knew: it was already too late.

# Chapter 21

Violet let a contented sigh escape as she eased into the bed. She hadn't been pampered like this in a long time. Gladys had treated them to a delicious meal of pot roast, glazed vegetables, and a rich and gooey chocolate cake.

Even better than the food had been the entertainment. Barney and Gladys had delighted them with stories about how they met at a butcher shop and how he proposed to her on the Ferris wheel at the county fair. Violet had laughed until her side hurt when he confessed he'd dropped the ring, and they'd had to shut down the ride so they could search the ground. It took three hours, but they finally found it.

They talked about more serious memories, too, including their teenage daughter's death after a five-year battle with cancer and the difficult period in their marriage that had followed. It had taken them several years to find their way back to each other.

As she talked about that time, Gladys had said something that made Violet reassess her whole life the past three years: "We finally figured out that holding onto past hurts was keeping us from experiencing future joy. Letting go didn't make the past hurt less; it just allowed us to recognize that it was only one thread in the tapestry of our lives."

Violet examined the stitches in the quilt on her lap. Was that what Cade had been? One thread in her tapestry? She had thought he was the entire picture, top to bottom, beginning to end. But now the whole thing had unraveled. How did she tie off that thread and graft in a new one? And what did that new thread look like?

An image of Nate popped into her head. Violet had found herself studying him as the older couple talked. He had laughed in all the right places, looked sympathetic when they spoke of the tough times, and yet Violet felt like he wasn't really there. He seemed lost in his own head, a haunted look fogging his eyes as if whatever he saw in there was too painful to bear.

But whenever he'd noticed her watching him, his eyes had cleared, and his smile had become genuine, kicking up a flutter deep in her insides.

Violet had felt her soul stir as she observed the love between Barney and Gladys. But it wasn't the same kind of jealousy-inducing stir she'd felt when Sophie and Spencer showed their honeymoon pictures. It was more of a nostalgia for something she'd never had, if that was possible. And a longing to have a future like that with someone, even if it couldn't be Cade.

Violet sucked in a sharp breath. She had never let herself think that before. She'd told herself that her future was as a single woman. That she'd be faithful to Cade until she joined him in heaven. Thinking anything else felt like breaking her marriage vows.

And yet, her vows had said "till death do us part," and death had parted them.

While that didn't change her love for Cade, it did change her situation. It made her alone—more than that, it made her lonely.

She had thought she was fine with that.

But spending so much time with Nate lately had made her less sure.

Had made her want more.

Violet tugged the pillow over her head. What would Cade think if he knew her line of thought? Would he want to punch Nate? Or would he shake Nate's hand and tell him to take care of her?

She wrestled with the question for hours before she fell into an uneasy sleep.

⁓

It seemed like only minutes later when her eyes popped open, straining to see in the pitch dark as her blood thundered through her. Where was she? And what had woken her up?

Slowly, her eyes adjusted to the dark, and Violet remembered she was at Gladys and Barney's. But that didn't explain why her heart had turned into a locomotive. She didn't think it had been a nightmare. Her skin was dry, not clammy, and she wasn't all tangled in the sheets like she was every time she dreamed about trying to save Cade.

A string of yells came at her through the wall, from Nate's room next door. Violet cocked her head, listening more closely. After a minute, the yelling picked up again. It sounded panicked.

Violet slid quickly out of bed and tiptoe-ran to the door. She clicked it open silently, then stood in the hallway, pressing her ear to Nate's door.

When the yelling started again, she grabbed the knob and shoved the door open.

Then she froze.

Nate was curled in a ball on his side, the blankets wrapped around him in a tangle.

He threw out an arm, palm outward, as if trying to stop someone. "No!" His voice was hoarse. "No! Not her!"

He pulled his arm back to his core, his whole body going limp for a second before it trembled under the weight of a huge sob. "NO!"

The word unfroze Violet, and she rushed to the bed, dropping to her knees at Nate's side.

"Hey," she whispered, her hand rubbing his bare shoulder. "Nate. Wake up."

Nate moaned. "Please."

Violet rubbed harder, spoke louder. "Nate, I'm here. It's Violet."

Nate's eyes flew open and skittered wildly around the room. Violet moved her hand to his rough cheek, turning his face toward her. His eyes stopped on hers.

It took a moment, but slowly he seemed to register who she was. He heaved a shaky breath. "Violet."

She was suddenly aware that she was still touching him. She scooted back a little but remained on her knees. "Bad dream?"

Nate scrubbed a hand over his face, wiping away a sheen of sweat, and sat up, extracting himself from the blankets. "Yeah. Sorry. Should have warned you I get them sometimes."

"Me too." Violet's eyes fell on Nate's bare chest. It was well-defined, but that's not what her gaze locked on. A long white scar ran from his left shoulder, across his chest, to the outside of his ribs.

He followed the path of her eyes and reached to grab his shirt, yanking it over his head.

Violet pushed to her feet and shuffled to sit next to him on the bed. "Do you want to talk about it? The dream?"

"I can't." His voice was raw, uncensored, and Violet knew he wasn't trying to put her off. He really couldn't talk about it.

"Mine are always about Cade. Except it's never about a car accident. There's always something else, some danger that I see just before it happens—a cliff he's about to fall off, a current that's about to sweep him away. I try to get to him, to warn him, but I'm always too late." Violet's throat burned just talking about it, and she tried to swallow, but her mouth was too dry.

"Sometimes I wake up before he dies. But sometimes I have to watch it. Have to go through the whole funeral, too. Every little detail of it is in place, except it's like it's in slow motion and it's never going to end." She almost choked on the last words, and yet she was grateful for the release of telling him. She'd never even told Sophie about the dreams. But knowing she wasn't the only one with nightmares had given her courage to share, especially if it might help Nate.

A warm hand gripped her fingers and squeezed. Before he could let go, Violet squeezed back. She needed this connection, this moment to tell her she wasn't alone, she wasn't the only one who hurt and didn't know what to do with it.

They sat like that, their breaths slowly matching one another, until Violet's head started to droop. "I'd better get back to bed."

Nate gave one last squeeze and let go of her hand. Violet fought off the wave of emptiness.

When she was to the door, she turned to look at Nate. He had lain down, his breathing now slow and even.

"Thank you," he said, his eyes closed.

Violet nodded. "Thank you," she whispered.

She fell back to sleep within seconds of climbing back into her own bed.

By the time she woke, a bright line of sunlight streamed in through the slight gap in the curtains.

She stretched, her heart lighter than it had been in ages. Something had happened during the night. The weight of memories hadn't been lifted, but it had changed so that she could start to see the light in them instead of only the dark.

She sat up and folded her hands, bowing her head.

*Dear Jesus, You are a great and a mighty God, and I thank you for this new day, for a renewed life, for the promise that you know all my hurts and have the ability to take them from me, maybe in ways I haven't seen or planned. Please bring the same healing you've brought me to Nate's heart, whatever his troubles may be. In your name I ask it. Amen.*

Violet sat and just breathed for a minute, paying attention to the air going into and out of her lungs. Somewhere along the line she'd forgotten that each day was a gift from the Lord and had started to look at the days as something to simply survive.

But not anymore.

As she got out of bed, she gave herself a cursory glance in the mirror. Her clothes from yesterday were rumpled but not too much worse for the wear. Her hair, on the other hand, stuck out in every direction. She ran a hand across her curls, attempting fruitlessly to tame them, then gave up. If unruly hair was the worst thing she had to worry about today, she'd count herself fortunate.

Homey smells and muted conversation drifted up the stairs, and Violet followed them to the kitchen. Nate was already there, chuckling at something Gladys had said as he scooped a forkful of eggs off his plate. The moment she walked into the room, his eyes went to hers, and he smiled, not that haunted, half-there smile from yesterday, but a genuine, heart-melting smile that Violet couldn't help but return.

"Good morning," she said softly.

He nodded and finished chewing, never taking his eyes from hers. "Good morning." Was it her imagination or did his voice have a new, tender note to it?

Violet scolded herself. Just because she'd had a revelation last night didn't mean he had. To him, she was still just his neighbor.

She slid her gaze to the table. Gladys obviously loved to cook. She'd laid out eggs, bacon, biscuits and gravy, and a pile of pancakes. "Wow, Gladys, you didn't have to do all this for us."

Gladys's smile was both wistful and filled with joy. "I haven't had anyone to cook for in a long time. Barney's diabetic, so no more pancakes for us." She passed Violet a plate. "Cooking's one of the things I'm going to miss most when we move into the new place. We have a meal plan there, so I won't even need to pour Barney his cereal."

Violet observed the older woman as she filled her plate. Somehow it had never occurred to her that she wasn't the only one entering a new chapter of her life—and there would be plenty more new chapters along the way. Perhaps it wasn't the changing of chapters that was so important but more what you did with the pages in them that mattered.

Violet pulled out the chair across from Nate and sat, bowing her head to give thanks for the food. When she lifted her head, Nate was watching her.

"Sorry I woke you last night."

Violet shoveled a forkful of pancake into her mouth, closing her eyes in bliss as the sweet tang of maple syrup and lightly browned pancakes hit her tongue. She waved her hand at Nate. She wanted to tell him that she was glad he had woken her, glad she had been there with him, glad they had shared that moment.

But with Gladys hovering over them, she said simply, "It was no problem."

The doorbell rang, and Gladys clapped as she had yesterday, making Violet grin. Someone had forgotten to tell the woman she was eighty-seven. "That'll be Sylvia's grandson. You finish up, and I'll get the door."

Nate stood and carried his plate to the sink. Violet started to follow, giving a remorseful look at her half-finished pancakes.

Nate waved her back into her seat. "You finish eating. I've got this."

Violet knew she should argue. But the pancakes were too good.

She kept an ear tuned to the other room as she ate. By the time she'd finished and entered the dining room, Nate and Sylvia's grandson were carrying the hutch toward the front door.

"Easy." She heard Nate's voice from the other side of the room.

She considered following him outside but changed her mind. He had this under control.

Instead, she approached Gladys, who was wrapping the last of the china. "Thank you again for allowing us to stay last night. That was more than was necessary. In fact—" She reached into her purse for her checkbook.

Gladys waved the checkbook off. "I did it as much for me as for you, dear. One last chance to entertain before saying goodbye to this house." To Violet's surprise, Gladys swiped at a tear.

Violet rubbed the woman's arm. "I thought you were happy to be moving somewhere more manageable."

"I am, dear, I am." Gladys patted Violet's hand. "But just because we're happy about the next part of our life doesn't mean we're not sad about leaving the last part behind."

Violet blinked hard so she wouldn't have to wipe away her own tears. Somehow Gladys had expressed exactly what she'd been feeling.

"All loaded up."

Violet and Gladys both jumped at the voice behind them.

Nate eyed them with concern. "Everything okay?"

Violet nodded.

"Perfect," Gladys said. "But I wonder if you could do me one more favor?"

Nate patted the older woman on the back. "After a breakfast like that, I'll do anything you ask."

Gladys rested her hand on the box of china she'd so lovingly wrapped. "Could you load this into your car as well, please?"

Violet already had stacks of unsold china in her shop, but she couldn't say no to a woman who had been so generous to them. "How much would you like for it?"

Gladys reached a leathery hand to stroke her hair, then let her arm drop. "I don't want you to buy it, dear. I want to give it to you." She looked at Nate, then at Violet. "To both of you."

"Oh, but—" That was too generous, on top of everything else. Plus, Violet didn't want to assume the older woman was getting forgetful, but they'd already told her they weren't a couple.

"I won't take no for an answer," Gladys cut in. "And before you think I'm senile, I know you aren't together. So you can each take half of the china. Who knows, maybe you'll join the set back together someday. But this way you can each remember the little old couple you brought joy for an evening."

Violet pretended not to know what Gladys meant about putting the set back together. "That's very kind, but—"

"I told you, I won't accept no. You'll be doing me a favor, anyway. Otherwise, I have to haul this to the thrift store, and it's mighty heavy."

"You could sell it."

"It's not worth anything. Just the cheapest set Barney's grandmother could find." She snapped her fingers toward Nate, then pointed to the box. "Now. Load it up."

Nate looked from Gladys to Violet. Violet gave a subtle shake of her head, but apparently Nate decided Gladys was the more formidable of the two because he crossed the room and picked up the box with a grunt.

Gladys winked at him. "That's a good boy."

Nate studiously avoided Violet's eyes as he slid past them and out the front door. Violet let her gaze follow him for a moment, trying to decide whether she should be angry or amused.

She settled on grateful. "Thank you, Gladys, for everything." She leaned down to give the small woman a hug.

"I know your heart's been broken," Gladys whispered as she held her. "But that doesn't mean it will never feel again. And when it does, you make sure that young man out there knows."

Violet scrunched her eyes shut and nodded against the huge lump that had formed in her throat.

"All set?" Nate called from the doorway.

Violet released her hold on Gladys and nodded. She wasn't sure if she was yet.

But she would be.

# Chapter 22

Nate fastened the last button of his shirt and tucked it into the waist of his jeans. He couldn't figure out exactly how he'd let himself get talked into the concert. It was the last place he wanted to go, the last place he told himself he'd ever go again. But when Violet had asked, the *yes* had come out in a nanosecond. In the few weeks that had passed since their trip to Barney and Gladys's, something had shifted between him and Violet—in a good way. That night, as he'd clutched her hand after his nightmare and she'd shared her own horrifying dreams, they'd forged a connection.

Since then, they'd stopped pretending that they weren't seeking each other out. They spent nearly every evening together, and he'd taken her out for dinner to celebrate when she sold the hutch a week after they picked it up. It was only pizza, but still—it was something. He'd been spending more time with her friends, too. He couldn't deny that it felt good to finally belong somewhere again. The last time he'd had that feeling was with his band.

Nate shoved the memory away. He couldn't let himself dwell on his lost dreams tonight.

Tony followed at Nate's feet as he padded into the kitchen. He gave the dog a scoop of food and waited absently for him to eat it. His eyes fell on the saucer from Barney and Gladys's china set that Violet had compelled him to take. He had told her to keep the whole set, but she'd insisted that he take at least one piece because Gladys had wanted them to share it.

He hadn't mentioned that Gladys also wanted them to share more—a life together—since she didn't seem to have picked up on that part of Gladys's ploy. Or if she had, she had pretended not to. As had he. In the end, he'd agreed to take one saucer because he'd figured if her set were permanently one tiny plate short, it would be no great loss.

And if they did happen to reunite the set someday—

Tony nudged Nate's hand with his cold nose, pulling Nate out of his daydreams before they could go too far.

"Okay, buddy." Nate locked Tony in his kennel. "I'll probably be home late tonight. So no parties." Nate almost bit his tongue as the words came out. They were exactly the same words his parents had said to him every time they went out. And he had always obeyed. Until that last night. When he hadn't.

Nate shoved a hand through his hair but then immediately tried to smooth it down.

The knock at the door made him jump, and in spite of himself, his heart picked up speed. It shouldn't react this way to a concert with a friend. But apparently no one had told it that.

Nate threw a treat into Tony's kennel and crossed to the door. He took two deep breaths before opening it.

But the sight on the other side stole those breaths right back.

Violet was wearing a flowing blue dress that hung longer on the sides than in the front and back. She'd gotten her cast off a few days ago, and her dark curls cascaded over her shoulders and onto her bare upper arms. Her lips glistened with a wine-colored gloss that made Nate want to touch them.

"Hi," Violet finally said, making Nate realize he'd been staring.

"Hi. Sorry." Nate swallowed. "You look great."

Violet's smile grew, making her lips even more inviting. Nate glanced over his shoulder, pretending to check Tony's kennel, before turning back to Violet.

But that smile was still there.

"Ready to go?" She sounded slightly breathless and excited.

Nate nodded and followed her to her car.

As Violet drove, they fell into the easy conversation that had become so familiar over the past few weeks.

But ten minutes later, Nate threw Violet a quizzical look as they pulled into the parking lot of the church. The place was jammed with cars, and people dressed in everything from ripped jeans and t-shirts to formal dresses were pouring toward the building.

"Are we picking Dan up?" Nate asked as Violet pulled into one of the few remaining parking spots at the far end of the lot, near Dan's house.

Violet looked away and tapped her fingers against the steering wheel.

Not good. She had something to tell him, and he wasn't going to like it.

"No." She looked away and continued in a rush, "The concert is at the church."

All the air disappeared from the car. She had tricked him into coming. She knew how he felt about church, and she had deliberately not told him she was bringing him to one. Well, she could forget it. There was no way he was going in there.

"Don't be mad." Violet gave him a pleading look.

He told himself he wouldn't be swayed by the genuine compassion in her eyes.

"I didn't tell you because I knew you wouldn't come otherwise. And I really think you'll like the music."

Nate tensed. It wasn't a question of if he'd like the music. This kind of music had been his life once. But it had almost been his death, too.

"If you don't like it, we can leave." Violet laid her hand, smooth and soft, on his. "Please. It would mean a lot to me."

Violet's eyes hadn't left his face, and he both dreaded and loved the hope he saw there.

"Okay." The word scraped up against his will.

"Thank you." Violet squeezed his hand, and in spite of himself, he let out a tight-lipped smile. Making her happy always did that to him.

Violet popped her car door open and bounded out, greeting a young couple who had gotten out of the car next to them. She waved to an older man across the parking lot. Nate watched her in wonder. She seemed to genuinely fit in here, to enjoy and care about these people. And they seemed to return the sentiment.

Of course, she hadn't committed any big, public sin to earn their wrath and scorn.

But as far as they knew, neither had he.

Nate fell into step next to Violet, trying to ignore the churning in his stomach that intensified the closer they got to the door, until it felt like he had swallowed a whirlpool.

An older man opened the church door for them, offering a cheerful hello. Nate mumbled a greeting, pushing past as fast as he could. He was in no mood to make small talk.

Inside, groups of people mingled around the spacious lobby, and the sound of laughter filled the space.

"The sanctuary is this way." Violet steered him past the people, and Nate was grateful when she only waved to a few groups but didn't stop to talk.

Inside, the church floor sloped toward the front, where a large open area held an assortment of instruments, from a drum set to half a dozen guitars and a baby grand piano.

Nate's fingers twitched. He could almost feel the smooth keys, feel the vibration of a perfect chord ringing out.

He shoved his hands in his pockets and scanned the crowd with Violet.

The seats were already half filled, but after a second Violet pointed. Sophie, Spencer, Tyler, Ethan, Ariana, Jared, Peyton, and Leah took up almost an entire row halfway to the front of the church, right in the center of the sanctuary.

Nate followed Violet toward them, his feet heavier with every step. He kept his head down, eyes trained on the floor.

When they reached their friends, everyone stood up to greet them. Their warmth helped Nate relax. This was just a night with friends. No one was going to grill him about his band or his failure. When Sophie leaned over to hug him, he hugged back. After a minute, they all settled into their seats. Nate jammed himself into the space between Violet and the end of the row. Their arms were pressed together, and her flowery scent wafted over him.

"Are we going to have room for Dan?" Nate peered down the length of the row, but he was pretty sure they couldn't cram in another person if they tried.

Violet's laugh startled him. "I don't think he's going to sit with us."

Nate felt his brow wrinkle. Clearly, there was some kind of joke going on here, but he wasn't in on it. "Why not?"

"Well, the pastor usually sits up front." Violet was still chuckling.

"The pastor?" Nate felt his mouth dip into a frown. This didn't make any sense. "Dan is a pastor?"

Violet stopped laughing. "I thought you realized. This is his church. He and his dad are co-pastors here."

Which would explain why he lived right next door. And was always talking about his members. Nate had figured he ran some sort of gym or something.

At that moment, the man himself emerged from a hidden door behind the front wall of the sanctuary. He was dressed in simple khaki pants and a button up shirt without a tie. Not Nate's typical image of a pastor. Dan scanned the crowd. When his eyes fell on their row, he made his way toward them.

As Dan held out a hand to him, Nate thought about the conversations he'd had with the other man. He hadn't held back his opinion that church was a waste of time at best and a fraud at worst. He felt suddenly awkward around this man he had come to see as a friend.

But Dan didn't seem to notice. "Hey, Nate, glad you could make it."

Before Nate could come up with a reply, a panicked looking teen ran up to Dan and whispered something. Dan turned to his friends. "Sorry. Problems with the sound system. I'll see you after the concert."

At the front of the church, the band members began to warm up.

The sharp chords pulled Nate back to the life he'd had before. He'd been so full of himself then, thinking he was someone special. That God had big plans for him. That the Big Guy had his back.

Look how wrong he'd been.

The pianist played a short riff, and Nate found himself leaning forward, eyes fixed on the guy's fingers. They were sure on the keys, just as his had once been.

Nate's gaze moved to the guy's face. His eyes were closed, and he seemed to be feeling the music, living it. Nate knew exactly what that was like. Playing was the only time he had really felt alive in those days—like he was doing what he was put on this earth to do.

"Nate?" A soft hand landed on his arm.

Nate ripped his eyes off the pianist and looked toward Violet, who was clearly waiting for him to say something. He gave her a blank stare, his thoughts still on the feel of piano keys beneath his fingers.

"Sorry, what was that?"

"Are you angry that I dragged you here?"

"What?" Nate forced his attention to her.

"You look kind of . . ." Violet trailed off. "Tense."

Nate glanced at his hands, which were fisted in his lap. His clenched jaw ached, too. He concentrated on loosening his muscles. How could he be angry when she looked at him with that soft gaze?

"No." He gave her what he hoped was a gentle smile. "I'm not upset."

Violet's features relaxed. A second later, the lights in the sanctuary dimmed, and the crowd grew silent.

Nate's stomach lurched. He wasn't sure he could handle this after all.

A spotlight flashed onto the band as the first chord rang across the auditorium. The gathered worshipers cheered and rose to their feet as the band broke into a familiar praise song.

Violet leaned toward Nate and pointed to a large screen behind the band, which showed the words of the song so the audience could sing along. But Nate didn't need the words. He'd sung this song more times than he could count, first as a child in church and then as his band grew large enough to tour.

But Nate's throat was too full to sing. He simply gave Violet a tight nod.

She smiled and closed her eyes, swaying as she sang along to the music.

Nate closed his eyes, too.

But instead of being lifted to the heights of worship, he sank into the past.

As song after song rolled by, Nate saw his band playing in venues just like this one, his hands on the piano keys, a microphone at his mouth.

He'd loved the energy of these events, the communion of worshiping together with so many people who believed in the same God, believed that he was all-powerful and the very definition of love. He'd wanted to dedicate his life to that God.

Of course, that was before he'd discovered it was all a lie. Maybe there was a God; he wasn't ready to go so far as to say there wasn't. But that God was not all-powerful. And he certainly wasn't all-loving.

Nate had learned that the hard way.

No matter how much he fought to resist the memories, they forced their way through. That last night, Nate and his band had played to a packed crowd at his hometown church. They had heard rumors that someone from a Christian record label would be in the audience. The added pressure spurred them on, and they played a flawless set. Afterward, the producer approached them and offered to set up a meeting for the next week.

The offer seemed to prove once and for all that Nate was on the right track with his life, that his father had been wrong about business school, and now he could drop out and do what he was really meant to do.

The producer insisted on taking them out to celebrate. Nate almost said no. He rarely partied, and he was exhausted after the grueling schedule they'd been keeping. But finally making it big felt like a milestone that needed to be celebrated. He didn't want to look back at this moment and realize he'd failed to appreciate it as it happened. Plus, he worried that declining would seem ungrateful. This guy had the chance to make or break his career.

The producer took them to an upscale bar and offered them all a round of drinks.

Nate said no at first.

But he was parched. And he'd turned twenty-one two months before. It was no big deal for him to have a drink.

Only there'd been another round after that. And then another.

Being out had felt good. Finally, he could let go of all the pressure and tension that had been building up for the past several years. For his whole life, maybe, with his dad's constant demand for success.

There was no more need for pressure.

He had made it.

The alcohol went down easier and easier the longer the night went on.

Around midnight, his phone rang. It was Kayla, calling from her own party, begging him to drive her home because she was too drunk to drive, and she was going to miss her curfew.

Nate had lectured Kayla a thousand times about not drinking. She was only sixteen. But he was also realistic. He knew his little sister wasn't a saint. So he'd made her promise that she'd never drive drunk. He'd promised he'd always come pick her up.

So he had downed his last drink, shaken the producer's hand, and congratulated his bandmates again.

Then he'd pulled out his keys and gone to pick Kayla up.

He never gave a thought to the fact that maybe he didn't belong behind the wheel of a car.

Nate's thoughts snapped to the present as someone tugged on his arm. He opened his eyes to find Violet pulling him gently down as all around them people sat. The band had stopped playing, and the lead singer was taking a long swig of water as Dan approached the front of the church. He wore a headset microphone and looked totally at ease in front of the packed church. The same way Nate had felt once.

"How's everyone doing tonight?" Dan called out.

The crowd roared its approval.

Nate swiped a hand over his damp forehead, trying to relax. Violet leaned closer to him, and he tried to use the contact to anchor himself to the present.

"You know," Dan was saying from the front of the sanctuary. "I'm not going to talk long because I want to hear some more of this incredible music. But I wanted to take a minute to talk to you about what an awesome God we have. Maybe you know him already, maybe you don't. Or maybe you knew him once, but you've decided you don't want to know him anymore." Dan wasn't looking anywhere near him, and yet Nate felt as if the words had been directed right at him. His shoulders tensed.

"The thing is, whatever you might know or think you know about God, he knows everything about you."

Nate's insides churned. What business did God have knowing everything about him? Some things were too horrible for anyone—even God—to know.

"But—and here's the important thing," Dan went on. "He loves you anyway." A few people clapped at that, and at least one person whistled. "No matter who you are. No matter what you've done. God loves you. He forgives you."

The weight of Dan's words throbbed against Nate's temples.

"Do you hear me?" Dan turned toward the other side of the church, but Nate could still feel the sear of his openness. "There is nothing—nothing—God cannot forgive. Nothing—not one single sin—Jesus did not die for. So whatever you're holding onto tonight, whatever burden you're carrying, leave it at the cross."

Dan directed one more look Nate's way, then walked to his seat at the front of the church as the band broke into another song.

Nate tried to inhale and focus on the music, but the room had gone airless. He stumbled to his feet, tripping over the end of the row, barely seeing what was in front of him. He charged down the aisle, through the sanctuary doors, and across the lobby.

As he slammed his body through the church doors, the clean night air pulled him up short, and he stood heaving, trying not to choke on the memories that swirled around him, an angry current fighting to pull him under, to drag him to where he couldn't breathe. To where he deserved to be.

The too-sweet scent of lilacs in the air when he picked up Kayla.

The too-loud click of his blinker against the pounding that had started in his head.

The too-wavy center line.

The too-bright lights coming straight toward them.

His too-slow reaction.

The too-high screech of metal on metal, followed by the grinding silence.

The empty seat, where Kayla had been. The broken window. The scramble from the car to find her crumpled in the road, blood spreading around her like watercolor paint.

Collapsing next to her as his own injuries overtook him. A final plea to God: "Take me. Please, take me, not her."

The strength of the memory dropped him to his knees.

He didn't want to hear that God was good, that he could forgive anything.

He didn't deserve to be forgiven for this.

# Chapter 23

Violet told herself not to follow Nate, to give him some space.

She managed to listen to herself for all of ten seconds.

As she walked deliberately toward the doors, she tried to work out what she would say when she got to him, how she would apologize. She had known how he felt about church, and yet she'd roped him into coming—by deceiving him, no less.

It was just that he'd obviously known the love of God once, if he knew those songs on the Christian radio station and had been in a band that played them. She'd wanted so badly for him to know God again that she'd thought it wouldn't matter how she'd gotten him here; she figured once he heard God's word again, his heart would be mended.

She'd been naive. Clearly, his issues with God ran deeper than she'd been willing to see. Which meant that whatever feelings she'd been developing for him—and she had to admit they were there—would have to be reined in. She could never be in a relationship that didn't have God at its center. She knew God was the reason her relationship with Cade had worked; and he was the only way a relationship between her and Nate would work as well.

Not that he'd come out and said he'd like to have a relationship with her. But she couldn't deny the spark between them anymore, the desire to spend every waking moment with him. She'd finally accepted—started to hope, even—that it could be leading to something more.

She pushed down her rising sorrow that it couldn't. That wasn't what this was about right now. It was about apologizing for dragging him here.

When she reached the glass doors that led outside, she stopped short. Nate was kneeling in the middle of the sidewalk, his head in his hands.

Violet raised a hand to cover her mouth. He was obviously still fighting with whatever it was that had driven him out here. She should leave him. Let him have the space he so obviously craved.

But he'd been there for her so many times. When she'd broken her arm. When she'd needed someone to talk to about Cade. And when she'd needed help saving her store. Without Nate, she wouldn't be halfway to paying off her back rent already.

She owed it to him to help him through this—whatever it was.

Steeling her shoulders, Violet slipped quietly through the door and hurried over to Nate, dropping to the ground next to him. She let her fingers graze his back lightly. He trembled slightly, and she planted her hand more firmly on his back. "Nate?"

He drew in a shuddering breath, then dropped his hands to his knees and pushed himself into a more upright position. She let her hand fall from his back.

"Sorry about that," he rasped, not looking at her.

"No, I'm the one who's sorry." Violet rubbed at the pale spot on her ring finger. "I tricked you into coming here even though I knew how you felt about church. I should have told you the truth."

A muscle in Nate's jaw twitched as he stared out over the parking lot. "I appreciate that. But I think I'll wait out the rest of the concert in the car." He held out his hand, palm up. "Give me the keys and go inside. I don't want to ruin your evening."

Violet shook her head. She was the one who had ruined the evening.

"I'm not going back in there without you, and you're definitely not going back, so how about we call it a night?"

Nate ran a hand through his hair, making the top stick up in funny tufts that Violet had an urge to run her fingers through. Finally, he nodded, and she took his elbow, leading him across the parking lot to her car.

Violet left Nate to his thoughts during the short drive home, but when they reached their building, each standing outside their own apartment doors, she turned to him. "You seemed to enjoy the concert at first. Was it something Dan said?"

Nate's eyes darted around the landing, as if trying to find anywhere to look but at her. "Let's just say I disagree with his assessment that everything can be forgiven."

Violet waited for him to add more. When he didn't, she said, "It might help to talk about it. I could make some coffee." She ached to take whatever this burden was from him. Or at least to help him carry it.

His eyes finally came to rest on hers, filled with an anguish she recognized only too well. "I can't."

"That's what I thought, too, for a long time." What she'd thought until only a few weeks ago, when she'd found herself opening up to Nate. The least she could do was offer him the opportunity to do the same.

For a second, she thought he was going to say yes. She watched the warring desires in his eyes, praying that for once openness would win out.

But the moment passed, and his guarded look fell back into place. The one she thought he had dropped as they'd grown closer.

"It's too much," he said finally, opening his door.

But Violet wasn't going to give up that easily. "Part of friendship is sharing." She took a step closer to his door. She tried to keep her voice steady, but it hurt that he didn't trust her enough to open up. "But I feel like I'm the only one who's sharing all the time. Every time I ask you anything, you put me off with vague half answers. I don't know why you left your band or why you're so angry with God or what you dream about for the future. None of it."

Nate's face contorted, and she took an involuntary step back.

"You want to know about my past?" His voice was laced with a hopelessness she'd never heard from him before. "My past is dead. You want to know what I dream for the future? Fine. I dream of—" He stopped abruptly and clamped his mouth shut.

"You dream of what?" Violet asked softly. In her heart, he said *you*.

But his eyes traveled from her face to her feet, then to the stairway. "I don't dream of anything for the future. My future is dead, too."

He turned and disappeared into his apartment, the click of the door ricocheting around the landing.

Violet stood staring at the closed door, feeling as if her future had somehow died as well.

# Chapter 24

Monday morning, Violet rolled over with her eyes clamped shut when the alarm went off. She'd been finding it easier to get out of bed lately, finding herself actually looking forward to the days. But after last night, she had to face the fact that today held no promise.

She scooted closer to what had been Cade's side of the bed and hugged his pillow to her body, inhaling deeply. But only the clean scent of laundry detergent reached her nose. Cade's sea-spray scent had long since faded.

The fabric grew damp under her cheek as the ache that had been starting to fade reared again in all its brutal glory. Her insides burned with it. She needed Cade here. Needed his arms around her. Needed his hand cupped against the back of her head, stroking her hair and telling her it would all be okay. More than anything, she needed to talk to him, needed the closeness of having someone to share everything with.

She'd almost thought she was finding that again.

With Nate.

But it turned out that had been an illusion, wishful thinking.

What she'd had with Cade was a once-in-a-lifetime intimacy.

She wouldn't find it again with anyone else. So she would stop looking. Focus on the store, maybe get more involved in church, and forget she had almost dreamed of more.

As the alarm blared for a second time, Violet groaned but pushed the pillow away from her face and dried her eyes.

After dressing in sweats and pulling her hair into a messy ponytail, she sent Sophie a quick text asking if they could meet for breakfast. She'd been trying to let Sophie and Spencer adjust to married life without too many interruptions, but she really needed her best friend right now.

She tried not to dwell on the irony that she had always been the one to dispense relationship advice, not the one needing it.

Sophie replied with an immediate yes, and twenty minutes later, Violet was seated at their usual table at the Hidden Cafe, nursing a cup of coffee. The restaurant was bustling today, and every few minutes, someone stopped at the table to say hello. Violet thought she'd done a pretty good job of keeping up the happy pretense so far, but if one more person asked her how she was doing, she was going to bolt.

Fortunately, Sophie breezed through the door just as one of the older ladies from church spotted Violet. Violet gave the woman a quick wave, then got up to hug Sophie.

"Sorry it took me so long to get here." Sophie squeezed her lightly. "Spencer wanted my opinion on the gazebo he's building in the garden."

Violet ignored the pang that shot through her middle. It wasn't Sophie's fault that she was living in wedded bliss while Violet was fighting to get through the day.

"What happened to you guys last night? Is Nate okay?" Sophie let go and settled into her seat.

Violet shrugged. "I have no idea if he's okay." Her voice contained a bitterness that she didn't like to hear from herself. But she didn't know how to make it go away.

"What do you mean?" Sophie's face reflected genuine concern, and Violet realized once more how good moving back to Hope Springs had been for her friend. The hardness that used to keep her from opening herself to others had softened into a kindness that came out in everything she did.

"I mean he shut me out. I found him crumpled on the sidewalk, Soph, completely—" She searched for the word. "Broken." There was no other way to describe it. "But he wouldn't tell me what was wrong. I thought maybe it was because I tricked him into coming to the church."

"You tricked him?" Sophie's voice held a reprimand, but she couldn't be more disappointed in Violet than Violet was in herself.

"I know I shouldn't have." She pressed a hand to her heart. "It's just, he used to be in a Christian band and I thought—"

"He was in a band?" Sophie's mouth fell open.

"I know, hard to believe, right? But for some reason, he stopped going to church somewhere along the line. And I thought if I could get him inside a church, he might, I don't know—"

"Come back?"

Violet nodded. "But I don't think that was the only thing, Soph. I think it was—" She broke off in frustration. "I don't know."

"What makes you think it was more?" Sophie took the coffee the waitress handed her and added cream and sugar.

"Have you ever looked into his eyes?"

"I guess. They're blue, aren't they?"

"They're—" Violet stared out the window at the lake. "They're like the lake in a storm, all churned up and conflicted and almost . . . haunted."

She could feel Sophie watching her, but she couldn't return her gaze. Sophie had been close to Cade, too. What must she think about the fact that Violet had noticed another man's eyes?

"And he has scars," she continued. "One on his knee. And one across his chest."

Sophie's coffee cup clanked to the table harder than normal.

"I mean—" Violet's face warmed. "He had a nightmare that night we went to pick up the hutch. I went in to see what was wrong, and he had his shirt off, and he had a scar from here—" She touched her shoulder and drew a line diagonally across her chest. "To here."

"It sounds like—"

"And that's another thing." Now that she had gotten going, Violet couldn't stop. "That nightmare really shook him. But he couldn't tell me about it. Even though I told him about mine."

"You have nightmares?" Hurt flashed in Sophie's eyes for a second but then was replaced by concern.

Violet reached across the table to grab her friend's hand. "Not so much anymore. I wasn't trying to keep them a secret from you. I just didn't want to worry you when you had all the wedding stuff to deal with."

Sophie laid her other hand on top of Violet's. "I always want to know, Vi, no matter what's going on with me."

"I know." She'd been silly to keep the dreams from Sophie. She was still getting used to her best friend being here for her again.

"Anyway." Sophie gave her a gentle smile. "He may not have come out and *told* you a lot about himself. But he's let you learn a lot about him in other ways."

Violet gaped at her friend. What other ways were there?

"Think about it, Vi." Sophie took a long drink of coffee, watching her over the rim.

Violet fidgeted under her scrutiny. Okay, fine, she knew Nate liked cookies and that he claimed not to like antiques, though she was pretty sure she was bringing him around on that one. She knew he was kind and protective and loved his dog. She knew he had a big heart that he kept guarded most of the time. She knew he had problems with his family and with church. But that was the thing—she didn't know why.

"I get your point," she finally said. "But there are so many pieces missing. And he's not willing to fill them in."

Sophie looked thoughtful. "You know his *character*, Vi. That's not something to take lightly. The rest is just details. And maybe those details are too painful right now. Sometimes people's scars run so deep that they can't see the only way to heal them is to share them."

Violet turned that over in her mind. Nate did seem to be deeply scarred—not only physically but emotionally and spiritually.

"Be patient." Sophie's voice had a gentle quality. "If you're still there when he's ready, he'll tell you."

Violet ignored the strange looks from passing tourists as she speed walked toward Nate's office building. After saying goodbye to Sophie, she'd spent the entire morning walking around town. Walking and thinking.

And she'd realized that Sophie was right. It wasn't important for her to know all the details of Nate's life. What was important was that she *knew* him. Knew his heart.

And she'd come to care about him, much as she'd tried not to.

So she'd be patient with him. Wait for him to be ready to talk to her. And in the meantime, she'd give him the cookies she'd stopped at Peyton's bakery to pick up.

Their mouth-watering aroma drifted from the bag. Maybe she'd stay and eat one with him. If he wanted her to.

She paused in the building's entrance and read the small directory sign. Instead of slowing now that she'd stopped walking, her heart rate kicked up a notch. She pressed a hand to her stomach. It was silly to feel so nervous and excited to see Nate when she'd seen him every day for the past few weeks. But seeking him out at work felt like she was taking things a step farther.

A baby step, maybe.

But still a step.

According to the directory, Nate's office was on the second floor. She wandered down the hallway until she came to a staircase. She climbed it slowly to give her heart a second to calm down.

The second-floor hallway was empty, with two doors leading off it. Neither was marked. She passed the first—she couldn't picture Nate decorating with the big vase of fake flowers that stood outside it.

Inside the next office, a young woman sat at a reception desk. Violet startled. Nate had never said anything about having a receptionist, but then, he didn't talk about his work much, aside from the occasional updates on things with her lease. So far Talmadge had rejected every other property Nate had shown him. Which was why she had to figure out a way to make up the rest of the back rent she owed—and soon.

But she could deal with that later. For now, she just wanted to see Nate. To reassure him that his aloofness wasn't going to scare her away.

"Can I help you?" The receptionist was gorgeous, with blond hair that flowed in a sleek line to her shoulders and high cheekbones defined by perfect makeup. Violet ignored a pinprick of jealousy as she glanced at her running shorts and tried to tuck a stray curl into her messy ponytail.

"I'm looking for Nate Benson." She tried to keep her voice professional.

A young guy emerged from behind the wall that separated the reception area from the rest of the office. "His office is down the hall on the left side. The one with the big vase. But you might want to knock first. I think he's in there with his girlfriend."

Violet's heart faltered.

*His girlfriend?*

She worked to cover the shock she was sure showed on her face. "Thank you."

She slipped out of the room into the hallway, heart thudding dully against her ribs. Nate had a girlfriend?

The guy had to be wrong. Nate wasn't the kind of man who would string two women along.

Or was he? Maybe she knew him less than she thought she did. Which was barely at all.

She should just go.

But before she could take a step, the office down the hall opened, and Nate ushered a woman through it. Violet recognized her as the same woman who'd visited his apartment right after he'd moved in. He'd said she was a business associate.

But she was carrying a pizza box and a water bottle.

They were facing the other direction, and neither of them noticed her.

"You did not seriously do that." The woman's laugh carried down the hallway, and Violet's hand tightened on the bag of cookies.

"I promise you I did." His rich voice was warm and uninhibited. Unlike last night, when it'd taken all her effort to get two words from him.

"I'd better get going." The woman pulled her keys out of her purse. "Lunch was a brilliant idea, by the way. It was nice to have a few minutes to stop and eat for a change."

Nate laughed. "No problem. See you next time."

The woman set off down the hallway, and Violet stood frozen. She'd been stupid to come. Stupid to think anything was developing between her and Nate. She'd let her own loneliness convince her there was something there that wasn't. It wasn't that his past was too painful to share.

It was that he didn't want to share it with her.

189

So she'd wait until he went into his office and then slink away and enjoy the cookies herself at home. She tried to loosen her grip on the bag, but it slipped from her hands. The fall wasn't far, but the sound of the bag hitting the floor was enough to make Nate turn his head.

A smile lifted his lips, but it didn't reach his eyes, which were still guarded. Or rather, guarded again. She imagined they'd been plenty unguarded when he'd been talking to his "business associate."

"Hey." He strode toward her. "What are you doing here?"

He leaned forward as if he was about to hug her but then pulled back.

Violet tried to mask the hurt lancing her heart. He'd never offered her anything more than friendship. If she'd come to expect more, that was her own fault.

His eyes widened as they fell on the bag. "Are those cookies from Peyton's?"

She passed them to him. "Just my way of apologizing for dragging you to the concert last night."

She moved to step around him, but he laid a hand on her arm. "I'm the one who should be apologizing. I'm sorry for ruining the evening."

She shrugged. The best thing she could do right now was be indifferent. Or at least pretend to be. "It was no big deal."

Confusion and hurt clouded his expression as he studied her. He grabbed a cookie out of the bag and held it out to her.

"No thanks." She pushed past the outstretched cookie and sped down the hallway.

She couldn't stay here one second longer.

# Chapter 25

Nate stared after Violet's retreating form. He must have done something wrong. But he had no idea what.

He took a bite of the cookie he still held in his hand, but he barely tasted it.

What did it mean that she'd sought him out like this? After last night, he'd been sure she'd never want to see him again.

He'd shown her his weakness. His most vulnerable side. And he'd noticed the hurt in her eyes when he'd refused to talk to her about it.

He'd left early this morning so he wouldn't have to run into her, wouldn't have to face her questions about why he'd had a minor breakdown over a concert of all things.

He took another bite of cookie, then dropped it into the bag. It was delicious as always, but he was too stuffed from the pizza he'd shared with Officer Jensen.

He drew up short outside his office door.

Was that what this was about? Did Violet think there was something going on between him and Officer Jensen?

That was ridiculous. But also . . . touching.

When was the last time anyone had been jealous for his attention?

Nate stood in the doorway, undecided.

Should he go after her, tell her she'd misunderstood who Officer Jensen was? But the moment he'd decided he should, another thought came

191

crashing in to smash the plan. If he told her that, he'd have to tell her who Officer Jensen really was.

And he wasn't sure he was ready to do that.

He shuffled slowly into his office.

Maybe this was for the best anyway. He'd let his heart get too far into this already.

Worse, he'd let her heart get into it, too. He didn't deserve a woman like her, and he knew it. He should let things end before he risked hurting her more than he already had.

A part of him refused to agree, arguing that he owed it to her to tell her how he felt. To sweep her off her feet and promise he'd care for her forever.

That was the part he wanted to listen to.

But before he could follow her, the office phone gave the shrill ring Nate had come to despise.

He sighed, resigned. If that wasn't a sign that he'd been about to do the wrong thing, he didn't know what was.

He returned to his desk and picked up the receiver. Lately, Dad had only been calling every few days. Could be that he was starting to trust Nate again. Or could be that he was sick of hearing Nate's voice every day. It didn't really matter to Nate. Either way, not having to check in with Dad every day was a plus.

"Did you look at that clause yet?" Might as well get right to the point. Nate had sent Dad Violet's lease weeks ago, with the unclear clause highlighted, but so far Dad hadn't said what he was going to do about it.

"I had my attorneys look into it." Dad did not sound happy. "They agree that according to that clause, if they make up their back rent, they have until the end of this month to renew."

Nate allowed himself a brief fist pump. "Great. I'll take Talmadge out to a few more places, then. He wasn't willing to look at them before, but—"

"Slow up, Nathan." Dad's voice was controlled, as always. "Talmadge still needs to get into that building. Do you think these people—this Cade and Violet Somers—are going to make the back rent?"

"It's just Violet. Her husband Cade died a few years ago."

Dad was silent, and Nate took it as a sign that he didn't care.

"And, yes, I think there's a good chance she'll be able to make the back rent. She's more than halfway there already."

"That can't happen, Nathan." Dad's voice was hard. "Talmadge wants that spot, and he's going to get it, one way or another."

"If she pays the rent, you can't—" Nate forced himself to stop and take a swig from the water bottle on his desk. He needed a second to get control of the anger boiling low in his stomach.

"You're not hearing me, Nathan. Whether she pays the rent or not, whether she wants to leave or not, whether you're sleeping with her or not, she needs to be out of there."

Nate choked on his water. "Sleeping with her?"

"Talmadge told me what's going on. Said he saw you groping her in the middle of her store. I would have thought your family would have meant more to you than a few cheap thrills, but I guess some things never change."

Nate chomped down on his tongue, hard, and counted to ten before answering.

"First of all, we are not sleeping together." How dare his father imply that? "And I was not groping her. We're friends and I was giving her a hug."

"Frankly, Nathan," Dad continued as if Nate hadn't said anything, "I'm surprised you would jeopardize your chance to see your mother and sister like this. All for some—"

"Don't say it." Nate shoved to his feet, his voice hard and firm.

"Don't say what?" Dad feigned innocence.

"Whatever you were about to say, don't say it. Violet is a kind and wonderful woman, and I'm not going to sit here and listen to you drag her name through the mud."

"If you care about her that much, I'd suggest you convince her to find a new location for her store. Because she's going to be out of there one way or another come next month."

"Why?" Nate dropped into his chair and scrubbed a hand down his cheek. "Why does it have to be this spot?"

Dad didn't say anything for a minute, and Nate figured he wasn't going to deign to answer.

"It's the spot Talmadge wants. And he's offering a lot for it. I don't think I have to remind you that we have some pretty large medical bills to pay off. Or had you forgotten?"

Nate dropped his head to the desk. Of course he hadn't forgotten.

"When can I see them?" He didn't know how much longer he could stand not talking to his mom or his sister.

"Stop yanking Talmadge around to all these other properties he doesn't want and get this done. Then we'll talk."

"And if she pays her back rent? You won't be able to cancel the lease then."

"Don't play hardball with me, Nathan. We both know I could plow her under in court. She doesn't have the resources to pay her rent, let alone deal with court fees. You don't want things to get ugly."

Nate shook his head. He was pretty sure they already had. "So you're going to kick her out of there, regardless of what her contract says?"

Dad hesitated, then spoke slowly and deliberately. "I'm not. You are."

Nate's feet dragged across the sidewalk. Even though he'd walked as slowly as he could, he'd arrived at Violet's store way too quickly. He'd debated coming. After the way she'd fled his office earlier, she obviously didn't want anything to do with him. And he didn't come bearing good news.

But she deserved to know that he was running out of ideas to save her store.

He didn't want to tell her to give up. But what else could she do?

He let himself into the back door of the apartment building, taking a second to steel himself. The light was on in her workshop, so he pushed the door open. But she wasn't back there. He continued to the front of the store. His breath got caught halfway to his lungs the moment he saw her. She was sitting on that Victorian couch she loved so much, the one she'd told him she imagined a young couple had spent hours sitting on, just talking, learning everything there was to know about each other. Nate had recoiled from the idea. The thought of someone knowing everything about him was too terrifying.

But at the same time, he'd been filled with a strange sort of longing for that kind of closeness. Not with just anyone.

With her.

He directed a disgusted grunt at himself. She was the last person he deserved to have that kind of relationship with.

And he was the last person she'd want a relationship with. Especially if she knew the truth about him.

He cleared his throat and stepped into the room.

The moment she turned to him, her eyes widened with surprise and something more—like hope. But a second later, they darkened. She looked away. "I thought you were at work."

"I, uh—" Nate's voice had suddenly dried up, like a desert stream that had gone too long without rain. "Could we talk?"

She pressed her lips into a line but nodded.

He moved closer, remaining on his feet and keeping the low coffee table as a barrier between them. "First of all, I wanted to clear things up." He licked his lips.

She was watching him closely, but her expression was nearly blank. She didn't encourage him to go on, but she didn't stop him either.

"I just thought, ah—" Okay, this was going to be harder than he'd thought. "I mean, I wanted to say that the woman you saw at my office— I'm not—" Why was this so difficult? "I'm not seeing her. Or anything. She's a business associate. We had a working lunch."

Violet shrugged and looked away. "There's nothing to clear up. It's none of my business whether she's a business associate or—" She blinked. "Or something else."

Nate's heart shriveled to a dehydrated lump. Much as he knew she was better off without him, he wanted it to be her business. He wanted her to care. He wanted her to want to be the only one he cared about.

Because she was.

But he forced himself to nod. To say, "Good."

She got up and walked toward her desk. "I should get back to work. I'm swamped today."

Nate swiveled to take in the empty store. It was Monday, so she wasn't even open today.

"Actually—" He followed her. "There's something else."

When she turned, her eyes, usually so warm, were shuttered. "What is it?"

He swallowed. He'd do anything not to tell her this. But he didn't see any way around it. "I just spoke to my father. And I think you might need to start looking for a new space."

Her expression crumpled, but she didn't move, didn't make a sound.

"I'm sorry, Violet. I tried. I'm still trying. But this Talmadge guy isn't giving up, and for some reason my dad is determined to give him what he wants. I don't know—"

"It's fine." Her voice was strained but loud.

"I'll keep—"

"I said it's fine. I'll figure something out."

Nate took a tentative step closer, but she retreated. He dragged a hand through his hair. "Let me help, Violet. We have some other properties that might—"

"I said I'll figure something out, Nate. Thank you for letting me know." Her overly polite tone stabbed at him.

"Yeah, of course." He walked to the door.

When he reached it, he allowed himself a glance over his shoulder.

Violet was holding a small music box in her hands and didn't look up.

He let the door close behind him with a soft click.

# Chapter 26

In spite of herself, Violet glanced toward the back door of the workshop. It was Friday, and she'd caught herself doing the same thing all week at this time. The time Nate used to come home from the office and stop by to talk.

She'd barely seen him at all since Monday when he'd told her she might as well give up, and she suspected he was avoiding her as much as she was avoiding him. On the few occasions they'd accidentally run into each other, they'd said hello or made a bland comment about the weather.

But nothing more.

Every word between them was stilted and formal now. Too polite.

Violet felt like a part of her—the part that had started to thaw—had frozen over again, more solid than ever.

She told herself it was for the best. If she'd let it keep thawing, it would only have hurt more when she fell through.

She turned her attention to the silver she was polishing. At least she could rub the tarnish off of some things.

A clang from the chimes drew a groan. She should be happy to have a customer, but it wasn't going to do a lot of good at this point. Nate had as much as told her she was out of here after next month anyway. She didn't know if she had the energy to start her store again in a new location. Maybe it was time to give up Cade's dream. Even if it had become her dream somewhere along the line, too.

She gave the spoon one last rub, then wiped her hands and started for the front of the store.

But the moment she saw her visitor, she wished she'd run away instead.

Talmadge looked up from a display of muskets and gave her the smile that always made her think of a rodent. She held back a shudder. Something about the guy didn't sit right with her, but she nudged the feeling away. Just because he wanted the same property she wanted didn't make him a bad guy.

"Mr. Talmadge." Her voice wasn't exactly welcoming, but she worked hard not to sound rude. "How can I help you?"

Talmadge approached and held out his hand, as if he were greeting an old friend. She shook his reluctantly.

"Came to take some measurements. My designer needs them to draw up plans for my new space." His smile morphed into a leer. "I trust you'll have all this junk out of here by the time I'm ready to start work."

Goosebumps rose on Violet's arms, but she refused to flinch. "To my understanding, no agreement has been finalized. I'll be staying here until I receive word otherwise."

"Look—" Talmadge lowered his voice. "I don't know what your boyfriend has promised you. But let's just say, this space is going to be mine one way or another. You should take a hint and move out. Before anything forces your hand."

Violet drew back. Was that a threat? Something hardened in her gut. She wasn't going to let Cade's dream go to this man. Not if she could help it.

"I wouldn't get too comfortable here, Mr. Talmadge. I have a lease with Benson Properties, and I intend to hold them to it."

Talmadge's barking laugh bit against her ears, but she didn't move. He held up his tape measure. "You and your intentions can do what you want. I'm going to go take some measurements." He swaggered toward the workshop, still chuckling to himself.

Steam boiled through Violet's blood. Who did this guy think he was, marching into her store and treating it as his own? She was tempted to call the police, but she didn't want to let him know he'd gotten to her.

For half a second, she wished Nate would show up to rescue her. But then she reminded herself that Nate wasn't on her side anymore. He'd probably tell her Talmadge was right and she should start packing.

She prayed for the clock to move faster. In ten minutes, the store would be closed, and she could ask Talmadge to leave. She tried to sort through the day's mail, but she had no idea what she was looking at. Every few seconds, her eyes darted toward the workshop. She could hear him shuffling around back there, but she couldn't see him. And she wasn't about to give him the satisfaction of thinking she was curious about what he was doing.

Finally, with one minute to go before closing time, he emerged. "Got everything I need." His voice was jovial.

She gritted her teeth, eyes still on the mail.

But a second later, she had to look up as he invaded the space right next to her. She resisted taking a step back. She couldn't let him think he was intimidating her.

"This is the last time I'm going to say this. Make things easy on yourself and get out now. Believe me when I say you'll regret it if you don't."

"You'll forgive me if I decline." Violet pushed past him toward the front door. "Now, if you'll excuse me. My store is closed for the day, and I'd like to lock up."

"Of course." Talmadge offered an oily smile and followed her. Halfway to the front of the room, he stopped. "Almost forgot my tape measure."

Violet waited at the front door as he disappeared into the workshop again. Her teeth were clamped so tight, she was afraid her jaw would be locked like that forever. Half a minute later, Talmadge emerged, whistling and tossing his tape measure from hand to hand as if it were a baseball.

He winked at her as he passed through the door. "Have a good evening."

The moment his feet cleared the threshold, she slammed the door and twisted the lock. Then she stood for a moment, her breath heaving.

When she finally managed to walk away from the door, it was on shaky legs.

She had no idea what Talmadge thought he was going to do to get her out of the shop. But seeing him in here had convinced her: She wasn't going to give this place up without a fight.

⸎

Nate shut down his computer and shuffled toward his office door. He was a coward, and he knew it.

All week he'd been leaving for the office by six in the morning, long before Violet would be up. He'd been coming home after her store closed, too, slinking past her workshop like a kid sneaking in after curfew, just in case she was still there.

Every time he saw her was like a punch to the gut. A reminder of the life he couldn't have. He needed the distance to help him get over his feelings for her.

Not that it was helping.

Behind the scenes, he was still working to find a way to keep her in the store. But Talmadge had refused to look at the last three properties Nate had proposed to him. And he was getting impatient. The other day he'd threatened to hire movers to come and remove the pieces from Violet's store.

Nate had finally talked him out of it.

He was pretty sure.

The sigh that slipped out as he locked up his office building felt like it would never end. The late September nights had started to cool, and a light breeze blew in off the lake. It was a perfect night to share with someone special. Maybe at dinner. Or maybe a walk on the beach. Or just sitting side by side on a couch.

He picked up his pace.

He had to come to grips with the fact that he would never have that. He kept his head down and walked.

A sharp scent caught at his nose as he approached the back door of the apartment building. He inhaled, trying to place the smell.

Was that smoke?

He looked up and down the street but didn't see any signs of fire. Someone nearby could be grilling out. But the scent wasn't quite right for that.

He gave one last look around before opening the door. The odor hit him full force the moment he stepped inside, and panic flooded his system at the haze of smoke that hung over the stairs. Blood roared in his ears as his hand instinctively flew to cover his mouth and nose. His eyes watered as he swiveled, searching out the source of the fire.

There.

The workshop was supposed to have dim security lights, but it was pitch black now, aside from a faint orange glow in the far corner. Nate's heart kicked up another gear. There were all kinds of chemicals in the workshop.

Flammable chemicals.

And Violet's apartment was directly above it.

Not pausing to think, he tore up the stairs three at a time and rushed her door. But it was locked.

He pounded on it—hard. When she didn't come after a few seconds, he pounded again, then ran to Mrs. D'Angelo's door.

No one answered there, either.

"Come on!" Nate ran back to Violet's door, pounding until his hand throbbed.

The prayer came instinctively. *Please, Lord, let her be okay. Let her answer this door and get out of this building. I don't care what happens to me, but please save her.*

He waited a second, as if he actually thought God might answer his prayer this time.

But when the door still didn't move, he decided he'd have to take things into his own hands. He backed up three steps and charged the door.

He was half a step away from it when it opened, and he went careening through, right into Violet.

He managed to get an arm under her to soften the blow before they both hit the ground.

"Oof. Nate, what—"

"There's a fire. Downstairs." He pushed himself upright but had to stop to cough, and she watched him as if she thought he'd lost his mind. He waved her toward the door, but she didn't move.

He swallowed down the rest of his cough so he could talk. "You have to go. Get outside and call the fire department. I'll get Mrs. D'Angelo."

Her eyes widened in fear, and she scrambled to her feet. A slow stream of smoke had started to filter into the room. She reached a hand to help him up.

But he didn't want her help. He wanted her to get out.

He jumped to his feet. "Go, Violet, now." He grabbed her arm and dragged her into the hallway and toward the stairs, then turned to Mrs. D'Angelo's door.

He pounded on it with two hands.

When he stopped, Violet was right there next to him. "Get out, Violet. Now. Some of those chemicals are explosive."

Violet trembled, but she didn't move away. "Give me your keys."

"What?" But he knew what she was asking. And he wasn't going to let her stay here and risk her life for his dog. He'd get Tony in a minute. After he got Mrs. D'Angelo.

"I'm not leaving without you, Nate, so give me the keys so I can get the dog and you can get Mrs. D'Angelo, and we can all get out of here."

"Why do you have to be so stubborn?" But he was already digging the keys out of his pocket. They didn't have time to stand here and argue. The moment the keys hit her hand, Violet flew across the hall.

Nate gave one more pound on Mrs. D'Angelo's door. When she didn't answer, he barreled at it with his shoulder. It didn't budge. But on the second attempt, he got through.

There was more smoke in here than there had been in Violet's apartment, and he pulled his shirt up over his nose.

"Mrs. D'Angelo?" He ran through the apartment and into her bedroom. She was lying in the bed, eyes closed, and Nate's heart lurched. Had she been overcome by the smoke?

"Mrs. D'Angelo?" He shook her shoulder, but she didn't respond.

He slid one arm under her knees and the other behind her shoulders and lifted her, then careened through the apartment to the landing. The smoke was thicker now, and he fought to see through his watering eyes. "Violet? Tony?"

He moved toward his apartment, but a voice called from the bottom of the stairs. "We're down here, Nate. Get out."

He followed the sound down the stairs and into the night.

# Chapter 27

Violet had never seen anything more beautiful than Nate emerging from the building carrying Mrs. D'Angelo. She ran to them and wrapped her arm around Nate's back, steering him to the grassy hill.

Nate laid Mrs. D'Angelo on the grass, and she dropped to the older woman's side. Tony hovered close to them.

Next to her, Nate gasped around coughs. "Is she—"

"She's breathing. And she has a pulse." Her heart eased a little as she felt the faint rhythm in Mrs. D'Angelo's wrist. "The fire department is on the way." Already sirens had cut through the quiet of the night, drowning out the crickets and the waves below.

Nate moved closer to kneel at her side, and they both stared toward the building. From out here, everything looked almost normal, aside from the smoke drifting out the back door. "How bad do you think it is?" she whispered.

A hand slid into hers and squeezed, and she leaned into him. Tony pressed up against her other side.

"It will be okay." His voice was hoarse, but its low rumble was reassuring. "Everyone's safe."

Violet nodded against his shoulder.

A second later, the first fire truck rumbled into the parking lot, an ambulance close behind it.

"Stay with her." Nate jogged toward the rig, where firemen were scrambling to roll out hoses and flip switches. With their equipment on, there was no way to tell if any of them were Jared or Ethan. Violet sent up a prayer for the firefighters' protection, whoever they were.

A few seconds later, Nate returned, along with two firefighters carrying a stretcher between them.

"It's going to be okay, Violet." She couldn't make out Ethan's face in the dark, but she recognized his voice, and a wave of reassurance washed over her.

As Ethan dropped to the ground next to Mrs. D'Angelo, Violet scrambled to get out of the way. Nate moved to her side. The arm he wrapped around her was solid and reassuring. She didn't care about anything else that had happened between them. Right now, she was grateful to have him here.

She bowed her head. She wasn't going to stop praying until this whole thing was over and all those firefighters were out of there safely. She'd meant to pray silently, but she couldn't stop the words from reaching her lips in a whisper. She half expected Nate to drop his arm once he realized what she was doing, but he only pulled her in closer.

After a few minutes, Ethan and the other firefighter lifted the stretcher with Mrs. D'Angelo. Her eyes were open now, and she had an oxygen mask over her face.

"Is she going to be okay?" Violet's voice shook. How would she live with herself if a fire that had started in her workshop took the dear old lady's life?

"We'll know more once we get her to the hospital, but I think so. I really should lecture you two about how you're supposed to get out and leave the saving others to us, but if she'd been in there much longer . . ." He grimaced. "What about you two? Did you inhale any smoke?"

Violet shook her head. "I'm fine. Nate inhaled a bunch, though. He was coughing and—"

"I'm fine." Nate cut her off. "Just get Mrs. D'Angelo to the hospital."

Ethan set off toward the ambulance. "I'll send someone over to examine you," he called over his shoulder.

As she watched Mrs. D'Angelo's still form, Violet's knees went weak. If Nate hadn't gotten them out . . .

She sagged against him, and he lowered her gently to the ground. "You okay?"

She tried to nod, but she was shaking all over now.

"You're in shock. Just a second." Nate passed her Tony's leash and jogged toward the fire trucks. Beyond the trucks, firefighters entered the building, hoses unwinding behind them. She prayed harder.

Nate talked with a firefighter standing next to the fire truck, then jogged back to her carrying a blanket. He wrapped it around her shoulders, then sat next to her and curled his arm around her, moving it up and down her back.

"Thank you." The words were way too small, but there was nothing else she could say.

His arm tightened around her, and she risked a look at his face. His teeth were clenched, but a muscle in his jaw jumped.

"I was in the shower. I had no idea there was anything wrong until I heard you pounding on the door. And then it took me a minute to get dressed." She glanced down, realizing for the first time that she was wearing her kitten pajamas.

"I'm sorry I knocked you down up there." Nate's voice was low. "When you didn't answer the door, I just . . ." That muscle in his jaw jumped again. "I was desperate to get to you."

She shuddered as all the emotions of the night washed over her. "How did you know there was a fire? Was there smoke in your apartment?"

"No. I just got home. I thought I smelled smoke when I was outside, but I couldn't place it. And then I opened the door and realized where it was coming from. I was—" His swallow was audible. When he finally finished the sentence, his voice was barely a whisper. "I was scared."

Violet angled so she could see him better. "But you ran into the building instead of out?"

His eyes met hers in surprise. "Of course I ran in. I wasn't scared for me. I was scared for you."

"Oh." Their eyes held, and her heart jumped. He had risked his life for her. Even after the cold way she'd been treating him all week. She'd been unfair. It wasn't his fault his dad was insisting on leasing the space to someone else.

She didn't know how long they sat like that, but she couldn't make herself look away. After a while, a paramedic came over, insisting that they be examined for smoke inhalation. Even as the paramedic listened to her lungs and examined her nose and throat, Violet couldn't take her eyes off Nate.

When they were finally given a clean bill of health, they walked hand-in-hand toward the fire trucks, where the firefighters were wrapping up their hoses.

One of the firefighters pulled off his helmet and approached them. As he got closer, Violet recognized him, and she let go of Nate's hand to run and hug Jared. "Thank you for being here."

He returned her hug. "The fire is out. It's not as bad as it looks. There's a lot of soot damage, but the structural damage is minimal. It looks like something was smoldering for quite a while before it flamed up. I'd say you caught it just in the nick of time."

Violet's heart jumped. If it weren't for Nate, she could be dealing with a whole lot more than soot damage. "What caused it?"

"Hard to say right now. We'll have an inspector check things out in the morning. In the meantime, you two are probably going to need somewhere else to stay tonight. Just until we can get someone in there to make sure everything is safe."

"Yeah, of course. Thank you again. I'm so glad you're all safe." She squeezed his arm, and he went back to help the crew finish cleaning up.

She pulled out her phone and dialed Sophie's number. She hated to intrude on her friends, but she knew Sophie would never forgive her if she sought help anywhere else.

As she lifted the phone to her ear, she turned to Nate. But he wasn't where she'd left him. She scanned the parking lot. He was at the far end, rounding the building into the narrow alley that led to the street, Tony following obediently.

Where on earth was he going? She set off after him at a run.

"Hi, Violet." Just the sound of Sophie's voice brought tears to Violet's eyes. She was so fortunate to have friends she could count on.

"Hey, Soph." She panted as she ran. "Can you hold on a second?"

"Sure. What's going on?"

But Violet lowered the phone as she closed the distance to Nate. He must have heard her footsteps because he turned toward her a few steps before she reached him.

"Where are you going?" The words came out in little gasps.

"Jared said we couldn't stay in the building tonight, so I figured I'd sleep at my office."

She stared at him with her mouth open. Was he kidding? The guy had saved her life, and he thought she was going to let him sleep in his office?

"No one's sleeping in an office. You'll come stay at Spencer and Sophie's with me."

"But I—"

She held up a hand, then lifted the phone to her ear. The moment she told Sophie what happened, Sophie insisted that they both stay there.

"Let's go." She hung up the phone and grabbed Nate's hand, tugging him toward her car.

But his feet remained planted. "I couldn't expect them to do that."

Violet rolled her eyes. And he thought she was stubborn? "They want to do it, Nate. They're your friends. They care about you." She almost added, *I care about you*. But she managed to swallow the words at the last second.

There would be plenty of time to sort out her feelings for him later.

For now, they both just needed a place to sleep.

# Chapter 28

"How'd you sleep?" Sophie passed Violet a cup of coffee, and Violet took it gratefully.

"Good, thanks." Better than she'd expected, actually.

Before she'd climbed into bed, thoughts about what could have happened and what would happen next had jostled for position of number-one worry. But the moment her head had hit the pillow, she'd been out.

And she'd begun her morning with a deep, long prayer about everything she had to deal with today.

She was as ready as she ever would be to handle whatever this day held.

"Is Nate up yet?" She tried to keep her voice casual, but the moment she looked at her friend, she knew she hadn't succeeded.

But all Sophie said was, "He's out in the shed with Spencer. I don't think he slept much."

Violet nodded and took another sip, but when she put the coffee cup down, Sophie was watching her.

"What?"

"Nothing." But the soft smile on Sophie's lips said it was something.

"Don't go getting any ideas, Soph. There's nothing going on between us."

Sophie laid a hand on her arm. "The man ran into a burning building to save you, Vi. That's not nothing."

Violet's whole body warmed. "He would have done that for anyone." But she couldn't deny that she'd thought the same thing. "Anyway, I can't really think about that right now. I want to get over to the store and see how bad things are."

"We're coming with you." Sophie dumped the last drops of her coffee into the sink and grabbed her keys. "Come on."

Violet didn't want to take her friends away from their day. But she couldn't say no. She was going to need all the support she could get.

As they stepped outside, Violet let herself pull in a breath of the fresh morning air.

The trees had taken on the brilliant hues of fall, and there was a bite to the air this morning, but she relished the feel of it in her lungs.

She should be depressed and scared after what had happened to her store.

But this morning, she felt blessed.

Blessed to be alive.

Blessed to have such amazing friends.

Blessed to have such an amazing . . . whatever Nate was to her.

It didn't mean seeing her store wasn't going to be hard. It didn't mean figuring out what to do next would be easy. But it did mean she knew she'd get through it, whatever happened.

Tony ran to greet them the moment they opened the door of the pole shed Spencer used as a woodworking shop. Violet crouched to pet him, her eyes searching the space until they found Nate.

He was bent in half, his head under a patio table Spencer had built. "That's some great craftsmanship."

The moment he stood, his eyes fell on her, and she could have sworn they brightened a shade. The light played on his face as he crossed the shed to her, accentuating his chiseled jaw, which was lined with stubble this morning.

It was a good look on him.

"Hey." He stopped just far enough away that Tony could stand between them. "How are you doing?" The concern in his eyes made her heart squeeze.

"I'm good." She squatted to pet Tony again, mostly to break the intensity of the gaze they shared.

"Violet." His voice was so quiet it made her look up. "How are you really?" He searched her face.

She stood and touched a hand to his forearm. "I promise. I'm good. When I take stock of what could have happened and what did happen—"

She swallowed past a fresh knot of emotion at the way God had spared them all. "I'm good."

He gave her an uncertain look but nodded.

"Should we go?" Sophie's voice from behind her made Violet jump. She'd almost forgotten that she and Nate weren't alone.

She made herself look away from Nate. "Yeah. I'm ready."

"Everyone else is going to meet us there. We should be able to make a good dent in the cleanup today." Sophie took Spencer's hand as they led the way out of the shed.

"Everyone else?" Violet stopped in her tracks. "I don't expect everyone to give up their day to do that."

Sophie waved off her comment, so she turned to Nate to protest.

But he smiled at her. "They're your friends. They care about you." She read in his eyes the words he left off—the same words she hadn't let herself say last night.

He cared about her, too.

Violet stared at the clothes iron the fire inspector held out toward her.

The initial shock of seeing her workshop covered with soot and partially destroyed hadn't worn off yet. And now he was telling her he thought the iron had started the fire.

"I don't understand how . . ." She spoke loudly to be heard over the industrial vacuum Dan was using to suck up soot particles.

The inspector passed her a piece of charred fabric. "This is all that was left, but I'd guess the iron was left on top of it, and the fabric smoldered for a while until it caught fire and spread." He gestured to the burned-out remains of a table, a bookshelf, two wicker chairs, and a shelving unit.

"But—" She tried to recall what she had ironed last. "I haven't used this iron in at least two weeks." She'd been working on a particularly stubborn set of drapes then, but they were on the sales floor now.

The inspector's brow furrowed. "It couldn't have been smoldering that long. Maybe you accidentally threw some fabric over it yesterday?"

Violet scrunched her face, trying to remember what she'd done yesterday. "I didn't touch any fabric yesterday. Actually—" She rubbed at the fabric in her hand. Through the char, she could make out a faint pattern of stripes. "This was on a roll on a shelf over there." She pointed across the room to where the rest of the fabric she used for reupholstering jobs rested on a shelf, all blackened by soot.

"You're sure?" The inspector's expression hardened.

"Absolutely sure. I haven't reupholstered anything in months."

Nate came over from where he'd been scrubbing soot off the walls with the special cleaning solution they'd picked up at the hardware store. "Is there anything else that could have caused it?" His voice was sure and firm, and Violet felt again the reassurance of having him near.

"Not that I've seen." The inspector grimaced. "I'll do some more digging, though."

Nate turned to Violet. "In the meantime, what do you want to do with these things?" He gestured to the blackened remains of the furniture that had been destroyed. "Is there any reason to save them?"

Violet shook her head. "No, they're not salvageable. But I should probably take some pictures first for insurance."

When they came to the burnt-through table where the inspector said he'd found the iron, Nate gave a low whistle. All that was left was a leg and half of a bottom support beam.

Violet frowned at the table. Why would she have put her iron here? She always used the ironing board Cade had built into the end of one of the shelving units. And she always put the iron away when she was done with it. Cade's tendency to leave out his tools had driven her crazy for that very reason.

An image of Talmadge rummaging around back here yesterday hit her, and she gasped.

"What's wrong?" Nate's head jerked up.

"Talmadge came in yesterday. He said he had to take some measurements back here."

Nate waited, obviously not picking up on where she was going with this.

"He said if I didn't move out of the store, I was going to regret it. I thought he wanted to intimidate me, but—"

"You think he did this?" Nate sounded incredulous.

"I don't know." She didn't particularly like Talmadge, but did she really think he would have burned down her store?

Nate dropped the table leg and moved closer to her, putting a hand on each of her shoulders. "That seems unlikely. Why would he destroy a building he wants to move into?"

Violet bit her lip. She had to admit it didn't make a lot of sense, but something about the way Talmadge had acted yesterday stuck in her gut.

"Or maybe he was trying to destroy some of my inventory. Make me give up. I'm telling you, he was ready to do whatever it took to get in here."

Nate scrubbed a hand over his face. "Okay. We should at least mention this to the fire inspector. And I'll talk to my dad. We'll get to the bottom of this. I promise."

Nate threw the table leg in the back of Spencer's pickup truck, then edged around the building and pulled out his phone. He didn't want Violet to stumble on this conversation. Not until he was sure.

He hated to think his dad was capable of it, but he had to ask.

The phone rang five times, and Nate was starting to contemplate what kind of message to leave, when someone picked up.

"Hello?"

He sucked in a sharp breath at his mother's voice and blinked back the heat behind his eyelids. He pressed his forearm to the building's brick wall and rested his head against it.

He could barely speak through the well of emotion building from his core. "Mom," he managed to croak.

"Nate?" Mom's voice sounded unsure.

He sniffed and cleared his throat. "Yeah, Mom, it's me." He swallowed past the burn. "It's so good to hear your voice."

"Yours, too." He could hear the tears behind her words.

"Mom, I'm so sorry, I never—"

But she was talking over him. "Where are you?"

He paused. What did she mean, where was he?

Before he could answer, he heard his father's voice in the background, followed by a low murmur from his mother.

"Mom?"

"I thought I told you not to call your mother. Do you have that much trouble following simple directions?" Dad's voice was as uninviting as ever.

Nate stiffened. "I wasn't calling to talk to her. I was calling to talk to you." Anger drew him up taller, as if he were face-to-face with his dad instead of hundreds of miles away. "What did you do to Violet's store?"

"First of all, you'd do well not to talk to me like that. And second, what are you talking about? I told you I was going to get her out of there. And that's what I'm doing."

"By having her building set on fire?" Nate was practically yelling, and he lowered his voice so no one would overhear. "She could have died." He could have died, too, for that matter. But he didn't bring that up. It wasn't like Dad would care anyway.

"Why I what?" The shock in Dad's voice was unmistakable, but Nate wasn't convinced.

"Don't play dumb, Dad. Were you after the insurance payout? Or was this all to get Talmadge what he wanted? Because either way, you failed. The fire is out, and Violet still has a store."

"Nathan. Have you been drinking again? You're not making any sense."

Nate closed his eyes and clutched the phone tighter. There was no *again*. He'd only had alcohol one time in his life. "So you're saying you didn't know there was a fire at Violet's store last night? The store she happens to live above. And so does a sweet old woman, who is now in the hospital with smoke inhalation." He broke off but then decided he might as well go for broke. "Oh, and so do I, by the way. In case you care about the fact that you almost killed your son. Whether you still want to call me that or not."

"Nathan, I didn't— I don't know what you're talking about. You're saying there was a fire at the property Talmadge wants?"

"Yes." Nate bit the word off. He could only take so much more of this game.

"But everyone is okay? You're okay?" Was that genuine concern in Dad's voice?

Nate hardened his heart. He wasn't going to fall for that. "Like I said, Mrs. D'Angelo is in the hospital. But she'll be okay. Violet is okay, although the back of her store is pretty damaged. It could have been a lot worse if I hadn't happened to come home when I did. Her apartment is right above where the fire was."

"And you're okay?" Dad repeated.

"I'm fine." Nate clamped his teeth together. He would not convince himself Dad cared. Not this time.

Dad's exhale crackled over the phone. "And you really think I had something to do with this?"

"Did you?"

"Of course not! For Pete's sake, Nathan, I'd think you'd know that without asking. Why would I set fire to my own building?"

"You were pretty adamant the other day that she had to be out of there one way or another."

"I meant that I was sending an eviction letter for you to sign and give to her. Not that I was going to commit a felony. I leave that to you."

There it was. Nate had known they wouldn't be able to get through a conversation without his past coming up. He forced himself not to react. "Do you think Talmadge could have done it?"

"What makes you think someone *did* it? Couldn't it have been an accident?"

"Maybe." Nate had to concede that. Violet's theory that someone had used an iron to burn down the store seemed pretty far-fetched. "But Violet is sure the iron that caused it was unplugged and put away, so someone had to get it out. And Talmadge was the last person in the store before she closed yesterday."

Dad snorted. "That's thin. She's probably afraid she won't get the insurance payout if she admits it was her fault."

"She's not like that, Dad."

"Everyone's like that for the right price."

Nate shook his head. This was going nowhere. But he needed to ask one more thing before he hung up. "Could I talk to Mom for a few more seconds? Please."

"You already know the answer to that."

"Does she even know where I am? Have you even told them where you've banished me?"

Instead of answering, Dad hung up.

# Chapter 29

Nate wrung the sooty water from his sponge and attacked the wall yet again. Violet had sent everyone else home two hours ago, but he'd insisted he wasn't leaving until she did.

She'd wanted to argue. He could see it in her eyes. But he'd picked up his sponge and gotten back to work, and a minute later she had fallen in beside him.

He wished she didn't have to go through any of this, but he had to admit that it was comfortable working together. Neither of them said much, but that was okay. Somehow, they seemed to be sharing something deeper.

"Phew." Violet dropped her sponge into the bucket and swiped the back of her wrist across her forehead. Nate grinned as her efforts to keep her face clean failed. A light stripe of soot crossed her face. He resisted the urge to wipe at the smudge only because his own hands were even dirtier.

"I'm hungry. How about you?" Her smile went right through him.

He didn't understand how someone who'd been through everything she'd been through in the past twenty-four hours could come out of it smiling like that.

"I could eat."

"Hidden Cafe? My treat?"

There was no way he could say no when she looked at him like that.

"We should probably change first." He pointed to her t-shirt, which had been the lightest shade of pink this morning but was now tinged gray.

Fortunately, they'd been given the all-clear to return to their apartments. And it sounded like Mrs. D'Angelo would be able to come home tomorrow.

Twenty minutes later, Nate had showered and changed and was ready to go. Unlike the first time he'd knocked on her door to go to dinner with her friends, he wasn't the least bit nervous this time. Being with Violet felt more natural to him now than being without her ever had.

When she didn't come to the door right away, he opened it a crack. "Violet?"

"I need ten more minutes," she called from the back of the apartment. "Come on in."

Music filtered to the living room as he stepped through the door, and he found himself humming along without the pang he usually felt. He moved to the couch and patted his back pocket. She may think she was treating, but she was wrong about that. Except his wallet wasn't there.

"Hey, I think I left my wallet down in the store. I'm going to grab it. Be right back."

He jogged down the steps and into the workshop. They'd made good progress today. She'd probably be able to reopen the store in a day or two. For the hundredth time, Nate was swamped by the staggering reality of how much worse it could have been. Of what could have happened. He could have lost Violet. Every time he thought about it, his body had a visceral response, his chest tightening, his throat catching.

But he hadn't lost her.

She was still here. Still alive. And still in one piece.

He couldn't pretend he hadn't prayed for that. Couldn't pretend God hadn't heard him. Couldn't pretend God hadn't answered.

But he didn't know what to do with that information. So he pressed it down and pushed it to the back of his mind. He could process it later.

Or not. One answered prayer didn't necessarily mean he and God were all good again.

He grabbed his wallet off the workbench where he'd left it this morning and turned to go, but something made him stop. He moved toward the sales floor. He didn't know exactly where he was going until his feet stopped in front of it.

The Bosendorfer.

He stared at it. It was a beautiful piece, rounded in all the right places, the keys gleaming and just crying out for someone to play them.

But it couldn't be him.

He'd promised himself.

Still, he found himself settling onto the bench and resting his fingers on the keys. Their cool smoothness tingled through his fingertips. All he'd have to do was apply the slightest pressure.

Nate closed his eyes, letting the silent war between his fingers and his brain rage.

His fingers won out.

A G minor chord resonated across the shop, and something stirred in his soul.

He tried a few more chords. It felt right and wrong at the same time to be playing again.

But this was the language of his heart. His soul.

He adjusted himself on the bench and brought both hands to the keys, picking out the first notes of a song he'd written years ago. It was the song that had brought his band to the attention of the record producer, but that's not why he played it.

He played it because it was the song that expressed the deepest longing of his heart, a longing to know that he was loved unconditionally, a longing to know that whatever he had done, God had prepared a place for him. He couldn't deny that he'd felt that longing again lately. But he hadn't known how to soothe it.

Now, he closed his eyes and let the words of the song do what nothing else could. As he sang, a slow trickle of relief flowed over him.

He let the chords carry him, let the song lift him until he didn't know where he was anymore.

Violet swiped on a light layer of lip gloss and emerged into the living room, still humming along to the music she'd just turned off. Today had been hard, there was no denying that.

But her friends had made it easier. They'd dropped everything and spent all day getting soot-covered and dirty to help her.

Especially Nate. He could have walked away. He could have said it was her problem. But he'd stayed, long after she'd insisted he leave.

"Okay, I had to wash my hair three times to get rid of the smoke smell, but I'm finally ready." She stopped as she entered the living room. It was empty.

She glanced around the apartment, but unless Nate had decided to play an epic game of hide and seek, he wasn't here. He'd said he was going to run downstairs to grab his wallet, but that had been at least ten minutes ago.

She grabbed a light coat from the hook next to her door and stepped into the hallway. "Nate?" Had he gone back to his apartment to wait? But when she knocked there, all she heard was a faint snuffling from Tony.

She started down the steps. No one had worked harder than him in the workshop today—maybe he'd gone back to it. Though she hoped not, since then he'd have to clean up again, and she was starving.

The moment she opened the workshop door, the lingering smell of smoke hit her nose. But that wasn't what stopped her in her tracks. A rich melody filtered to her from the front of the store.

The song was somehow familiar even though she'd never heard the words before. She stepped into the workshop and followed the music toward the sales floor. She knew exactly where it was coming from.

After a few more chords, a deep male voice joined the lilting music.

Violet's hand lifted to her heart.

She'd never heard Nate sing before, but that was his voice.

She inched closer, afraid if he heard her, he'd stop. Finally, she came to the alcove where the piano had sat for so long.

Nate's eyes were closed, and his face wore an expression she couldn't place. He bowed his head as he began to sing another verse.

*Can your love really be so great, so vast*
*Can you really love me, no matter my past*
*No matter my future, or who I am right now*
*Are you the one I need, or are you a dream somehow*
*An ache in my heart that will never cease*
*Or the one who can fill me—fill me with peace?*

The song drew her closer, but she bumped against a floor lamp that let out a metallic clang.

Nate's eyes snapped open, but his fingers continued to play over the keys.

His eyes latched onto hers and didn't let go.

Violet couldn't look away.

It was as if her soul was being tugged up from all the layers of grief and pain she had cradled it in the past three years.

She felt raw and exposed and yet also alive.

As Nate's voice picked up the song again, she was drawn closer to him, until she stood only steps in front of him. His eyes were still locked on hers.

Every part of her body seemed to sing with the connection between them.

After another minute, Nate's voice grew quiet and dropped out. The piano, too, softened, then faded.

And still their gaze remained locked.

Violet felt the steady in and out of her breath. Felt the slow thump of her heart.

Finally, she dragged her eyes from his, down to the piano. "You wrote that?" The song had been so raw, so open. Not at all how she thought of Nate.

There was something in his smile she couldn't place—longing, maybe?

"A long time ago."

Something in his voice tugged her closer, and he slid over as she moved to sit on the piano bench next to him. She lifted her hands to the keys. "Can you teach me?"

He watched her fingers for a second, then moved his hand slowly to touch hers, shaping her fingers to the keys. The simple connection of their hands made her feel more awake than she had in years. He pressed gently on her thumb until a note rang out. "C," he said.

He moved to the next finger. "D."

After he'd run through a scale, he lifted his hand off of hers. "We should probably get that dinner now."

She swallowed. Nodded. But neither of them moved.

His head tipped closer, and Violet's heart went wild. He was going to kiss her.

She should turn her head, run, move out of the way. But she didn't want to. She wanted to know what his lips would feel like on hers.

She waited, her breath caught in her lungs.

After a second, Nate slid off the bench. "You were starved an hour ago. You must be famished by now."

He threaded his way through the displays toward the back room. By the time Violet caught up, she'd almost managed to convince herself that it was for the best that they hadn't kissed.

Almost—but not quite.

# Chapter 30

The wind cut through Nate's coat, but he didn't care. The weather may have darkened as they'd entered October, but his days had brightened. Ever since that night on the piano bench when he and Violet had been within heartbeats of kissing. He'd kicked himself a thousand times for pulling away. Even if he knew it was what was best for Violet.

In the week since then, he'd been looking for another opportunity to bring his lips to hers. But though they spent nearly every second he wasn't at work together, he hadn't found the right moment yet. He wanted it to be perfect. And he was willing to wait to find that.

She'd invited everyone over for dinner tonight, and he'd promised to help get things ready. Not that he had any idea how to cook, but that didn't matter. He wasn't going to pass up any chance to spend time with her. He'd been foolish enough to waste those opportunities before. Not anymore.

He jogged up the stairs and found Mrs. D'Angelo just emerging from her apartment.

"Hey, Mrs. D. Thanks again for the pie." He patted his stomach. "Though I probably shouldn't have eaten it all in one night."

Only a day after she'd returned from the hospital, Mrs. D'Angelo had brought him an apple pie to thank him for saving her. He'd been embarrassed and yet at the same time, filled with a sense of something larger than himself.

"You're welcome, dear." Mrs. D'Angelo gave him her crinkly smile. She reminded him of his own grandma, and the longing for his family that always hovered in the background flared up.

"God sure knew what he was doing when he brought you to Hope Springs." Her voice was scratchy from the smoke she'd inhaled, but her words were clear.

Nate froze. He could admit that perhaps God had answered his prayer to save Violet. But it wasn't God who had brought him to Hope Springs. It was his own mistakes. "Actually, I moved here to work for my father."

Mrs. D'Angelo shook her head. "That might be the circumstance that brought you here. But do you really think God didn't have a bigger purpose in mind? Look what he's done with you since you've been here. Don't think I haven't seen how you've changed in the past two months. You're not the same surly, feeling-sorry-for-himself man you were then."

"I—" But Nate had no response to that. He wasn't sure if he was supposed to take it as an insult or a compliment.

"God has softened your heart, young man." Mrs. D'Angelo stooped to pick up the paper on her welcome mat. "And if I'm not mistaken, he's used your Violet to do it." She winked at him.

Nate opened his mouth to protest, but by the time he'd come up with a response, she'd already disappeared into her apartment.

"She's not my Violet," he finally whispered to the empty hallway.

He moved slowly to Violet's door and knocked, still contemplating Mrs. D'Angelo's words.

Violet opened the door, greeting him with the warm smile he'd come to love.

*There she is.* He couldn't stop the thought. *My Violet.*

"Hey." Violet resisted the urge to hug Nate the moment he stepped into her apartment. Much as she wanted to feel his arms around her, she'd never greeted him with a hug before, and it'd be weird to start now.

"Hey." Nate's answering smile made her stomach flutter. She could step closer right now and just kiss him. There was no use pretending she hadn't been thinking about doing just that every moment since they'd almost kissed on the piano bench last weekend.

But he clearly hadn't been ready, and she didn't want to scare him off.

"So, you ready to cook?" She wiped her hands on her apron, more to have something to do with them than because they were dirty.

"As long as you tell me exactly what I need to do." He gave her a self-conscious look. "I may have neglected to mention that I'm not exactly a top chef."

"That's okay." Violet led the way to the kitchen, that nervous fluttering in her stomach still in full force. "I'll go easy on you. You can make the graham cracker crust for the cheesecake."

She passed him a package of grahams. "The food processor is over there." She pointed to its spot in the corner of the kitchen counter.

"Um, okay. Do you have a recipe?"

Violet grabbed a spoon from the antique juice pitcher that held her kitchen utensils. "You're kidding right?"

Nate was staring at the package of graham crackers as if they were a grenade that might explode in his hand.

She couldn't hold back a laugh. "Okay, you weren't kidding. Haven't you ever made a graham cracker crust?"

Nate passed her the grahams. "Literally, the extent of my kitchen experience involves pushing buttons on the microwave."

She opened the package. "Didn't you ever help your mom in the kitchen?" It was a dangerous question, she knew. He always shut down when she asked about his family. But she'd found herself wanting to know everything about him lately, from how he preferred his eggs to what his family was like.

"Not really."

Violet looked up at the edge in his voice, trying not to show her surprise that he'd volunteered even that much information about his family.

"Why not?" She dropped the grahams into the food processor, waiting for him to change the subject like he did every time things turned personal.

"My parents were very traditional. He worked. She took care of the house and cooked. I guess she figured I'd get married and have that kind of relationship, too." He rubbed his chin.

Violet stilled as she listened. "And is that what you thought, too?"

Nate looked toward the window. "I suppose at one time it was." He shook himself a little. "Anyway, that was a long time ago. It's about time I learned how to make something other than a frozen dinner. Teach away." He gestured to the food processor.

Violet watched him a moment longer. He'd ended the conversation but not before revealing more about himself and his life than he ever had before. His face wore a trace of the vulnerability he'd allowed himself to show. It made her want to reach up and touch his cheek.

"Now, you process them, until they're fine crumbs." She pointed to the controls on the food processor and stepped aside to let him do it as she picked up the mixer and turned her attention back to the filling.

As she switched the mixer on, she heard the steady whir of the food processor. He'd done it—taken his first steps into the world of cooking.

A second later, a gritty dust of graham spattered Violet's arms and rained down onto her head.

She spun, lifting the beater out of the bowl as she did.

Cheesecake filling joined the graham crumbs cavorting in the air. A glob splattered her cheek, and another landed smack in the middle of Nate's chest.

Violet gasped and quickly switched the mixer off. But graham pieces were still dancing in the sunlight.

"Turn it off," she shouted to Nate over the sound of the food processor.

"How?" Nate looked like a panicked deer.

Violet reached past him and flipped the switch to off.

In the sudden silence, they stood staring at each other.

A dusting of grahams covered Nate's shirt, which had a blob of filling right over the heart. Another, smaller dollop of filling perched on his shoulder like a flat parrot.

Violet could feel the sticky cream cheese slipping down her own cheek. She lifted a hand to wipe it away.

Nate started laughing first, but it was only half a second before Violet gave in, too. Soon, they were both letting out deep belly laughs, holding the counter for support. Every time Violet slowed down, she took another look at Nate and was attacked by another fit of giggles.

Finally, her sides hurt too much to laugh anymore.

She wiped her eyes as Nate's laughter slowed, too.

"How'd I do?" he asked innocently.

"Perfect. That's exactly what was supposed to happen." Violet raised a hand to her hair, shaking out pieces of graham, then grabbed the towel off her shoulder to wipe the rest of the cheesecake away. She passed it to Nate so he could wipe up his shirt as she grabbed the broom.

"How have you survived this long on your own?" Violet teased as she worked. Her face hurt from all the smiling, but it was worth it.

"No one's ever tried to kill me with exploding graham crackers before."

"Yeah, usually we put the cover on the food processor before we turn it on. I haven't seen your technique before."

Violet set the broom aside and surveyed the room. The counter was covered with crumbs, but that would be easy enough to clean up. The bigger problem was that she had no more grahams to make a crust. "Guess we'll have cheesecake filling for dessert. We'll call it a cheesecake mousse."

"Sounds fancy."

"Oh, yeah, totally five-star." Violet returned his grin as her eyes fell on the blob of cheesecake still sitting on his shoulder. She grabbed the towel from his hand and instinctively wiped at the spot.

Only when his shoulder jumped under her touch did Violet realize what she was doing.

But she didn't stop.

She didn't want to.

Under her hand, his shoulder was firm. Solid. Strong.

"Violet." His voice was low, slightly strangled.

She raised her eyes to his.

They were burning with something she couldn't name.

Something she could only feel.

Her hand stilled on his shoulder, but she didn't drop it.

"You have a little . . ." He raised a hand to her cheek. The feel of his fingers against her skin made her forget everything else.

His hand lingered, his thumb trailing back and forth slowly over her skin.

Violet closed her eyes and lifted her chin, leaning toward him.

The air between them grew thick.

Violet's hand tensed on his shoulder.

His thumb stopped moving as he pressed his palm into her cheek, drawing her closer.

Violet sighed as his breath brushed her lips.

Her heart had run away with her, and she didn't care.

She wanted to feel his lips on hers.

Her whole body tingled as time slowed down.

She could feel him millimeters away.

And then there was a knock on the door.

# Chapter 31

Nate jumped back, dropping the hand that had been pressed to Violet's smooth cheek.

Violet looked flustered, and she smoothed her shirt as she strode toward the door.

Moving deliberately in an effort to get his still-hurtling heart under control, Nate grabbed a rag and brushed the graham cracker crumbs from the counter into his hand.

He heard voices at the door, and then Sophie was greeting him with a hug. "Violet's been bragging about your excellent cooking skills. Can't wait to try your graham cracker floor pie."

Nate grinned. He loved how this group could make him feel instantly at ease. "Yes, and did she tell you about her course of cheesecake filling a la shirt?" Nate winked, and Sophie burst out laughing.

Violet joined in, too, the joy in it stirring Nate's heart. Her laugh had become one of his favorite sounds.

"All right, fine, you got me. We make quite a team." She smiled at him, and Nate's heart fumbled. They did make a good team.

"At least dinner itself isn't a bust." Violet pulled a pan of lasagna from the oven. "I didn't let Nate help with that."

As everyone filled their plates, Nate just watched. If anyone had asked him two months ago if he planned to make friends and become part of the community here, he'd have slammed the door on them. But this group had welcomed him in, no questions asked, and they made him feel like he was one of them. Like he belonged.

The apartment was too small for the number of people in it, but it didn't feel cramped. It felt warm and inviting. The small kitchen table was full, and people sat on the couch and the lone chair in the living room. Nate waited until Violet was settled, then moved to sit next to her on the floor in front of the coffee table.

He folded his hands as the others prepared to say grace. To his surprise, he looked forward to it.

Violet's inviting voice lifted over them. "Dear Lord, thank you for bringing us together tonight for good food and even better friendships. Thank you for giving us one another, that we may celebrate our joys and share our burdens and that we may serve as reminders to one another of the perfect love you have for us. In Jesus' name. Amen."

"Amen," Nate murmured. Her prayer had made him unexpectedly emotional, and he had to keep his eyes closed for an extra second.

"You okay?" Violet leaned close enough that her shoulder brushed against his. "You seem like you're—" She gestured in that cute way she always did when she was looking for a word. "Somewhere else, I guess."

The smile he gave her was genuine. As hard as he'd tried to keep a lock on his heart, she'd broken right into it. "I'm here." He bit into his lasagna. "And this is delicious."

When he looked up, Sophie caught his eye. She shot him a conspiratorial wink, and his face warmed.

After dinner, the friends ate cheesecake "mousse" by the bowlful before Violet suggested a game of charades. Nate groaned. He didn't understand the appeal of a game in which you had to make a fool of yourself in front of others.

But he ended up having a great time, acting out the game-winning charade of Snow White by pretending to be every one of the seven dwarfs. Violet made the winning guess, sealing the victory for their team, and he scooped her into a hug without thinking. She squeezed back, burying her face in his neck for a moment. He could have stayed like that all night, but he made himself let her go. When she pulled away, her cheeks were flushed, and her eyes sparkled. He almost moved in for a kiss right then and there. But the room full of their friends stopped him.

After a while, Sophie started to yawn. Spencer wrapped a protective arm around her shoulders. "Time to get my wife home to bed. Thanks for everything, Violet."

An attack of longing hit Nate as he watched the newlyweds. He wanted to have that closeness with a woman. To know that she trusted him completely. And that he would never do anything to break that trust.

The rest of the group followed shortly after Spencer and Sophie.

Nate knew he should go, too.

He wasn't sure he could trust himself not to do something stupid if he was alone with Violet. Like act on his growing desire to kiss her.

But his eyes fell on the small mountain of dirty dishes in the kitchen. He couldn't leave her to clean everything up alone.

"Do you prefer to wash or dry?" he asked, leading the way to the kitchen.

"Oh, you don't have to—"

"I helped make the mess, didn't I? With my gourmet cooking skills?" He grabbed a dish rag and a towel, holding both up so Violet could choose which she'd rather use.

She weighed the options for a minute before grabbing the dish rag. "This way I get done first and get to watch you slave away while I relax," she explained, drawing an unexpected laugh from him. He loved how she could do that.

They worked side-by-side in silence for a while, the only sound the clanking dishes.

Just as the sounds were starting to lull him toward drowsiness, Violet spoke abruptly. "Nate, are you a Christian?"

Nate studied the plate he'd been drying, then set it on the stack next to him, cringing as it clattered more loudly than he'd intended. He hadn't expected the question, and he wasn't sure how to answer it.

He set the towel down and leaned against the counter.

Violet dropped her rag into the water and turned to face him.

"I used to be," Nate said slowly. "I mean, I grew up Christian, went to a Christian college, was in a Christian band."

He glanced at Violet, then let his gaze flit away at her earnest expression.

"But that was a long time ago," he continued. He couldn't bring himself to look at Violet. He knew how important her faith was to her and that she'd likely be disappointed—maybe even angry—that he didn't feel that way anymore.

"And now?" Violet's voice was low but not judgmental. She simply sounded as if she wanted to know him better.

"If you had asked me a month ago, I would have told you in no uncertain terms that I had no use for God," Nate said. "But in the last few weeks, I've felt this—" He didn't know how to put it into words. "I don't know—this pull."

Like maybe God was trying to call him back—but he wasn't sure how to say that without sounding crazy. "I guess I would say I'm open to the possibility of God again."

Violet nodded, seemingly satisfied. "I don't know what I would have done without my faith after I lost my mom and Cade and everyone important to me," she said softly.

Abandoning the few remaining dishes, she led him to the living room, and they settled on the couch. She angled her body toward him but looked lost in her own thoughts.

He lifted an arm and slid it behind her shoulders. He wanted to pull her close and make everything she'd gone through all better, but he knew only too well that wasn't the way it worked. "Do you mind if I ask what happened? With your family, I mean? You said you don't have one anymore."

Violet tucked a stray curl behind her ear. "I don't mind." Her voice was soft. "My dad left when I was a little girl. I barely even remember him, really, and I never knew his parents. I remember my mom's parents. They were great. They lived down South, but whenever they came to visit, they'd take me to the Chocolate Chicken for ice cream." A slight smile played over her lips. "But they both died when I was in middle school. First my grandma, and then my grandpa a couple months later. And my mom—" She blew out a quick breath. "She died when I was in college—"

"I'm so sorry." Nate rubbed her shoulder. "That must have been awful." He could barely handle not having seen his mom in years, but at least he knew she was still alive.

Violet tilted her head to the side so that it almost rested on his arm. "It was hard. I was the older sister, and I tried to take care of Jade, but I was pretty wrapped up in Cade and our plans for the future at the time. I should have done more. Maybe she would have stayed."

"Where'd she go?" He ached to pull her in closer but resisted. He needed to let her talk about this.

"She decided she wanted to be an actor. Never mind that she'd never been in so much as a school play in her life. I tried to talk her out of it, but she thought I was trying to hold her back. She took off for L.A. the day after her high school graduation." Violet directed her eyes to her lap. "I haven't talked to her since." Her voice was small and nearly broken.

"You've tried. I've seen you." She had to realize that none of this was her fault.

"I know. I just feel like there must have been something more I could have done. But then I got married and we got busy with the antique store and everything was a rush. Until—"

She broke off, and her throat bobbed as she swallowed.

"Until Cade died," he finished for her.

She nodded, blinking rapidly as moisture collected on her lashes. "Sometimes I feel like everyone I've ever cared about has left me. I've spent days—years, really—praying that God would help me understand why he's taken all these people from me."

"And did he answer you?" Nate leaned closer, finding he needed to know the answer more than he wanted to admit.

She managed a wavery smile. "He showed me that he was in control even in all of these losses. That he's bigger than I am and stronger and that he has a plan for me even in this."

"How can you believe that?" Nate wanted to understand. Wanted to believe she was right about God. But how could he place his faith in a God who would allow this amazing, generous woman to suffer like this? "How do you know it's not that he doesn't care about you and what happens to you? About what happened to your mom and Cade and everyone else you love?"

Instead of giving him the flippant answer he expected, Violet considered his words. When she spoke, her voice was firm. "Only the Holy Spirit can give me that kind of faith." She touched her heart. "It's something I know here, in my inmost soul. And some days I have to fight to remember it, but he always brings me back to the truth that his love for me is even greater than my mom's was, than Cade's was, greater than anyone's ever could be. And if he says that he's working for my good in all things, I trust that."

"Easy as that? You just trust?" If that was the case, Nate was doomed. He'd never be able to trust that easily.

Violet blew out a breath that rustled her hair. "It's not easy, believe me. My sinful nature keeps trying to heap the doubt back on me. That's why I spend so much time in prayer and in his word. It's the only way I get through the day."

Nate had felt that way once, a long time ago. He'd felt like Jesus was his best friend, like he could tell him anything. But those days were long past. Much as he might wish for that kind of closeness again.

"Would you like to pray together?" Violet's voice was tentative, like she wasn't sure if he'd explode at the question.

A few months ago, he would have.

But tonight, he felt a crack in the armor he'd built up to protect himself from ever getting hurt by God again. Tonight he could see that maybe it wasn't God who had hurt him. Maybe he'd hurt himself.

He allowed himself to nod, not trusting his words to carry the depth of his feelings.

Violet wound her fingers through his. "Dear heavenly Father." Her voice was strong and sure, even though Nate's hands shook in hers. "You have promised us that you are all-powerful and all-loving. And yet sometimes it's hard for us to reconcile these two things, especially when we face hurts that we can't imagine a loving God would allow to happen. But you tell us that you work all things for our good. Help us to trust this, even when—especially when—we can't see it through our own pain. Amen."

Nate clutched her hands tighter as the prayer ended, his eyes still closed. He needed a moment to catch his breath.

It was as if Violet had smashed down all his walls and seen right into his heart. Seen exactly what he needed to hear, exactly what had been weighing on his soul for the past seven years.

She knew him without his ever saying a word.

When he at last opened his eyes, she was watching him. "I'm glad you moved in next door," she whispered.

"Me, too. I like being your neighbor." He meant to keep the conversation playful, but she slid closer.

"Is that what we are? Neighbors?" She lifted a hand to his cheek.

It was only by sheer force of will that he didn't close the rest of the space between them. "Well, we live next door to each other, and that's kind of the defining characteristic of neighbors."

She nodded, but her expression was serious as she moved even closer, until they were only inches apart. His eyes went to her lips, and he felt the catch in his breath and in his heart.

Her eyes closed, and she tilted her head toward him. He let his eyes close, too.

He moved a fraction of a centimeter at a time, giving her a chance to stop this if it wasn't what she wanted.

But she moved closer to him, and then their lips were pressed together.

Hers were soft and smooth and felt like they'd been made just for him. He slid his hand from hers and lifted his fingers to tangle in her hair, letting himself fall into whatever this was.

Whatever it could become.

# Chapter 32

Violet felt as if she was on one of those rides that slowly hoisted you a hundred feet in the air and then let you hurtle to the ground. It was exhilarating and terrifying. All night, she'd relived that kiss with Nate. The sheer exhilaration of her lips on his, of his hands in her hair. And the terror of not knowing what it meant for her relationship with Nate—and, worse, what it meant about her love for Cade.

She'd waited as long as she could to call Sophie, but by six, she'd been unable to wait any longer.

A groggy Sophie had invited her to come over right away, even though they'd see each other at church in a few hours. But now Violet stood with her hand on her own apartment door, debating. What if she stepped into the hallway and saw Nate? Would things be awkward? Would he regret their kiss? Would he say it had been a mistake?

She drew in a deep breath and opened the door.

But the landing was empty, and the breath she'd been holding seeped from her as disappointment flooded her chest.

Apparently she'd wanted to see him more than she let herself admit.

But this was for the best.

This way, she could let Sophie help her sort out her feelings first.

Before she acted on them and did something she'd regret.

By the time she got to Sophie's house, she'd almost convinced herself that she already knew what to do. She had to stop things with Nate before they went any further. She was half afraid Sophie would confirm her feelings and half afraid she'd say Violet should go for it with Nate.

She pulled her jacket tighter as she crossed the frost-dusted grass to Sophie and Spencer's front door. Not bothering to knock, she slid inside silently.

Sophie and Spencer were sitting at stools in front of their kitchen counter. Each had a muffin in front of them, and Spencer leaned over to pop a bite of his into Sophie's mouth. Then he kissed her forehead before pushing his stool back.

Violet had to stop at the jolt in her heart. She knew everything about Spencer and Sophie. She'd been the one to set them up—twice—but still, it felt as if she'd walked in on an intensely private moment.

"Hey, Violet." Spencer caught sight of her first and gave her his easy smile. "Grab a muffin and some coffee." He dropped another kiss on his wife's head, then disappeared out the front door.

As soon as he was gone, Sophie turned to Violet. "All right, spill. I saw those looks between you and Nate last night, so . . ." Sophie waved a hand in the air, inviting Violet to finish the story.

Violet covered her face with both hands, suddenly afraid to tell her friend what had happened.

Sophie and Cade had been close. She'd be devastated at the thought of Violet kissing another man. Not to mention that she'd likely tell Violet it was a bad idea.

Which it was.

But that didn't mean she wanted to hear someone else say it.

"You know what?" Violet uncovered her face. "I was totally overre-acting. It was nothing." She grabbed a muffin and stuffed a big bite into her mouth.

"If you think you're getting off the hook that easily, you obviously haven't been paying very good attention during the last twenty-eight years of our friendship."

Violet dragged out her bite as long as she could, but finally there was no more avoiding Sophie. There was no way she was getting out of here without telling her friend everything.

"Fine." She worked to make her voice nonchalant. "We kissed."

"Obviously. I could have told you that was going to happen. It's about time." Sophie took a bite of her muffin, letting a smile play on her face.

"You knew we were going to kiss? How? I didn't—"

"The point isn't how I knew. It's how was the kiss?"

Violet closed her eyes, trying to figure out how to describe it.

"That good, huh?"

Violet shook her head, opening her eyes. "I mean, it was good." Really good. "But it was like— Remember that time when we were in fifth grade and we saw that tornado go through the cornfields to the west?"

The tornado had been too far away to damage any buildings in town. But even from that distance, she had been in awe of its sheer power and its destructive potential.

Sophie nodded, giving her a puzzled look. "He kisses like a tornado?"

Violet let out a little laugh. "No. It's just, I feel like I could be completely knocked over and spun around by the strength of it, you know?"

"Oooh." Sophie held the word out longer than necessary.

"What?" Violet knew that sound. And she had a feeling she wasn't going to like what Sophie had to say.

"I haven't seen you like this since you first realized you were in love with Cade." Sophie's voice was quiet, as if she was trying not to alarm Violet, but Violet jumped to her feet, agitated.

"I'm not in love with Nate." She stopped. Reexamined her words. Was she in love with Nate?

"I didn't say you are." Sophie's voice was calm, too calm, as she took another bite of muffin.

"No, you didn't say it, but that's what you think. You think I'm betraying Cade and falling in love with another man." Violet pointed an accusing finger at her friend.

Sophie dropped her muffin and pushed to her feet, looking truly shocked. "Violet, betraying Cade and falling in love with another man are not the same thing. Is that what you're upset about?"

Violet stopped pacing. "Upset? I'm not upset." But the crack in her voice gave her away.

Sophie crossed the room and wrapped her in a fierce hug. "Sweetie, having feelings for another man is not a betrayal. Cade is gone. He would want you to move on."

"No he wouldn't. At his funeral, I promised him I'd never love anyone else like I loved him. And now—" She swallowed the sob she felt building. "Every day, I feel the hole in my heart growing a little smaller. And someday, if I let it, it will disappear, and Cade will be really gone. How is that not a betrayal?" She couldn't hold back the tears any longer.

"Honey, I knew Cade. Almost as well as you did, remember? And he would never— Look at me." She waited for Violet to lift her head. Tears shone in her eyes, too, as she continued. "He would never in a million years want you to have a hole in your heart. He'd want you to have a full life. Including someone to love."

A sob tore loose from deep in Violet's soul, rocking her body and sending shudders through her frame. It took a moment for her to calm down.

But in that moment, she felt cleansed, as if she'd been given a new chance at life. A chance to release her hold on the past and move toward the future.

# Chapter 33

Violet's hand shook as she reached behind her neck and tried to work the clasp of the white onyx Cade had given her on their first anniversary. He'd put it inside a huge box, laughing as she dug through piles of packing peanuts to get to it. Then they'd had a snowball fight with the peanuts. It had made such a mess. But the joy of sharing that moment was totally worth the time they'd had to spend cleaning up afterward.

She finally succeeded with the clasp and raised a hand to her lips at the memory of the kiss they'd enjoyed after the clean-up.

Lips that for the past week had been kissing another man.

Lips that wanted to kiss him again.

She could finally admit that letting herself feel this way was okay. It was better than okay.

It was a sign that she still had a heart somewhere in there under all the layers and cushions she'd built up around it.

Violet tried to read over the speech she had prepared for the assembly at the high school. But every time she did, the familiar images of Cade morphed into Nate. It felt like her two worlds—her past and her present—were colliding.

Maybe she should call off her visit to the school. She'd agreed to it more than six months ago. When she was in a very different place emotionally.

But she'd been asked to share the story of Cade's death as part of a campaign to prevent drunk driving among teens. And though she felt sick at the thought of sharing her pain publicly, if it could help prevent even one family from going through what she had, it'd be worth it.

Sophie had offered to go with her, but Violet had said she preferred to do this alone. Now she was starting to rethink that. But it was too late. She was supposed to be at the school in fifteen minutes.

She gave herself a last look in the mirror, then grabbed her purse. If she didn't do this now, she never would.

She opened the door but immediately took half a step back. "Nate!" Her heart hammered and she pressed a hand to her chest. "What are you doing here?"

He lowered the hand that had been lifted. "Well, I was about to knock, but I guess you read my mind." He gave her a sneaky smile. "Since it's Monday and you're off, I thought I'd play hooky so we could spend the day together."

"Oh." She pulled out her phone to check the time. "I'm sorry. I have an appointment."

His face fell, but he leaned forward to peer at her more closely. "Hey. Are you feeling okay? You look really pale." He reached for her hand. "And you're shaking."

"I'm fine." She worked to steady her voice. "Just nervous."

Concern clouded his eyes. "Why? What's going on? Did Talmadge threaten you again? Because—"

"No, nothing like that." She tried to slide past him, but he was blocking the doorway.

"Violet." He lifted her chin with his hand. "Tell me what's going on. I want to help."

"I'm supposed to give a talk at the school. But I'm not sure I can." Her voice cracked on the last word, and he pulled her into his arms. She burrowed closer, letting his warmth cloak her.

"Is there anything I can do to help?"

"Would you—" She swallowed. She wasn't sure she could ask it of him. But she also wasn't sure she could do it without him. "Would you come with me?"

"Do you even have to ask?" He took her arm and led her down the stairs.

The chaotic chatter of teenage conversations filled the high school auditorium. Nate shifted in his seat next to a group of giggling teenage girls. He didn't take his eyes off Violet, who was seated in an uncomfortable looking chair on the stage, even paler than when they'd left the apartment.

She'd barely said two words on the drive here, but from what he had gathered, both she and Cade had gone to school here, and they'd asked her to speak about his death. They were probably establishing a scholarship in his name or something.

Nerves twisted in his gut for Violet's sake. It was obvious she wasn't comfortable with the idea of public speaking. But when he'd asked why she'd agreed to do it, she'd simply said it was important and fallen silent again, so he'd left her to her thoughts.

He tried to catch her eye now, but she was reviewing a stack of index cards clutched in her hands.

A balding man in a suit approached the microphone and tapped it, sending a loud crackling through the space. The buzz of conversations slowed and died, although a couple of the girls next to Nate were still giggling.

"Good morning, students. As you know, we are bringing in a series of speakers this year to highlight the consequences of our choices. Our speaker this morning is a Hope Springs graduate, and so was her husband

Cade. I hope you'll give Mrs. Somers your full attention as she tells you about how one teenager's choice to drive drunk resulted in her husband's death at the age of twenty-five. Mrs. Somers?"

The room fell entirely silent as Violet walked tentatively toward the microphone, but a low buzzing had filled Nate's head. He fought to control the nausea rising in his throat.

In one horrifying moment, it all clicked into place. Cade hadn't just been in an accident. He'd been killed by a drunk driver.

By someone like Nate.

It took all of his willpower to remain in his seat. He couldn't get out of his row without stumbling over a dozen students. Plus, he wasn't certain his legs would hold him. And there was a part of him—the part that watched a cut bleed for a few seconds before putting on a bandage—that felt compelled to hear what she had to say. To subject himself to the torment he deserved.

Nate held his breath as he waited for her to speak, as if that could change what she was about to say.

"My name is Violet Somers." Violet's voice shook, but she let her gaze sweep the auditorium, making eye contact with each section. Nate glanced around at the students, but they all had their eyes fixed on the stage. When her gaze reached his row, she paused. Nate dropped his eyes to his lap before she could make eye contact with him. He couldn't handle that right now.

"I grew up here in Hope Springs and went to high school here. I even had some of the same teachers you have. Like Mr. Peterson and Mrs. Fox. And Mr. Jessup was still the principal. Although he had more hair then." There was a smattering of laughter from the students. "From almost before I can remember, I hung out with the same group of friends. We climbed trees together, ate ice cream together, pulled pranks together." She leaned away from the microphone and stage whispered, "But if Mr. Jessup asks,

I had nothing to do with the cow in the cafeteria." More laughter from the students. In spite of himself, Nate smiled. Violet had forged an instant connection with these students, and he knew whatever she said to them would have an impact.

"We were a group of boys and girls who loved life. Loved being together." Her voice lowered. "Loved each other."

She took an audible breath. "But then something happened. I don't really know when or how. But one of the boys became more than a friend. His name was Cade."

Nate was entranced by the slight smile on her face whenever she said her husband's name, even if it sliced his heart at the same time. He wanted to be the one to bring that look to her face from now on. But he couldn't be. Not after this.

The smile lingered as Violet kept talking. "We never really declared ourselves boyfriend and girlfriend. Not officially. But that's how everyone saw us. And I guess that's technically what you call it when two people only want to spend time with each other. At least that's what my best friend Sophie told me."

The girl next to Nate sighed.

"Our second year of college, Cade proposed. It was—" That smile again. "It was magical. He had no money at the time, of course, but he talked the art director at our school into letting him use one of the galleries where some of my work was displayed. And he blew up two hundred balloons with his own air. By the time I arrived, he was sitting with his head between his knees."

A gentle laugh went up around the auditorium. They all knew how this was going to end. Otherwise, Violet wouldn't be up there.

Nate clenched his teeth, not releasing even when the pain began to morph into a headache.

"I asked if he was okay, and he said, 'No.' And I was worried. He was all pale and sweating, and I thought, you know, we'd better get this guy to the doctor, he's really sick. And then he grabbed my hand." Violet held out her hand. "And he said—" She blew out a short breath.

Nate could almost feel everyone in the room leaning forward.

"He said he wouldn't be okay until I agreed to spend the rest of my life with him."

The whole room seemed to exhale at once, and nearly all the girls in Nate's row lifted a hand to swipe at their eyes. He pressed his lips together and swallowed down the hard lump that had clotted the back of his throat.

"I said yes before he had the ring out of his pocket." Violet ran a finger under her own eye, and Nate had to look away. He wanted to rush the stage and tell her to stop. Tell her not to hurt herself by reliving this story. Not to hurt him.

But she kept talking, building up to the inevitable.

"We got married the day after college graduation. Not long after that we opened an antique shop. It was—" Violet seemed to be searching for the right word. "It was perfect."

She fiddled with her index cards as she stared out over the heads of the students. For a moment Nate thought she wouldn't be able to go on. But then she shook her head and looked at the audience. "Actually, that's not true. It wasn't perfect. No relationship is. We fought sometimes. Sometimes I thought he was a slob. Sometimes he thought I was a control freak." She laughed a little, and so did the audience. "But it was just right for us, you know?" She sniffed. "We had actually just decided to start a family."

Nate's lungs constricted. He hadn't known that.

"But we didn't get a chance." Violet's voice was stronger now, though Nate knew this had to be the hardest part.

"On June twelfth, three years ago, we were supposed to pick up a piece for our antique shop. It was farther than we usually went, and I wasn't sure we should go at all. At the last minute, we had an argument, and I decided not to go."

Violet took a moment to scan every row of students. When her eyes stopped on his, Nate saw her shoulders rise as if she were drawing strength from him.

Still looking at him, she continued, "I was painting when someone knocked on the door that night. I thought maybe Cade had forgotten his keys. He did that all the time. By then, I'd had time to calm down from our argument, and I was ready to meet him at the door with an apology."

She directed her gaze to the other side of the room, and Nate's breath caught. He didn't want to hear this next part. He couldn't handle hearing it. And yet, he needed to hear it. If nothing else could convince him to let Violet go, this would. After all she had been through, she'd never be with someone like him.

"But it wasn't Cade. It was a policeman. And in that moment, I knew. I just stood there, completely numb, my stupid paintbrush still in my hand, until the officer asked if there was anyone he could call. Without thinking, I said he should call Cade." She closed her eyes for a moment, her face ashen under the stage lights. Nate looked away. He couldn't take much more of this.

"The officer led me into the house and sat me down and explained that he couldn't call Cade because Cade was dead. It was a drunk driver. A teenager who had been at a party." Her shaky inhale rattled the microphone. "Because of one person's mistake, Cade was gone."

Nate had known this was where the story was going. And yet, the words were a rock plunging into his gut.

He couldn't sit here any longer.

Couldn't pretend that he belonged here.

He belonged with the guy who had killed Cade.

He shoved his way blindly past the masses of legs and out the auditorium door.

# Chapter 34

Violet faltered as the auditorium door slammed. She tried to convince herself Nate had to use the restroom, but the way he'd plowed through the students told her otherwise. She'd obviously said something to upset him. She should have warned him that she'd be dwelling a lot on her past with Cade in her talk. But that didn't mean she didn't want a future with him.

She forced herself to keep talking, to tell the students that every choice they made had the potential to affect not only themselves but also the lives of people they'd never met, people they might never meet.

As she brought her talk to a close, the auditorium was silent, and nearly every student was either looking at her or looking into their laps. Several were wiping their eyes, and tears sprang to hers as well at the thought that maybe she had impacted them, at least in some small way.

Mr. Jessup came up beside her and spoke into the microphone. "Thank you for sharing your story, Violet. I remember Cade very well, and I know I speak for everyone who knew him when I say we all miss him and we're so sorry for your loss." He laid a hand on her arm. "Do you have a few minutes to answer some questions from our students?"

Violet's stomach dropped. Giving her prepared speech had been hard enough. But live questions were another thing altogether—what if she didn't have the answers?

But the whole room was silent, and Violet felt like the students were waiting for her. She nodded mutely.

A few hands went up across the auditorium, and Violet pointed to a young girl near the back.

The girl stood. "What happened to the driver who hit your husband?"

Violet closed her eyes. She'd left that out on purpose. She didn't like to think about it. But these kids deserved to know what could happen. She made herself look at the student who had asked. "Unfortunately, he was killed in the accident as well."

A collective gasp went up from the students.

"Someone said to me afterward that I must be glad about that." Violet's chest tightened at the memory as she scanned the room filled with kids the same age as the boy who had died with Cade. "How could I be glad that alcohol had taken another life? That's not what Cade would have wanted, and it's not what I wanted, either."

She gave the students a second to digest her answer, then pointed to a boy closer to the front.

"If the other guy had survived, would you have been able to forgive him?"

Violet pondered the question. She'd wrestled with the issue of forgiveness so many times. "Just because he died doesn't mean I don't need to forgive him," she finally said. "It took me a long time to see that I was holding onto my resentment and anger toward this kid. I didn't want him dead, but I did sometimes wish I'd have gotten justice for Cade's death. Or at least that the boy was around to apologize to me or show some remorse."

The student who had asked the question sat down, but Violet had more to say.

"The thing is, I couldn't have forgiven him on my own. But God worked on my heart and showed me that this resentment I was holding onto was poisoning me and hurting my relationship with God. Over time, he helped me see that no one is beyond his forgiveness. So no one should be beyond mine either. He helped me forgive that driver. And I pray for his family. Because they suffered a hurt just as deep as mine." She glanced at Mr. Jessup out of the corner of her eye. He'd always been careful not to bring religion into the school, but he gave her an encouraging smile.

He leaned over her to speak into the microphone. "I think we have time for one more question."

Violet gestured to a girl sitting close to Nate's still-empty seat. "Have you started dating again?"

The girl in the seat next to her gasped and hit her arm, but Violet smiled, even as her heart stuttered. "It's okay. I don't mind the question." She tried to gather her thoughts. "For a long time—until very recently, actually—I had no plans of ever dating again. I was sure that all my best days were behind me and I had no hope for a future. I was still living in the past, too busy looking at what had been to see what could be. But now—" She drew in a quick breath. "I guess I'm saying, I'm open to the possibility of a future again. And to the possibility of love."

The girl nudged her friend, and Violet smiled. They couldn't have failed to notice that Nate was a little old to be a student here.

After the students had applauded to thank her for being there, Mr. Jessup steered her off the stage and into the hallway.

"One of our student journalists was wondering if she could do a quick interview with you for the school paper." Mr. Jessup spoke loudly to be heard over the clamor of students filing past.

"Sure. I just need to find my friend first." Violet peered through the milling students, trying to spot Nate.

"Great. Why don't you meet her in the courtyard in five minutes? You remember the way, right?"

Violet nodded. Of course she remembered the way. On sunny days, she and Cade had always had their lunch out there.

Mr. Jessup got swept along in the tide of students, and Violet offered him a last wave before turning in the other direction, watching for Nate.

She roamed the emptying hallways for a few minutes, but there was no sign of him. Maybe he'd ducked into a bathroom or was waiting by the car. She'd have to find him after the interview, which hopefully she could make quick. Her speech had left her completely wrung out.

The moment she opened the door to the courtyard, her eyes fell on him, hunched at a picnic table in the middle of the open space.

She breathed out a breath she didn't know she'd been holding and moved toward him.

"You did good." He didn't look up.

She took a seat next to him. "You left before I was done."

Nate turned his head, until Violet could see the pain that always lurked under the surface of his gaze. Except today it was right at the top.

"I'm sorry, I—"

But Violet grabbed his hand, lacing her fingers through his. "I understand why it would be hard for you to hear about my past. About my life with Cade. But—" She squeezed his hand. "I'm not stuck in that past anymore. I've realized that I want a future."

"Violet—" Nate's voice was hoarse.

But before he could continue, the courtyard door swung open. A dark-haired girl stepped through and walked toward them.

Violet waved to her and leaned closer to Nate. "Sorry, I said I'd do a quick interview before we go."

Nate slid his hand out of hers and stood. "That's fine. I'll go wait by the car."

"No, wait." She grabbed his arm. "Will you stay with me? I'm not sure I can handle much more of this on my own."

She could see him wrestle with the answer, but finally he sat down.

"Thank you," she whispered as the girl reached them.

"I'm May. Thanks so much for sharing your story." The girl flipped through the screens on her phone. "You don't mind if I record this, do you?"

"Of course not."

"Great." May set the phone on the table between them. "So I think you did a great job covering everything in there, but I have a few questions that you didn't talk about in your speech." She flipped open the notebook she carried with her and scanned a page. "First, I know the boy who hit your husband died, but if he hadn't, do you know what kind of sentence he would have been facing?"

Nate stiffened next to her, but when she looked at him, he was staring at the brick wall of the school, whole body rigid.

"I'm sorry, I really don't. I never looked into it."

"Sure, no problem." The girl jotted a note. "I know you said you forgave him, but what kind of punishment do you think would have been fair if he had lived?"

Nate climbed over the seat of the picnic table. "I'll be over there," he murmured, taking off for the other side of the courtyard. Violet stared after him for a second. She shouldn't have asked him to stay. More talk about her past was the last thing he needed.

Violet turned over May's question in her mind, searching for the right answer. But the truth was she didn't know what would have been fair. She certainly wouldn't have wanted the kid to spend the rest of his life in prison, but she didn't think a couple days would have been enough, either. "I guess just enough to ensure he would never do it again," she said. "Though I don't know how anyone would ever know what that number would be."

"Fair enough." May made another note.

After a few more questions about some of the specifics of her friendship with Cade and their wedding day, May stood. "Thank you so much for your time, Mrs. Somers. I'm sure it's not easy to talk about."

"You're very welcome. I only hope it makes a difference."

"I think it will." May took two steps toward the door, where Nate was hovering, waiting for them to finish.

Gratitude flooded Violet's heart. He had probably been dying to get out of here, but he'd stayed for her sake.

"Oh, one more thing." May turned back to her and lowered her voice. "You said you were open to the possibility of love again. Did you mean with the hot guy that's with you?"

Violet laughed. She certainly found Nate attractive, but she hadn't known high school girls would consider him hot. She toed at the grass. "It's possible."

May smiled. "Is he a lot like your first husband?"

Violet tugged on a strand of hair, thinking. "In some ways yes, but mostly no."

"Any examples?"

"You sure are a thorough journalist." She considered the question a minute. "Okay, well, Cade was kind of larger than life, you know? Loud and playful and always laughing. But Nate is . . ." She gestured toward him. "Well, not. He's quieter, more sensitive. A musician."

"Yeah?" May's eyebrows went up, interested.

"Yeah, he used to be in a band."

May was scribbling furiously. "And how are they the same?"

"I guess . . ." Violet searched for the words to describe it. "Maybe it's not so much that they're the same but that the way they make me feel is the same. Cherished. Protected. Like they'd give up their lives for me."

May's pen flew across the paper.

"Actually—" Now that she was talking about it, Violet found she didn't want to stop. "Nate recently saved my life in a fire."

"Wow." May's pen stopped and she looked over at Nate again. "That's—just wow. Maybe I'll do a story about that, too. What's his last name?"

"Oh, you should." Violet got caught up in her enthusiasm. "His name is Nate Benson. And he's a hero." She felt herself blushing. "I mean, that sounds corny. But he is."

# Chapter 35

Three days.

For the past three days, Nate had been pretending everything was fine with Violet. But he knew she could sense that something was off. Every time she asked if anything was wrong, though, he forced a smile and dropped a light kiss on her lips.

But he felt like an imposter every minute they were together.

Today he couldn't pretend anymore. So he'd skipped out of the office early and slipped past the back door to grab Tony and drag him out to the Sugarbush in spite of the cutting temperatures and the sharp wind that gusted from the lake.

They started out at a walk, but soon Nate's feet picked up speed, and he pushed Tony to run harder. The tree branches above them whipped into a frenzy, dropping leaves all around them.

Nate tried to block out the thoughts that had been circling through his head in a constant loop since he'd heard Violet's story.

He had to tell her the truth about himself, he knew that. But the moment he did, any hope he'd started to have for the future would be shattered.

Every time he thought about it, a dull pain pressed against his ribcage.

A fresh, furious gust of wind whipped against him, and Nate pulled to a stop. Tony tugged on the leash for a minute, but when Nate didn't move, he stuck his nose to the ground and sniffed around.

Nate tipped his head toward the sky letting the sharp breaths stab into his lungs, relishing their sting.

He closed his eyes as the roar of the wind filled him.

He couldn't go through life like this anymore.

Couldn't deal with remembering who he was and what he had done.

Couldn't deal with an empty future of paying for his past sins.

Couldn't deal with the burden of getting through each day.

Nate turned, dragging Tony with him as he jogged toward town.

He knew what he had to do.

Still gasping from running all the way to Dan's house, Nate lifted his hand to knock. Next to him, Tony panted, his tongue lolling to the side.

The door opened, and Nate found himself straightening.

"Nate?" Dan looked confused to find Nate on his doorstep, but he offered a genuine smile.

"Are you busy?" Nate shifted from one foot to the other. Maybe this had been a bad idea. But he didn't know where else to turn.

"Of course not. Come on in."

"I have the dog. We can do this out here."

"Don't be ridiculous. It's freezing out. Bring the dog in, too."

Nate hesitated another half second, but his hands were stiff with the cold, so he led Tony into the house. He dropped onto the comfortable old couch in the living room, and Tony settled at his feet.

Dan plopped into the chair across from the couch and sat, waiting.

Nate opened his mouth, but he didn't know where to start. Didn't know what to say.

Dan slapped the arm of his chair and jumped up. "How about a game of pool?"

Nate nodded, grateful. He'd let off some steam with a game of pool, then tell Dan the truth about himself.

Dan led him to the basement, where a beat-up looking rec room contained a pool table and a foosball table.

"The table's kind of warped, just to warn you." Dan racked the balls. "We use it for teen nights. They don't seem to mind."

Nate's memories flashed to his own youth group and the pastor who had mentored him and encouraged him to pursue his music. Just one more person he'd let down.

Dan gestured for Nate to break.

But Nate's shot was off, and he ended up without a single ball in the pocket.

"That sounds about right," he muttered, offering a wry smile.

Dan studied him as he chalked his own cue, then bent to take his shot, sinking the five ball in the far corner.

"Nice shot."

"Thanks." Dan moved around the table to line up his next shot. "So, how are things with Violet?"

Nate's stomach turned. Dan apparently wasn't going to waste any time getting to the crux of the matter. "They're good. Everything's great."

Dan glanced up from his pool cue, and Nate looked away.

It was time to drop the pretense.

"Violet is wonderful. She really is. And I care about her." He licked his lips. "A lot, actually."

"But?" Dan prompted.

Nate looked him in the eye. "I'm not who she thinks I am." He refused to look away. "I'm not who any of you think I am."

Dan straightened, ignoring his shot, and leaned against the pool table. "And who do we think you are?"

Nate sighed. "I don't know. A good guy. A nice person."

"And you're not?" The hint of a smile tugged at Dan's lips, and Nate fought the urge to punch it off. Why did Dan insist on remaining so calm when Nate was about to obliterate the image his friend had formed of him?

"No, I'm not." His voice was hard. "I'm a—" He choked on the word but made himself say it. "I'm a felon."

He watched Dan's face closely, waiting for the disgust and revulsion. But aside from a flicker of surprise, Dan's expression didn't change.

"So am I," the pastor said, as if he were remarking on the weather.

That Nate had not expected. Did Dan think this was a joke?

"What? No—"

But Dan cut him off.

"Maybe not in the eyes of the state. But in God's eyes. We all are." Dan set his pool cue down and sat on the edge of the table.

"I'm not talking about God's eyes," Nate huffed. "I'm talking a felon. As in, I spent time in prison for a crime I committed."

"I understand that." Dan's calm was infuriating. "But it doesn't matter. Sin is sin."

Nate chucked his pool cue at the ground, the clatter of its fall dulled by the thin carpeting. "Fine. Sin is sin. How's this for sin: I almost killed my sister?" He spit the words at the preacher. There. Let him deal with that confession.

This time, Dan couldn't mask the shock on his face.

A flash of vindication washed over Nate, followed by a surge of shame.

The man he had come to think of as a friend now knew his terrible secret. Knew who he truly was.

And would hate him for it.

Nate fell into the vinyl chair next to the pool table and dropped his head into his hands. Tony's tags jangled as the dog padded across the room, then laid his head on Nate's lap. Nate dug his hands into the dog's fur.

The chair next to him creaked as Dan settled into it.

A large hand rested on Nate's shoulder, and he turned his head to look at Dan. Why hadn't he fled the room the moment Nate told him his secret?

"Do you want to tell me about it?" Dan asked quietly.

Nate swallowed. That was the last thing he wanted to do.

And yet he needed to do it.

He started talking, beginning with his band's success, the celebration at the bar, the beers. Through it all, Dan kept his steady gaze on Nate, nodding now and then to encourage him to continue.

When Nate reached the part where he got into the car, Dan closed his eyes momentarily. Nate could see that his friend knew what was coming. That it would devastate him and ruin whatever friendship they might still have after everything else he had confessed.

Nate hauled in a ragged breath and made himself go on.

"I didn't think twice about getting in that car." His voice cracked. "I had never been drunk before, and I didn't think I was then. But I was. I was drunk and I got in a car, and I crossed the center line."

Next to him, Dan let out a swift exhale. Nate waited for Dan to tell him to stop, to tell him he didn't want to hear the rest. But Dan sat silent, waiting.

"We hit another car head-on. There was only one person in that car, fortunately, and he had some injuries, but he was okay. But Kayla, my sister, was thrown from the car. When I got to her, all I could see was blood spreading around her. I begged God to make her okay." A silent sob racked his body, and he couldn't go on.

Dan gave him a minute, then asked quietly, "What happened to her?"

Nate lifted his head and stared at the pool table with its scattered balls. "I don't know." The despair closed off his throat, and he struggled for a moment just to breathe. When he could finally speak again, his voice was a rasp against his throat. "She's alive, that much I know. But my dad hasn't let me have any contact with her since that day. She was in a coma, and I don't know if—" Air rattled in and out of his lungs as he tried to regain control. "I don't know if she's ever woken up and if she has—if she's the same person she used to be."

He slumped forward, and Dan's big hand fell on his shoulder again.

After a few seconds, Nate lifted his head and pinned Dan with his gaze. "So you wanted to know where I was from. Prison. That's where. I came straight here from prison."

Nate sagged against the back of his chair, waiting for Dan's reprimand. Waiting for the man to tell him what he already knew—he'd gotten off too easy and deserved to be in hell.

Dan contemplated him, but Nate couldn't read his friend's expression. "You're still in prison."

Nate stiffened. That's exactly what he felt like, but how did Dan know?

"You've made this prison for yourself," Dan went on. "You've told yourself you don't deserve to be forgiven. You're so locked into that belief that you don't see the truth right in front of you: you *are* forgiven."

Nate jumped to his feet, a surge of anger and adrenaline propelling him to the other side of the room. When he got to the wall, he pushed off it like a caged animal.

"I don't want to be forgiven," Nate spat. "I want to know what to do to make up for it. How to make it right. I can't erase that night. But there must be something I can do."

Dan's infuriating calm smile was back. "That's the thing, though. There's nothing you can do."

All the adrenaline drained out of Nate, and he fell against the wall. That's what he had feared. He'd have to live with this weight, this guilt, for the rest of his life.

"Listen." Dan leaned forward, bracing his elbows on his knees. "There's nothing *you* can do. But that's because everything's already been done for you. Jesus paid the price for all sin." He held up a hand as Nate started to protest. "Even this sin. He promises he's removed it from you as far as the east is from the west."

"Well, he shouldn't have," Nate snarled.

"No, he shouldn't have. You certainly don't deserve it."

Nate's head snapped up. At least Dan could admit that he didn't deserve forgiveness.

But Dan kept talking. "I don't deserve it, either. No one does. That's what grace is. God's undeserved love."

That word.

Grace.

Nate knew that word. Once upon a time, he had believed in that word. Had believed that God loved him no matter what he'd done.

What had happened to the little boy, the young man who had believed that?

"You know what else is a sin?" Dan went on.

Nate stilled, waiting to hear how else he had failed.

"Holding onto your guilt. You're not bound by these chains anymore. God has released them. So now you need to let them go."

Something in Nate's heart cracked.

"I don't know how." His voice scratched against his throat.

Dan rose to his feet and crossed the room, pulling him into a tight hug.

"Good thing God has that covered for you, too." Dan released him but kept a hand on his shoulder. "Would you like to pray together?"

Nate nodded, not trusting himself to say anything else.

"Heavenly Father." Dan's prayer was strong and sure, as if he talked with God every day. Which he probably did. Nate used to do that, too, and he had an unexpected longing for that old intimacy with his heavenly Father.

"You know our sins. You know our hurts. You know our hearts." Dan squeezed Nate's shoulder. "We ask that you would soothe us when the guilt of our sins threatens to drown us. When we think we have to do something to deserve your love and forgiveness. Take us by the hand and remind us that there is nothing we have to do—nothing we can do—to deserve you. That you love us anyway. That you died for us. And that you forgive us. Unconditionally. Ease our hearts, calm our spirits, and draw us closer to you day by day. In Jesus' name we ask this. Amen."

Nate stood with his eyes closed, letting the peace of the moment wash over him. He felt as if his soul had been cleansed. As if he'd gotten a second chance at life.

Not that his heart didn't still ache. Not that he didn't still hurt for the past.

But in spite of all that, he knew he could go on. He could live as a forgiven child of God.

"Thank you," he finally whispered.

Dan clapped him on the back. "Any time." He bent to pick up Nate's pool cue and passed it to him. "Your shot."

Nate nodded, still feeling stunned by Dan's forgiveness—and by God's. He bent to line up his shot.

Just as he drew the pool cue back, Dan cut in. "I still don't understand what all of this has to do with Violet."

Nate picked up his head, ruining his shot.

"Oh, sorry." But Dan's eyes gleamed.

"You did that on purpose," Nate accused.

Dan didn't blink. "I'm waiting for an answer."

Nate let out a heavy breath that felt like it might pull his soul right out with the air. "I know how her husband died. If Violet knew the truth about me—" He rubbed roughly at a spot on the pool table. "I'm afraid every time she looked at me, she'd see the driver who killed her husband."

Dan nodded thoughtfully, and Nate's heart dipped. He had half hoped Dan would tell him he was wrong.

"I guess there's a risk of that." Dan lined up his shot. "But maybe you should let her be the one to decide. By not telling her, you're not protecting her. You're protecting yourself." Another ball dropped into the corner pocket.

Nate knew Dan was right. And yet— "She deserves better."

Dan leaned down for another shot. "Violet deserves to smile again. To laugh." He paused, seeming to see through Nate with his stare. "To love. If you're the person who can give her that"—Dan pointed his cue at Nate—"then you're exactly the person she deserves."

Nate's mouth went dry. Is that what he wanted? Love?

But he already knew it was. "How do I know she won't run when I tell her the truth?"

"You don't." Dan bent over, barely pausing to sight his shot, and hit the ball. "Just like you didn't know if you would win this game. But you started playing anyway."

Dan sank the rest of the solid balls, then dropped the eight ball in the side pocket, shooting Nate a wicked grin.

"Well, I hope things go better with Violet than they did in this game," Nate muttered.

But he couldn't stop the laugh that burst out of him. He felt lighter than he had since the night of the crash.

He may not deserve a future with Violet.

But by God's grace, he might get one anyway.
He only hoped it wasn't too late to try.

# Chapter 36

Violet couldn't shake the heaviness as she locked up the shop for the day. It'd been a good day, money-wise, and she was getting closer to being able to pay everything off.

But Nate hadn't come by this evening. She tried to tell herself he'd probably gotten caught up at work. He'd probably be home any minute, and he'd knock on her door and ask if she wanted to hang out.

But in her heart, she knew that wasn't going to happen. She'd been sensing him pulling away the past few days, ever since he'd heard her talk about Cade at the school. She was trying to respect the fact that maybe he needed more time and space to deal with everything she'd said. But it was hard. Now that she knew she was ready for another relationship, knew who she wanted that relationship to be with, knew how she felt about him, she didn't want to wait.

As she stepped onto the landing at the top of the stairs, her phone rang, and she paused to pull it out of her pocket. She didn't recognize the number. Frowning, she swiped to answer, just as she heard the door downstairs open.

"Hello?" she said into the phone as she spun toward the stairs.

"Hi, Mrs. Somers. This is May. From the high school?"

"Hi, May." Violet's gaze zeroed in on Nate. He had closed the door and was leaning against it, his eyes directed toward her. But he didn't smile. Instead he looked—

She wasn't sure how to describe it, but if she didn't know better, she'd say he looked almost scared. Her eyes went to Tony, panting at his feet as if he'd spent all day running.

"I was just calling with a couple of follow-up questions." May sounded hesitant, but Violet couldn't focus on that. She was too busy trying to figure out how to reach Nate.

"Sure, May. How can I help you?"

"Well, I was writing my article, and I wanted to see if I could get a little more background on that guy that was with you, so I wouldn't have to bother you, and . . ."

"Yes?"

Violet started down the steps. If Nate wouldn't come to her, she would go to him. Maybe he was hesitant because he didn't know how she felt. So she'd show him.

"Well—" May let out a quick breath. "You didn't mention that he had been convicted of drunk driving."

"What?" Violet jerked to a stop as the whole stairway tilted under her. She either had to sit or fall over.

Right now.

She dropped to the step above her with a thud.

Through the fog that closed in around her, she vaguely saw Nate move toward the stairs, his expression changing to concern.

"So I was wondering if you had anything to say about that? You know, given the way your husband died?" May sounded far away, and Violet was no longer sure any of this was real.

"I'm sorry, I can't— I don't— I have to go." Violet pulled the phone away from her ear and quickly hung up, afraid of what other venom might spew out of it if she didn't.

"Violet?" Nate crouched on the step next to her, and Tony sniffed her knees. "Are you okay? What was that about?"

Violet tried to figure out how to speak while she was drowning. "That was May. The girl from the school newspaper. She wanted to follow up on some things."

She looked away. She didn't want to say the rest. Didn't want to hear him say it was true. But she forced the words out. "She wanted to know how I felt about your drunk driving conviction."

# Chapter 37

This couldn't be happening. Nate had come home from Dan's fully intending to tell Violet everything. But not like this.

Her eyes refused to leave his, and he hated the hope shining in hers. She was waiting for him to tell her it wasn't true.

He looked away and held out a hand to her. She hesitated for a second, then took it and let him pull her to her feet and lead her into his apartment.

Inside, he steered her toward the couch. She sat, her moves mechanical.

Nate stepped away from the couch to pace in front of the window. He couldn't be next to her when he did this. It would be too hard not to touch her, not to seek her comfort. But he didn't deserve that.

He almost choked on a shaky breath, his stomach roiling at the thought of what he was about to do.

He loved this woman—he couldn't deny it any longer.

And he was about to ruin any chance that she could ever feel the same way about him.

"I'm so sorry, Violet." Nate swallowed against the burn that had already kicked in at the back of his throat. "I had no idea how Cade died until the other day. I never meant to hurt you."

Violet nodded, not looking at him.

But he knew he hadn't said enough. "I should have told you sooner. I just didn't want you to think—" His voice cracked. "I never meant for it to happen. It was the only time I ever drank, and—" He stopped himself.

She didn't need to hear his excuses. "I will regret it every day for the rest of my life."

"So that's what your scars are from? On your chest and your knee?"

He nodded and tried to think of anything else he'd kept from her. Now that she knew, she might as well know everything. "It's also why I can't drive. My license was revoked. And it's why I meet with Officer Jensen, the woman you saw me with that day you brought me cookies—" His eyes flicked out the window to watch a boy struggling to get a kite in the air. "She's my parole officer. I'm a felon, Violet. I just got out of prison."

"Did anyone die?" Violet's voice was so quiet he could have pretended not to hear her. But she deserved to know the whole truth.

"No."

He could see her let out a sigh of relief, but he wasn't going to let himself get off that easily.

"My sister almost did. I actually don't know—" He turned away as he felt himself choking up. He didn't deserve her sympathy, and she had such a soft heart, he knew she'd give it if she thought he was hurting. After a minute, he cleared his throat and turned toward her. "I don't know how she is. That's why I've been so desperate to meet my dad's demands. It's the only way he'll let me see her and my mom again."

Violet inhaled like she was about to say something, but he had to finish this or he never would.

"It was selfish of me to let myself get involved with you when I knew I could never be the man you deserved." He gave a wry laugh. "I tried not to, I really did. But you made me feel like someone else when I was with you. Someone who could be more than this huge mistake. And I let myself get wrapped up in that. I just fell so hard for you and your loving spirit and your—" He dragged a hand through his hair. "Anyway, I'm sorry."

He finally looked at her, but she was watching her thumb slide up and down her empty ring finger.

He moved to the kitchen to get himself a glass of water—and to give her the space he was sure she wanted.

After downing two glasses, he stood with his hands braced on the counter, his head tucked between his shoulders. How could he go back out there? How could he face her now that she knew who he really was?

*Please give me strength.* He whispered the prayer, then straightened.

But before he could return to the living room, he heard the click of a door opening and closing.

# Chapter 38

Violet leaned against the inside of her apartment door. She hadn't meant to flee Nate's apartment, but her thoughts had swarmed and knotted until she felt like she was going to split in two.

She just needed some space. Some time to process what Nate had told her.

She'd talk to him in the morning when she was thinking straight. When she'd worked out what she wanted to say. What she wanted to do.

Violet shuffled to her bedroom and climbed into bed, fully clothed. She closed her eyes and tried to sleep. But she could still hear what Nate had said.

He'd driven drunk. He'd almost killed his sister.

But beyond that, she could see the guilt and torture in his eyes. The shame and regret in his voice.

She'd seen his brokenness. He'd let her in.

Yes, he'd made a mistake.

About the biggest one he could have made.

But did that mean he didn't deserve to be forgiven?

Did she really mean what she'd said the other day at the school? That no one was beyond forgiveness?

She folded her hands and prayed for the strength to forgive. Her prayers continued long into the night, until she finally drifted into sleep.

In the morning, she sprang out of bed the moment her alarm went off. Without bothering to change out of the rumpled clothes she'd slept in last night, she sped through her apartment, out the door, and across the landing to Nate's. She had to catch him before he left for the office. She needed to tell him that she forgave him and that nothing he had told her changed the way she felt about him.

When he didn't come to the door, she pounded harder.

A few seconds later, a door opened across the hall.

Violet spun toward Mrs. D'Angelo, apologetic. She'd gotten so caught up in her emotions that she'd been thoughtless. "I'm so sorry, Mrs. D'Angelo, I didn't mean to wake you."

Mrs. D'Angelo tsked at her. "Please, child, I haven't been able to sleep past four in the morning since you were in diapers. Just heard you knocking there and thought you should know that no one's going to answer."

Violet's stomach dropped. "Why not?"

"Your young man left early this morning, before the sun was up. Had a suitcase with him, so I figured he was taking a trip."

"Did he—" Violet worked to control her voice. "Did he say how long he'd be gone?"

Mrs. D'Angelo gave her a gentle look, and Violet almost lost her composure right there. "I didn't get the impression he'd be back, dear. I'm sorry."

Violet pressed her lips together to stop the trembling.

When she turned to her apartment, her eyes fell on a note that had been taped to her door. She pulled it off with a shaking hand.

*Violet,*

*I am sorry for everything. I want you to know how much you mean to me. That's why I need to leave, so that you can have the future you deserve with someone who deserves you. I wish you only all the best.*

*Love,*

*Nate*

*PS Please take care of Tony. The key is in the super-secret hiding spot.*

Violet lowered the note, her heart thudding a rhythm of regret against her ribs. How had she let the one man who made her alive again leave without a fight?

# Chapter 39

It was better this way.

Nate had repeated the same thing to himself every ten minutes the entire bus ride, but he still hadn't managed to convince himself.

Leaving without saying goodbye to Violet was easier, but it had left him feeling hollowed out inside.

And the feeling only grew as he thought of the look Tony had given him when he'd shut him in his kennel. He'd miss that dog, but there was no way to bring him on the bus. And he trusted that Violet would take good care of him.

Maybe being with Tony would remind her of him from time to time.

The man in the seat next to Nate let out a honking snore, and Nate pressed closer to the window. He never would have guessed he'd miss Leah's bubbling chatter—the same chatter that had annoyed him on his way to Hope Springs.

Had that really only been two and half months ago? Somehow, in that time he'd gone from resenting his move to Hope Springs to falling in love with the place. He hated the thought of all his friends finding out what he'd done. Hated to imagine what they'd all think of him now. But Violet had made it pretty clear when she'd walked out of his apartment. She didn't want anything to do with him anymore.

He didn't know why he'd let a tiny part of himself hope that she'd be able to see past what he'd done. That she'd see the man he could be, the man she made him want to be. He should have known it was too much to ask. He couldn't blame her for not giving it.

Nate let his eyes drift over the now empty cornfields. He probably shouldn't have bought the ticket. There was no way Dad was going to let him in the house.

But when the woman behind the bus station counter had asked where he was going, the name of his hometown had just come out.

They were only twenty minutes or so away now, and Nate's stomach had become one of those rides at the fair that made little kids get off and promptly barf. He tried to come up with a strategy to get past Dad's objections.

But by the time the bus pulled into the station, he was just as empty as he'd been when he left Hope Springs.

He found his way to the Uber he'd ordered from the bus and gave the driver his former home address. He'd have to knock on the door and wing it.

The drive went way too fast, and when the Uber driver pulled into the driveway of his childhood home, Nate just sat. It looked almost the same, although the plum tree in the front yard was larger now, and they'd painted the door a bold blue.

"We're here," the driver pointed out.

"Yeah." But still Nate sat and stared at the house. For the past seven years, he'd dreamed of the moment he'd walk inside again. But now that the time was here, he wasn't sure he could do it.

"Look, I don't mean to rush you or anything, but I have another . . ." The driver circled his hands.

"Oh, sorry." Nate opened his door and forced his feet to the pavement, grabbing his suitcase and wheeling it behind him. "Thanks."

He'd barely slammed the door before the car was gone.

Nate hesitated. This was it. He either walked up to the door or—

No.

There was no *or*. He was going to do this. Right here and right now.

His feet carried him across the driveway, along the path in front of the house, and up the porch steps. It felt odd to reach for the doorbell when he'd opened this door a million times in his life.

But this wasn't his home anymore.

He pressed the button and listened as the bell resounded through the house.

He found himself needing to pray as he waited, but the words wouldn't come. He'd have to hope God got the message anyway.

He tried to peer in through the sidelight, but it was privacy glass, and he could only see faint shadows behind it. Was that someone coming toward the door?

Nate's heart pounded in his ears.

This was it.

He took a step back, staring at the fine cracks in the wood of the porch. He couldn't bring himself to lift his head as the door opened.

"Oh my— Nate!"

His head whipped up when he heard his sister's voice. But the moment his eyes fell on her, he dropped his suitcase and sagged against the doorframe.

"Oh no, Kayla. I'm so sorry." The words were strangling him.

How could he have done this to her?

Because of him, his beautiful, vibrant sister, the one who had been an all-state cross-country runner, was in a wheelchair.

# Chapter 40

This was a mistake. He shouldn't have come. Dad was right—he didn't deserve to be part of his family's life anymore. Not after what he'd cost his sister.

And yet she'd insisted that he come inside, and now she was maneuvering around the kitchen to get him a cup of coffee. He wanted to tell her to let him do it. It'd be so much easier for him. And yet, as he watched her, he had to acknowledge how capable she was, deftly wheeling her chair around obstacles and reaching into cupboards.

Even more striking was how grown up she looked. She'd been a gangly seventeen-year-old at the time of the accident, which made her twenty-four now. Twenty-five, he corrected himself. Her birthday was last month. Her face had matured in that time, and in place of her old ponytail standby, she wore her auburn hair in a sleek face-framing cut. Even her hands, with their practiced and sure movements as she added sugar to his mug, seemed grown up.

"Here you are." She set the coffee cup on the table. How could she smile at him and serve him coffee after everything?

"Thank you." He managed to rasp out. He didn't know what else to say, so he took a sip of the coffee. It burned his tongue, but he didn't care. He deserved far worse than a burnt tongue after what he'd done to her.

*You're forgiven for that.* But the reminder rang hollow now that evidence of what he'd done was right in front of him. Maybe Jesus had forgiven him, but how could his family ever?

"Kayla, I'm—"

But he had to stop as she wheeled up next to him and wrapped her arms around his shoulders. He stiffened for a second, then swiveled to bring his arms around her and pull her in as tight as he dared. Which wasn't very tight.

"You won't break me, Nate." Kayla's voice held both a laugh and a reprimand. "Give me a real hug."

He squeezed harder, closing his eyes against the rush of emotion. How could she want to be anywhere near him, let alone hug him?

"I'm so sorry." He whispered the words into her shoulder. "I never meant for you—"

"I know." She rubbed a hand up and down his back, the same way their mother always had when they were sick.

When she finally pulled back, Nate swiped a quick hand across his cheeks.

"Dad wouldn't let me—" He fumbled. This wasn't the time to blame things on someone else. "I didn't know you were—" The word stuck on his tongue.

"Paralyzed?" She said it gently, not an accusation. Just a fact. As if she were saying that she were tall or dark-haired or something that was a part of her.

He winced. "Yeah."

She touched a hand to his arm. "It's okay, Nate. Really. Remember, I've had a long time to get used to it. You've only had a few minutes."

"So, what—you're just okay with this?" Nate shoved to his feet. How could she just accept this? Why wasn't she angry at him? She should yell at him, scream that he was the worst brother in the history of the world, tell him to get lost.

"I wasn't at first." Her eyes followed him as he paced the room. "Not for a couple of years, actually. I was angry." She dropped her eyes. "Really angry."

He deserved her anger, he knew that. But his stomach plunged to hear her say it. "At me."

She raised her eyes and met his. "A little. But mostly at God."

Nate nodded. Don't get him started on being angry with God. He knew that feeling only too well. And though that anger had begun to fade in the past few weeks, it threatened to rear up again now that he was confronted with what had happened to his sister. He reminded himself that what had happened wasn't God's fault; it was his own.

"But," Kayla continued. "Mom and Dad kept bringing me to church, even when I didn't want to go. They kept reminding me of God's love for me. And God worked on my heart. I eventually got involved with a support group for young adults with injuries and disabilities. And now I'm actually working with kids with disabilities." Her eyes came to life. "It's like I've found my purpose, Nate. And it's a purpose I wouldn't have found without all of this." She gestured at her lap, where her legs sat perfectly still.

"You're saying this is a good thing?" Nate couldn't wrap his head around it.

Kayla looked thoughtful. "Would I have chosen for it not to happen, if I had a choice? Of course. But it did happen. And as terrible as it was, God used it to bring about good. We both know I wasn't exactly on a godly path before the accident. That was you, with your worship band and all your churchy stuff."

Nate let out an ironic laugh. Funny how things had changed.

"I didn't want anything to do with God then. But he used this to show me my need for him. And to show me how he could use me for his kingdom."

Nate was stunned into silence.

Was there a chance that God had used all of this for his good, too? Kayla was right that he'd been into all the churchy stuff, but looking back on it now, Nate could admit he'd been doing it more for himself than for God. He'd wanted the record contract not so he'd have a bigger platform to share God but so that he'd have a bigger platform for himself.

"But don't you miss running?" He finally asked the question that had been dragging on him since the moment he'd seen her in that chair.

"Of course." Her answer was immediate, and it sent a stab of guilt through him.

"Then how can you say—"

She held up a hand. "Running was only a small part of who I am. And anyway, I'm training for a race right now."

Nate stared at her. Was he missing something here?

"There's a big wheelchair marathon in Madison in a couple weeks. I finished in the top fifty last year. My goal this year is top twenty."

"Wow, that's amazing." Nate crossed the room to give his sister another hug. She'd always been spunky; he should have known nothing would stop her from competing.

"You can train with me now that you're here." Kayla slugged his shoulder. "If you think you can keep up. You always were a slowpoke."

"Slowpoke? Hey, I beat you that one time—"

"Yeah, because I had a sprained ankle."

"Oh, come on." But Nate's heart eased. He had missed the broth-er-sister teasing that used to drive their parents crazy. "You know I—"

But the words died on his lips as the door from the garage into the kitchen opened.

His mother stopped halfway through the door, her mouth half open.

He needed to say something, but nothing sounded right in his head. Finally, he got out the only word he could. "Mom."

It was enough. Mom unfroze and lunged toward him, tears spilling down her face. In a second, she had him wrapped in her arms. Nate lifted her off her feet and held her as tight as he could.

"Nathan, put me down." But her voice was full of joy and tears. Nate gave her another good squeeze.

"What's going on?" At the sound of Dad's voice, Nate set her down, and she moved to the side. Nate was left face-to-face with his father.

He tried not to wilt under Dad's hard stare. "What are you doing here?"

Nate swallowed against the dryness in his throat. This is where figuring out what to say ahead of time would have come in handy.

But as if he'd always known what he would say in this situation, the words started flowing. "This is my family. And I couldn't wait any longer to see all of you. To tell you how very sorry I am. How sorry I will be for the rest of my life. And to beg for your forgiveness." He held up a hand as Dad started to talk over him, and to his surprise, Dad fell silent. "Before you say anything, I know I don't deserve your forgiveness. But I'm hoping you'll consider giving it anyway. Out of sheer grace."

The words out, Nate fell silent.

"I forgive you, Nate." Kayla's words were soft, but they fell like a balm on Nate's soul.

He blinked rapidly and reached behind him to grab Kayla's hand. "Thank you." The words were barely a whisper, but it was all he could get out past the surge of gratitude for her unexpected gift.

"I just think," Kayla continued, her voice stronger. "That if Jesus forgives you for this, then we really have no right not to. Right, Dad?"

Nate couldn't bring himself to look Dad full in the face but watched him out of his peripheral vision. Dad's jaw worked, but he remained silent.

A second later, he fled down the hallway.

It was what Nate had expected, and yet he still felt deflated.

"Give him time." Mom's voice was gentle, and she pulled Nate into another hug.

Nate nodded. At least Dad hadn't asked him to leave. He supposed that was something.

He let Mom usher him to the table and pour him yet another cup of coffee. Then he sat with Mom and Kayla as they caught him up on everything he'd missed over the last seven years.

He told them about his life in Hope Springs, too. He meant to leave off the parts about Violet, but she'd become so wrapped up in every aspect of his life that it was impossible not to mention her. He pretended not to notice the glance that passed between his mom and his sister whenever he said Violet's name.

They didn't know that part of his life was over. That whatever thoughts he'd had about a future with Violet had died the moment she'd found out the truth about him.

After a while, their conversation wound down, and Mom sent him to unpack his suitcase in his old room. As he walked down the hallway, Nate's eye caught on the dozens of pictures hanging on the wall. Some were new—a picture of Kayla in her wheelchair at the finish line of a race, one of Kayla and Mom at the beach, and one of Kayla all dressed up next to some guy Nate didn't recognize. But there were old pictures, too. Even, to his surprise, some of him. He moved to the picture on the end, from the trip where he and Kayla had collected all those shells. That was the day they'd both decided they wanted to be marine biologists. He'd be a musician on the side, and she'd be a runner.

Nate slid a finger over Kayla's youthful face in the image. How could her life—their lives—have turned out so differently from what they'd planned?

A noise from behind the closed door to Dad's office across the hall caught his attention.

Without considering what he was doing, Nate lifted his hand to the doorknob. He eased the door open a crack, then immediately wished he hadn't.

Dad's back was to him, his head bowed and shoulders shaking. The sound of muffled sobs stabbed Nate right through the middle.

He'd never seen Dad break down before. Not even when he'd stood behind Nate as he'd pleaded guilty to the drunk driving charges.

Nate hesitated. Maybe he should go to Dad. Try to comfort him.

But he reminded himself he was the one who had caused this.

He closed the door silently and walked away.

# Chapter 41

Tony's whines woke Violet early. She winced as her bare feet hit the hardwood floor on the way to the living room, where she'd tucked his kennel next to the window.

The dog turned in wild circles as she approached.

"Ugh. Nate taught you to be a morning person, didn't he?" She shoved down the swoop of regret at Nate's name. She'd spent all day yesterday telling herself it was better that he'd left anyway. She wasn't about to undo that now.

The moment she let Tony out of his kennel, he raced to the door. She glanced at the window. The sun was barely peeking over the horizon. "Seriously? You want to go outside right now?"

But she padded to the bedroom to throw on some sweats. Tony shouldn't have to suffer just because Nate had left him. Had left them both.

Just like her mom. And her sister. And Cade.

She fought to push aside the loneliness and remember that she had lots of friends, lots of people who cared about her.

Her Bible was lying open on her bedside table. She'd been too tired after the emotional day yesterday to read much. On a whim, she grabbed it. Maybe she could read while Tony played outside.

But the mid-October air sliced at her face the moment she stepped out the door. Maybe she'd been too optimistic to consider reading outside this morning.

"Let's make this quick, Tony," she mumbled. She led the dog to the grassy hill behind the apartment, trying to shove away the memories of all the times she'd stood out here with Nate.

She waited for Tony to do his business, but the dog pulled on the leash, dragging her down the hill. She tried to tug back, but Tony was on a mission. She didn't realize where he was taking her until he stepped onto the beach.

Instinctively, she recoiled. She couldn't walk here.

But Tony didn't give her a choice. She either had to follow him onto the beach or have her arm ripped out of the socket.

The dog tugged her to the water's edge. At first she resisted, jerking back on the leash every few seconds to coax the dog to go back. But after a while, she gave up and let herself be pulled along.

Tony finally stopped at a rocky outcrop. Violet considered it. Her fingers had gone numb, and the wet sand had frozen her toes. But the sun was above the horizon now, and the entire sky was layered in shades of pink and red and orange. She couldn't remember the last time she'd seen a sunrise like this. It felt like an invitation.

She climbed onto a low rock, and Tony scrabbled up after her. He settled against her leg as she tilted her head and watched the colors play across the sky.

After a while, she opened her Bible. She'd been reading through the book of Deuteronomy over the past few days, and she picked up where she'd left off, with Moses giving his final instructions to the Israelites before they entered the promised land. But her heart was only half in the reading. Until she came to Deuteronomy 31:8: *The Lord himself goes before you and will be with you; he will never leave you nor forsake you. Do not be afraid; do not be discouraged.*

Tears filled Violet's eyes, and a soft peace washed over her.

No matter how many people in this world had left her, no matter how many more would leave her, God would never forsake her.

How had she let herself lose sight of that fact?

The cold had seeped through her sweatpants by the time she slid off the rock, but her heart felt warmer than it had in a long time.

God had brought Nate into her life for a reason, Violet knew that. And even if he was no longer part of her life, he'd been one of the threads pulling together her tapestry. He'd helped her realize that she didn't have to live in the past. That she was ready to move on and—if the right person came along—love again.

Next time she felt that pull toward someone, she wouldn't resist. She would tell them how she felt, as soon as she felt it. Like she should have done with Nate.

That was her biggest regret in all of this.

He'd left without knowing how she felt about him. Without knowing she loved him.

She'd thought about calling him. But something held her back. It wasn't that she didn't want to be with him. But she sensed he needed the space to work through things on his own. She only prayed that he'd know she forgave him. And, more importantly, that he would know the peace that could only come from knowing Jesus had died for his sins.

Violet was halfway up the hill to her building when her phone rang. She pulled Tony to a stop, trying to catch her breath. Had Nate sensed that she was thinking about him? Was he thinking about her, too?

But it was much more likely to be Sophie or Peyton. More likely to be anyone, really, than Nate.

Still, she couldn't stop the surge of hope.

She had to stare at the number for a few seconds before she believed it was true.

Then she answered quickly, before it could go to voice mail. "Jade?"

There was no reply at first, and Violet held her breath. Was she really going to get to talk to her sister for the first time in six years?

After a second, a small voice said. "Hi, Violet."

Violet closed her eyes and breathed out a prayer of thanks. "It's so good to hear you."

"You too." Jade sounded like she was crying, and Violet laughed as tears ran down her own face, too.

# Chapter 42

Nate made himself knock on Dad's office door. In the two days he'd been home, Dad had barely said a full sentence to him.

But he couldn't put this off any longer. It was time for him to stand up for what was right. He owed Violet that much.

"Come in." Dad's voice wasn't exactly inviting, but Nate pushed the door open.

He tried to ignore the way Dad's eyes hardened the moment they fell on him.

"We have to talk."

Dad sat silent. Apparently that was as much of an invitation as Nate was going to get. He crossed the room to stand in front of Dad's desk, feeling suddenly like a naughty schoolboy facing the principal.

"I don't know what Talmadge has over you, but you have to call off the witch hunt for Violet Somers's property. Before she gets hurt."

Dad crossed his arms in front of him.

Nate ignored Dad's look of disapproval and kept talking. "There are plenty of properties in Hope Springs. There's no reason to let Talmadge ruin Violet's life. She doesn't deserve that. Whatever he has over you, she shouldn't have to pay the price."

Dad's frown deepened, until his whole lower face was a map of downward slanting lines. Nate was reminded once again of how much his father had aged.

"You think he has something over me, Nate? That I'm trying to evict your friend for my own gain?"

Nate stuffed his hands in his pockets. "Tell me I'm wrong."

Dad's frown twisted. "It's not what he has over me, Nate. It's what he has over you. You want to blame someone for what's happening to your friend, blame yourself."

Dad's words fell against him like blows, and he grabbed at the edge of Dad's desk. "Me? What could he possibly have over me?"

Dad scrubbed a hand down his cheek, looking weary. "After the accident, when you were in the hospital and then afterward when you were in—" Dad looked away.

"Prison." Nate filled in. He didn't blame Dad for not wanting to say it. No matter how many times he said that word, he'd always hate the taste of it.

Dad kept going as if he hadn't heard. "We worked very hard to keep everything quiet. To keep your name out of the papers. But there were a lot of reporters at the concert that night because everyone knew that producer might be there." Dad's sigh carried a weight Nate wished he could lift. Everything Dad had been through in the past seven years was Nate's fault. "Anyway, Talmadge was the guy I hired to keep things quiet. He pulled some strings, called in some favors. Nothing illegal but definitely things that were distasteful. He managed to do a pretty good job of it."

"Why?" None of this made any sense. Dad hadn't cared what happened to Nate after the accident. He'd made that abundantly clear.

Dad lifted his shoulders. "To protect you. So you could have a decent life when you got out." He looked away for a second. "Anyway, a couple years ago, Talmadge began talking about how I hadn't really paid him enough for what he'd done. He started demanding more. But the more I gave him, the more he demanded."

Nate felt sick to his stomach. He had no idea Dad had done all of that for him.

"Why Violet's property, though? Why wouldn't he consider any of the other places I tried to show him?"

Dad shrugged. "At first, I think it was just the location. But when he realized that you were in a relationship with Violet, he saw targeting her store as a way to hurt you and hurting you as a way to hurt me, especially when I told him he could have any property but that one."

"But why would he want to hurt you?" Never mind the question of why Talmadge would think hurting Nate would hurt Dad in turn. He obviously didn't realize Dad detested Nate now.

Dad dropped his gaze to his desk. "You're not the only person who's done things you're not proud of. I cheated Talmadge out of a deal years ago. A pretty big one. He's never forgiven me. When I went to him about all of this, I knew something like this was a distinct possibility. But he's the best at this sort of thing."

Nate chewed his lip. "I don't care if people know. Let Talmadge tell everyone. Don't protect me at Violet's expense."

Dad studied him as if unsure who Nate was anymore. "Actually, I just got a call from the private investigator I hired to look into your suspicions that Talmadge started that fire."

"And?" Nate's hands clenched. If Talmadge had intentionally endangered Violet—

"He's passed the evidence he collected on to the Hope Springs police department. They should be picking him up any minute now."

Nate dropped into the plush chair behind him. "And in the meantime? What if he tries to hurt her again?" He never should have left her alone.

"He won't. My guy is on him twenty-four, seven."

Nate pushed to his feet. "And her store? You have no reason to evict her now."

Dad shook his head. "There's still the matter of her back rent."

"She's really close on that. I've got calls out to a couple of guys who might be interested in a Bosendorfer piano she has. And if that falls through—" Nate scrambled for something, anything. "If that falls through, I'll pay it off myself."

Dad snorted. "With what money?"

"I'll get a job flipping burgers. Or I'll work for you. Whatever. You can have my salary until her rent is paid off."

"You really want to do that for her?" Dad squinted at him as if suspicious of his intentions.

"Absolutely. I'd do anything for her."

"Why? What's in it for you?"

Violet's dark eyes and gentle smile popped into his head. "Because she's the best person I know. Because she reminded me who I really was when I couldn't see it. Because—"

Dad held up a hand. "I get it. You're in love with her." He rolled his eyes, but something in his features had softened. "I'll take that into consideration."

# Chapter 43

"Have a nice day." Violet smiled at the sweet older lady who had bought a Victorian wall sconce. The sale wasn't quite enough to meet her back rent, and she only had a couple days left before the deadline to pay it off and renew her lease.

She hadn't been able to bring herself to hold a going out of business sale. If it came down to it, she could always move her stuff into a storage unit and get a temporary job until she figured out what to do next.

She rearranged a small display case of porcelain dolls. The one with the tiny dimples reminded her of Jade, and she pulled it out of the case. Next time she talked to her sister, she'd ask for her address and send this to her as a surprise.

They'd talked on the phone once more in the past week. Jade told her about the various odd jobs she'd held down while looking for work as an actor. She'd worked as a waitress, a cell phone saleswoman, and even one of those people who dressed up as a hot dog to try to drum up business for a fast-food joint. Along the way, she'd managed to snag a couple of small parts in commercials but nothing like what she'd hoped to land.

She'd seemed thoroughly discouraged, and Violet sensed there was a lot Jade wasn't telling her, but at least it was a start.

Violet had found herself spilling to Jade about Nate as well. Although Jade hadn't offered any advice, just knowing she was listening made Violet feel less lonely.

After setting the doll aside, Violet picked up the day's mail. She shuffled the bills to the bottom of the pile but stopped when she came to a formal-looking envelope from Benson Properties. She frowned at it. She'd been wondering how Nate would tell her that she had to get out. She'd let herself hope he'd call. It'd been more than a week since she'd heard his voice, and she yearned to talk to him again—even if it was only to say goodbye.

But apparently a formal letter was all she was going to get.

She sat on the stool behind the counter and ripped the envelope open. She might as well get this over with.

She withdrew a thick sheaf of papers clipped together. Her heart accelerated as her eyes fell on the note on top. That was definitely Nate's handwriting.

*Dear Violet,*

*After further investigation, my father has uncovered evidence that Talmadge was responsible for the fire. He has contacted the Hope Springs police department, so you shouldn't have any more trouble. Please know how sorry everyone associated with Benson Properties is for this. We hope you'll accept the enclosed check as reimbursement for any expenses incurred in the cleanup and repairs.*

Frowning, Violet flipped through the packet. The tone of the letter made everything clear. Nate was contacting her as a corporate representative. Not as a friend. And definitely not as anything more.

When she came to the check, Violet gasped. It more than covered what she'd spent on the repairs. But she shook her head at the check, as if it could see her. She'd never wanted money from him. She wanted him.

She turned back to the letter.

*You will find enclosed a lease renewal agreement. We'd like to renew your lease for five years, if you are still interested in staying. Please consider any outstanding debt canceled as well.*

It was too much, and Violet knew she should be grateful. But it all felt empty without Nate here to tell her in person, to celebrate with her.

*If all this should prove agreeable to you, please sign and date the enclosed agreement and return it to the address below.*

She scanned the address. It was in Wescott. Was that where he had gone? Home? She hoped so. And that he'd found the peace he'd longed for.

The letter continued in smaller, messier handwriting, and Violet had to squint to make it out.

*I want to say again how sorry I am about how everything turned out. I want you to know that you changed my life. Really. I hope you are well. And Tony, too. Tell him I miss him.* ~~And~~

And what? Violet wanted to shake the letter. Did he miss her, too? Is that what he'd been about to write?

But he'd left the letter like that, signing it, *Yours, Nate.*

Violet's hand shook. He'd given her everything she needed to keep her dream alive.

Everything except himself.

# Chapter 44

Nate huddled deeper into his jacket as a gust of wind swept through the crowd lining the route of the Madison Wheelchair Marathon. He shifted anxiously from foot to foot. Mom had gone to the starting line with Kayla, and he and Dad had been standing out here for half an hour. So far, neither of them had said a word.

Although Dad seemed to now accept the fact that Nate was going to be part of their life again, the few conversations they'd had in the past week and a half had been strained. Thankfully, Dad hadn't let that get in the way of doing the right thing for Violet.

Still, that didn't mean things between them were easy.

Not by a long shot.

Next to him, Dad took a step away, putting more distance between them. "I'm going to go grab a coffee. You want one?"

It wasn't meant to be a trick question, Nate knew that. And yet he had to be careful not to let Dad think he was taking advantage of them. He was already living in Dad's house and eating his food.

"I'll grab you one." Dad didn't wait for an answer before he disappeared into the crowd.

Nate let out a long breath. He studied the map of the course in his hand. How was his little sister going to wheel herself twenty-six miles? She'd let him try the wheelchair the other day when he'd been watching her train, and it was *hard*.

But that was Kayla. Completely determined.

Nate tried not to think about what she could have done with that determination if she'd never been injured. He had to remind himself that Kayla was right. God had used her injury for good. Who knows where she would have ended up if she had continued her former lifestyle?

Still, some nights the guilt clawed its way back in, worming and twisting until it almost consumed him.

The only thing he could do those nights was to climb out of bed and spend the night on his knees in prayer.

Thankfully, praying was becoming familiar again, and he'd dug out the old Bible tucked into the drawer of his nightstand. As he read it again, he enjoyed revisiting his old notes and highlights. He felt like that young man again, full of all his new discoveries of God's love in Scripture. And at the same time, he felt like a seasoned veteran, someone who had seen that life wasn't always pretty but that God was there through all of it.

"Here."

Nate jumped as Dad thrust a coffee at him. "The race just started. She won't get to this spot for at least fifteen minutes, though."

Nate nodded stiffly and took a swig of the coffee, burning his tongue. He ignored the pain and kept his eyes on the empty road.

"Look, Nate—" Dad cleared his throat.

Nate waited, shoulders tensed. He'd known it was too good to believe that Dad would let him stay indefinitely. He'd probably been waiting to get Nate alone so he could tell him to get lost.

"I wanted to apologize—"

"Wait, Dad, before—" Nate stopped as Dad's words registered. "What?"

"For what I said when I picked you up that day. About wishing you weren't—"

"Born?" Nate said the word without a hint of resentment. "No problem. I've wished it plenty of times myself." He stuffed his left hand in his pocket and took another sip of the scalding coffee.

"I don't wish that." Dad's voice was low. "I was angry and hurt and holding onto that. You have to understand, I felt like I'd lost two children. Thinking about what you were going through in that place and what Kayla was going through out here—it was too much."

Nate kept his eyes on the route, even though no racers had appeared yet.

"I felt like I had failed to protect you. Both of you. Before all of this, I had such visions for the future for you and for Kayla, and in that one moment, they all came crashing down. It took me a long time to get to grips with the new future."

"And have you now?" Nate found that he really wanted to know. Because he wasn't quite sure he'd come to grips with it himself.

Dad's sigh was ragged. "I'm working on it, son." His hand fell on Nate's shoulder, and Nate didn't dare to move for a second. Then he pulled his hand out of his pocket and lifted it to cover Dad's.

A second later, the crowd around them broke into cheers, and Nate leaned to see past the tall guy who'd stepped into his line of sight. A group of wheelchairs rounded the corner. Nate squinted into the sun, trying to make out Kayla.

"There she is." Dad pointed.

With her neon pink helmet decorated with a purple cross, Kayla was easy to pick out leading the pack.

"Go Kayla. Push it." Nate screamed like he used to scream at her cross-country meets. He'd never been prouder of his little sister, not even when she took the state championship.

When the wheelchairs were past, they followed the crowd toward the finish line so they could catch the end of the race as well.

They met up with Mom halfway there, and Nate found himself comfortably walking between his parents for the first time in nearly a decade. He'd expected it to feel strange to be home again. But nothing felt more normal or more right.

They spent the next hour talking comfortably as they waited for the racers to reach them.

"Oh, Nate." Dad dropped the comment casually during a lull in the conversation. "I almost forgot. Your friend sent in her lease renewal yesterday. She included a very nice letter thanking me."

A wave of simultaneous relief and regret washed over Nate. He was glad Violet was going to be able to keep her store. He only wished things could have been different and he could be there with her.

"She sent a note for you, too." Dad pulled a crumpled piece of paper out of his jacket pocket. He gave Nate a look as he passed him the paper but didn't say anything else.

Nate smoothed the paper on his leg, then tried to read it discreetly, painfully aware of both of his parents watching him.

*Dear Nate,*

*I just wanted to say thank you for what you did to save the store. If it weren't for you, I would have given up a long time ago. The thing is, I used to look at the store as a way to hold onto my past. But now I see it as a way to move into the future. And because of you, I'm ready for that future, whatever it brings.*

*One thing I didn't get to tell you before you left was that I forgive you. I saw how deeply what happened scarred you and how sorry you were for it. So I want you to know that I don't hold your past against you—and neither does Jesus, just in case you were wondering.*

Nate closed his eyes and dropped his hand to his side. For her to say that, after everything. He didn't know what to do with it except cherish it.

After a second, he lifted the letter again, greedy for every single word she had to say to him.

*I noticed that your letter came from Wescott. I hope that means that you've gone home to your family and that you've found peace with them. If you ever decide to come back to Hope Springs, I'll be here. And if you don't, I wish you every blessing.*

*Love,*

*Violet*

Nate reread the last two words. *Love?* As in *love?*

"Is this the same Violet you've been telling Kayla about?" Mom leaned her shoulder into him.

So much for secrets between siblings. But he laughed. "Yeah, it is."

Mom looked like she was about to say something else, but the crowd sent up a roar, and cowbells clanged all around them. Nate's heart leaped as his eyes searched the course. Kayla was still in the lead, but a guy with a green helmet was close to pulling ahead of her. He shoved to the front of the crowd, his parents right behind him. All three of them screamed for her. As she pulled even with them, she shot them the same triumphant smile she'd worn before she'd taken the state cross-country championship. Nate's heart lifted. Despite all that had changed, despite the wheelchair, his little sister was the same Kayla. She had this.

Her wheelchair crossed the finish line a fraction of an inch ahead of the other guy's.

Nate jumped up and down and pumped a fist into the air. He spun to hug Mom. After he let her go, he hesitated a second, then hugged Dad, too. Dad clapped him on the back.

The three of them hovered together as Kayla was presented her medal and gave a few interviews. Nate had been the center of attention once, the cameras and interviews directed at him.

But seeing his sister beam in the spotlight, he didn't miss it at all. What he had now was so much more precious than that.

Finally, Kayla made her way over to them.

"Why don't you guys go get the car?" Kayla told their parents. "Nate and I will wait here." She led Nate to a picnic table in the park where the race had ended.

"So—" Kayla pulled up next to the table as Nate sat on top of it. "I see you got Violet's letter." She gestured to the piece of paper he'd pulled in and out of his pocket a dozen times since reading it.

"Good to know some things are private around here." Nate ruffled her hair in the way she'd hated when they were kids.

But she ignored it. "And?"

"And nothing. That's over now. I messed everything up pretty big."

"Doesn't sound over, judging by the letter. It sounds very much like she wants you to come back."

Nate shook his head. That didn't matter. Even if Violet thought she wanted him in her life, she was better off without him. And anyway, he'd already decided what he was going to do with his future.

"I'm going to stay here. With you." Nate folded the letter and tucked it into his back pocket, as if he were putting thoughts of Violet away forever. As if that were possible.

"And do what? Babysit me? In case you haven't noticed, I'm pretty capable." She held up her medal.

"I did notice. And congratulations." Nate shoved her shoulder.

"Well, then don't use me as an excuse to hide out here."

"It wouldn't be right." Nate scanned the street for Mom and Dad's van. He was ready for this conversation to be over.

"Wouldn't be right how?" Now Kayla's persistence was downright annoying.

"I'm not going to leave you here. Like this." He gestured to her wheel-chair. "While I go off and have a relationship. A life."

The glare she shot him made him look away. "You don't think I can have a life?"

"No, of course not. That's not what I meant. But—"

"Because I'll have you know I have a very full life. And a relationship, too."

Nate spun toward her, suddenly finding himself in protec-tive-big-brother mode. "What relationship? With that guy in the picture? Why haven't I met him?"

Kayla played with her hands. "Well, *had* a relationship."

Nate's shoulders tightened. When he found the monster who had hurt his sister, he would rip his face off.

"Relax." Kayla smirked at him. "I'm the one who broke it off. Garrett was a good guy, but I wanted to focus more on my racing and my ministry right now. Maybe someday I'll be ready for a serious relationship but not yet."

Nate exhaled.

"You have to stop defining me by my disability, Nate. I can have just as full and rich a life as anyone. I'm not dead. Now you need to stop living like you are."

Nate stared at his little sister. When had she grown so wise?

"Go back to Violet." Kayla gave his leg a double pat, then wheeled her chair away from the table. "Have a life with her. I promise I'll be fine. I'll even come to visit."

# Chapter 45

When the bus finally pulled into the Hope Springs station, relief filled Nate.

He was home.

Despite the assurances of Violet's letter, a flurry of nerves worked through him. Did she really want to see him again? Or was that only something she'd written, knowing he was hundreds of miles away? And what about everyone else? Would they welcome him back now that they knew who he really was?

There was only one way to find out.

Nate squared his shoulders, grabbed the two suitcases he'd brought with him this time—his parents had promised to ship the rest of the stuff he'd spent the past two days packing—and set off through the dark to Hope Street.

The moment he walked into the building, all the memories from the past three months bubbled up, and he couldn't wait another second to see her. He charged up the stairs and knocked on her door.

No answer. He tried not to be crushed by the disappointment. It was Saturday night. She was probably at Sophie's or Dan's or whoever had invited everyone over this weekend.

He dragged his suitcases into his own apartment, which looked the same as when he'd left—except the dog kennel was missing. A pang hit him at the realization of all he'd walked away from. He paced the empty apartment for a few minutes, but if he stayed here all night, he'd go crazy.

Without pausing to consider where he'd go, he made his way down the hill toward the beach and the rocky outcrop that had become his favorite thinking spot.

His breath puffed in front of his face in the cool evening air as he crunched across the seashells. The moon was full tonight, casting a white glow on top of the water, and he watched the waves as he walked, letting their monotonous back and forth motion lull him.

He was almost to the rocks when he heard wild footsteps scrabbling over the shells, followed by happy barking.

Nate's head swung toward the sound, and he squatted just in time for Tony to barrel into him. As the dog planted joyful kisses on his cheek, Nate searched the dark.

The moment his eyes fell on her, a tsunami of hope slammed into him. Violet followed Tony, her footsteps barely making a sound. The moonlight bounced off her dark hair and lit the soft smile on her lips. Nate caught his breath as his eyes met hers. There was a trace of uncertainty there but also hope.

He straightened as she reached him.

"Violet?" his voice was barely a whisper, lighter even than the breeze that played with the tendril of hair on her face.

But somehow she heard him. "Nate."

They looked at each other a beat longer.

Then she stepped into his arms.

Without thinking, Nate pulled her tight against his chest. She felt right in his embrace. He never wanted to let go.

He moved his hands to her cheeks, which were red with the cold. "What are you doing out here?" He stepped back to pull off his sweatshirt and passed it to her.

She pressed her face into it for a second, then put it on. Nate's heart almost burst at the familiar movement.

"I've been coming out here to think. And pray." Violet hid her hands in the sleeves of his sweatshirt.

He brushed a curl off her cheek and tucked it behind her ear. "It's a good spot for that."

He couldn't take his eyes off her lips. He wanted more than anything to kiss her right now.

But first he had to say something.

He took a step back so he'd have a clear head. Or at least clearer.

The hope in her eyes dimmed a little, and he almost stepped forward to take her hands again. But he had to do this first. "There's something I have to say. And I don't want you to stop me. Okay?"

She bit her lip but nodded.

"First, I want to say again how sorry I am that I didn't tell you everything sooner. Not telling you was as good as lying to you. And I don't ever want to do that." He swallowed. "Lie to you I mean."

Violet opened her mouth as if she was going to answer, but he raised a hand, pressing on. "I know you already said you forgive me for that, and I believe you. And—" He took half a step closer. "Thank you. You don't know what that means to me."

He gazed out to the lake, where the waves continued to roll in. "And thank you for reminding me of God's forgiveness. I tried to push it away for a long time. But you and Dan—and even my family—have helped me see that I don't get to decide what God forgives. Jesus did that for me."

Violet raised a hand to rub a finger gently under each eye.

Nate wanted to gather her to him, but he had more to say. "And I'm sorry that I ran away from you. I know you feel like so many people in your life have left you, either on purpose or because of circumstances they couldn't control. I never wanted to be one of those people."

She was crying openly now, and Nate moved closer but didn't let himself touch her, no matter how badly he ached to wrap her in his arms. That had to be her choice.

"And I want you to know that I'll never be one of those people again. I'm here to stay." His eyes locked on hers. "If you want me to."

With a choked cry, she stepped forward. And that's all it took. His arms went around her, and he cupped his hand against the back of her head.

She nestled closer, and Nate sighed.

Somehow, through all the horrible things that had happened, through everything he'd been through and put others through, God had brought him to this point. To this perfect place with this perfect woman.

After a few minutes, she lifted her head, and her eyes landed on his.

He brought his head down slowly, watching every change in her expression. Surprise. Joy. Hope. Love.

He felt all of it echo in his own heart.

He let go of everything except this moment and pressed his lips to hers.

When they finally pulled apart, they whispered the words at the same time: "I love you."

# Epilogue

Nerves surged through Violet's whole body as the lights in the sanctuary dimmed. Nate stepped to the front of the church with the rest of the worship band. Down the row, all their friends were applauding and cheering. To Violet's left, Kayla was leaning forward in her wheelchair, an expression of sheer glee on her face. Violet knew the feeling. Nate had been playing with the church worship band for six months now, but this was their first concert. Violet was overcome with a mix of awe and joy and amazement at what God had done in Nate's life. And in hers.

If anyone had told her when he moved in across the hall last summer that she'd soon find herself looking forward to every moment with him, she'd have called them crazy. Not only because he wasn't the friendliest new neighbor of all time. But even more so because she hadn't thought she could ever love another man the way she'd loved Cade.

But, then, she didn't love Nate in exactly the same way she'd loved Cade.

Her love for Nate was just as strong, but her relationship with him was different than her relationship with Cade had been. Where she and Cade had grown up together and knew everything about each other, she was still learning new things about Nate every day. And where she and Cade had matching outgoing personalities, Nate was much quieter and more reserved. Where her love for Cade had been youthful and exuberant, her love for Nate was more mature—quieter but no less certain.

Nate's eyes met hers as the opening chords of a praise song rang through the church. Violet kept her eyes on his as she broke into the chorus with the rest of the audience. She wondered if anyone else in the crowd sensed the energy that pulsed between them as they praised their God together—the God who had given them both a second chance.

Halfway through the concert, Kayla leaned over to give her a hug. Violet squeezed back. Nate's little sister had only arrived for a visit the day before, but already Violet loved her.

"He's always been good," Kayla said into her ear. "But there's something different about him now. It's like he's—" She gestured as if searching for the right word. "Real now, I guess."

Violet nodded. She could feel it. In everything he did, Nate made it clear that he'd experienced God's grace firsthand. And he wasn't going to hide that from anyone.

When the concert came to a close, Violet was exhausted but in a good way, as if she'd poured everything she had into worshiping her Creator. The band waved to the cheering crowd and then exited the church.

All except Nate.

A lone spotlight picked him out on the piano bench.

The audience fell silent again as soft chords floated up from the Bosendorfer Nate's father had purchased from her, then turned around and donated to the church.

Nate's voice picked up the melody of a song she'd never heard.

*I thought my life was over,*
*Thought that I was done*
*Planned to live out my days*
*Never knowing the warmth, the warmth of the Son.*
*But then you opened up my eyes*
*Told me I was blind but now could see*

*That you had more in store*

*That you had plans, that you had plans for me.*

Violet closed her eyes, swallowing against the lump in her throat. She knew Nate had written the song based on his own experiences, but it seemed he'd taken the words right from her soul. When Cade died, she'd thought her life was over. But God had used Nate to show her that he wasn't done with her yet.

*And so today I thank you*

*For the life you've given me*

*It's a life I don't deserve.*

*It's a life that makes me, a life that makes me free.*

Violet swiped at the tears on her cheeks, noticing that most of their friends were doing so as well.

A few minutes later, Nate was at her side, pulling her into a hug.

"Hey, it wasn't that bad, was it?" He dropped a kiss on her forehead.

She shook her head. "That good, actually. These are good tears."

He smiled as he wiped away a teardrop she'd missed. "They're cute on you. I'll have to try to make you cry some more of those sometime."

As if that was some sort of cue, all their friends gathered up their coats and bags.

"Anyone want to grab a bite at the Hidden Cafe?" Sophie slipped her arm into her jacket.

"We'll be there in a little bit." Nate pressed another kiss to Violet's head. "I just have to clean up first, or it's going to be a mess for worship tomorrow morning."

"We can give Kayla a ride over there." Sophie rested a hand on the back of Kayla's wheelchair. Kayla giggled, and Violet could have sworn the younger woman winked at Sophie.

Nate gave his sister a stern look, and she tried to straighten her lips for a second before they tipped into a smile again.

"Yeah, get out of here." Nate shooed her away.

"Maybe I should go along." Violet started to follow. She didn't want Kayla to be uncomfortable sitting at the restaurant with a group of people she'd only met a couple of hours ago.

Nate grabbed her hand and tugged her toward him. "One thing about my little sister. She can handle things just fine on her own."

He lifted Violet's hand to his lips and brushed a light kiss onto her knuckles. "Anyway, I'll get lonely here if you go without me."

She laughed at him. "You'll have the rest of the band." Except the front of the church was empty. She swiveled to search the sanctuary, but that had cleared out, too. Even their friends had disappeared. "Where'd everyone go?"

"It's just us." Nate tugged her toward the piano, which gleamed in the single spotlight that still shone on it. "Come here."

She tilted her head but let him pull her onto the piano bench with him.

"Do you remember when you asked if I'd teach you to play?"

She nodded. Why was he bringing this up now? When they had a whole church to clean up, all by themselves apparently?

"I thought this could be the first song I teach you." He positioned his hands on the keys and started to play. After a couple of notes, Violet recognized the melody as "Canon in D."

Nate played a little more of the song, and then his hands stilled, and he turned to her with a soft smile she couldn't quite read.

She did want to learn the piano, and she was sure he was a good teacher, but—

"That sounded kind of complicated. Shouldn't I start with 'Hot Cross Buns' or something?"

Nate smiled gently and swept up both of her hands in his, holding them to his heart. "Maybe. But I think that would be an odd song to play at our wedding."

"Our—" The electricity of the word traveled through her whole body.

Nate took one of his hands away from hers and reached behind a piece of sheet music, pulling out the saucer she'd given him from Barney and Gladys's set. A small black box sat in the center of it.

His face swam in her vision as her eyes filled, but she was pretty sure he was smiling.

"Are those good tears?" He lifted his hand to wipe one that had fallen onto her cheek.

She sniffed and half laughed. "Very good."

"In that case—" He slid off the piano bench, pulling her to the edge of the seat. Then he bent slowly to one knee, releasing her hands so he could open the ring box and hold it out to her.

"Violet, you helped me find my life again. And now I know that it won't be complete without you. Will you marry me?"

Violet's eyes traveled from the simple solitaire to her finger, where the white band that had once stood out so starkly had faded. Was she ready to put a new ring in that spot?

But she already knew.

She held out her hand to him and let him slip the ring onto it.

Before she could admire it, Nate had gathered her in his arms, almost crushing her with the force of his hug. "You are an amazing woman, Violet. Do you know that?"

Violet shook her head, raising her eyes to meet his. "You said I helped you find your life. But the truth is, you gave me mine back. I was holding onto a past that could never be again. I didn't think I had a future."

She lifted a hand to his face, ran it over the rough stubble on his cheek. "I didn't think my heart would ever be whole again."

Nate dropped his forehead to hers, his breath a whisper on her lips.

"Neither did I," he said. "Not until you."

Thank you for reading NOT UNTIL YOU! I hope you loved Nate and Violet's story! Catch up with them and the rest of the Hope Springs friends in Not Until Us—this time it's Pastor Dan's turn to find love!

And be sure to sign up for my newsletter to get Ethan and Ariana's story, Not Until Christmas, as a free gift.

Visit https://www.valeriembodden.com/gift or use the QR code below to join.

～

## *A preview of* Not Until Us (Hope Springs book 4)

### Chapter 1

How had she messed up again?

Jade swiped at her cheeks as she slid the key into the lock of her apartment door. If the God her roommate Keira kept telling her about had any decency, Keira would still be in bed. She wasn't in the mood to be reprimanded by her squeaky clean friend right now. She already knew last night had been a mistake.

One she'd made far too many times.

She inched the door open slowly but let out a frustrated breath as her eyes fell on her roommate, perky as ever, sitting on the couch with some kind of kale-soy-banana-protein drink in hand.

Apparently God didn't have any decency. Or he had one wicked sense of humor.

"Good morning." Keira eyed Jade's clothes—the same ones she'd been wearing when she'd left for work last night.

Jade held up a hand. "Don't say it."

"Say what?" Keira took a long sip of her drink, still watching Jade.

"Fine. I screwed up. Again." She tried to sound defiant, but even as the words came out, a bone-crushing weariness descended on her. She was trying to be a better person. She really was. But old habits were hard to break. Last night had been just one more name to add to her list of lifelong mistakes. Or it would be if she knew his name.

She buried her face in her hands. She was an awful person. "I don't know why I keep doing this." When the guy had walked into the bar, she'd told herself to ignore him. But she'd been bored. And he'd had nice eyes and witty banter. Plus, he was only passing through town on business. There was no chance things would get messy or complicated. He'd go on his way, she'd go on hers, and neither of them would worry about it again.

Besides, he'd practically challenged her to go back to his hotel room with him. What was she supposed to do?

*Walk away.* The voice in her head sounded an awful lot like her big sister Violet. Not that Violet had any idea what Jade's life was like, aside from the sanitized version Jade fed her on their weekly phone calls.

Keira crossed the small space and pulled Jade's hands away from her face, holding the protein drink out to her. Jade wrinkled her nose and pushed it away. After eight years in Los Angeles, she still had no interest in the stuff that passed for breakfast around here. Give her a donut and a strong cup of coffee any day.

"Change is hard." Keira wrapped an arm over her shoulder and steered her to the couch. "You should pray about it."

Jade shook her head. If there was anything she was less interested in than protein shakes, it was prayer. "I need to pack. My plane leaves in a couple hours."

She still wasn't sure what had compelled her to give in to her sister's pleas that she spend the summer in Hope Springs. But maybe it would do her some good to get away from this town of broken dreams for a while.

Besides, the way Violet talked about Hope Springs made Jade almost homesick for it.

Almost.

Mostly, though, she was going because she owed it to Vi. After six years of completely cutting her sister out of her life, Jade didn't deserve the second chance Vi had given her. The phone calls they'd been exchanging for the past couple years weren't enough. The least she could do was spend the summer helping her sister finalize plans for her wedding.

"Well, look at it this way." Keira sucked down the last of her shake. "Maybe you'll meet a nice, wholesome man in Hope Springs, and you'll get married and live happily ever after."

Jade snickered. "You read too many small town romances. Trust me, there's no one in Hope Springs I'd consider dating, let alone marrying. Besides—" She flopped onto the couch. "I'm not really the happily ever after kind of girl."

Keira tipped her head to the side, studying Jade. "Everyone's a happily ever after kind of girl. It just takes some of us longer to get there than others." She moved to the cramped kitchen to rinse out her glass.

Jade stared after her. Keira could dream about happily ever after all she wanted. But Jade knew the truth. There was no such thing. She'd learned that lesson early, and she wasn't going to forget it anytime soon.

## Chapter 2

Dan hadn't known it was possible to sweat this much.

This had to be the hottest Hope Fest parade on record. Of course, that might have something to do with the heavy lion costume he was wearing. Grace had borrowed the local high school's mascot, insisting that if they were going to have a Noah's ark float, they needed the animals too. Lucky for him, he was exactly the right size for the costume.

Despite the sweltering heat, Dan had to admit that the float had turned out better than he could have imagined. And judging from the crowd's cheers as they walked past, he wasn't the only one who thought so.

Dan swiveled to catch a glimpse of the others marching with him. There had to be nearly one hundred people representing Hope Church in the parade—all of them in some sort of animal costume or another.

His heart filled. He knew many of them were there in tribute to his father, who had been their spiritual leader for nearly forty years. Dan had almost canceled the church's entry in the parade this year. His grief over Dad's death was still too raw for him to dedicate the time needed to plan it. But when he'd brought it up to the church board, they'd reminded him that the congregation was looking to him as their new head pastor for guidance in how to move on. He was glad now that he'd listened to them. The parade seemed to have brought his members together in a way nothing else had lately.

"Hey. This turned out really well." His sister Leah sidled up to him, decked out in a colorful parrot costume. "Dad would have loved it. I could totally see him hamming it up in that costume."

"I was just thinking that. Thank goodness Grace came through with all this stuff." It was almost a miracle, considering he'd asked her to be in charge of the parade only two weeks earlier. And she'd done it all with a smile.

"Speaking of which—" Leah poked him in the side, and Dan knew what was coming. "How was your dinner last night?"

"You mean the one you tricked us into?"

Dan, Leah, and Grace had worked on the float until late the night before, and afterward Leah had suggested they grab a bite at the Hidden Cafe, before conveniently remembering she had to take care of a friend's cat.

"How was the cat, by the way?"

"What cat?" Leah waved to the cheering crowds. "Oh, yeah. The cat was good."

Dan gave her a little shove. "There was no cat."

Leah laughed, completely unashamed. "Nope. But you didn't answer my question. How was dinner with Grace?"

Dan sighed into his costume, then wished he hadn't, as his breath only made the small space steamier. "It was fine."

"And?" Leah poked him, as if waiting for more.

He lifted his hands, the claws of his costume clacking. "And that's it."

There'd been no fireworks. No amazing revelation that this was the woman for him. Just some good food, a bit of conversation, and a wave goodnight.

Which was fine.

Just fine.

"You should ask her to the fireworks tonight."

This time Dan managed to contain his sigh—barely. "I just don't see this going anywhere, Leah."

It wasn't like he was looking for a relationship anyway. Sure, he'd been performing marriage ceremonies for his friends more frequently lately, and every once in a while, he longed for what they had. But mostly, he was too busy with his ministry to consider marriage and a family.

"Famous last words." Leah flitted away to pass out candy to the parade goers.

Dan shook his head at her. His sister was a meddler, there were no two ways about it. Her heart was in the right place, but sometimes he sure wished that place was somewhere else.

By the time they reached the final stretch of the parade, Dan was tempted to pull his lion head off. But he forced himself to wait until they'd gone past every last spectator.

When he'd finally taken the costume off, he grabbed an abandoned water bottle from the float and poured it over his head. The few kids whose parents hadn't yet plucked them from the realistic-looking ark giggled, and he grabbed another half-empty water bottle and gently tossed a few drops their way. They shrieked but laughed harder.

"You're good with them." Grace came up next to him, looking cool and comfortable in her shorts and t-shirt. She'd ridden along in the truck to manage the speaker system. She started pulling decorations off the float.

"Ah, kids are fun." Dan lifted a little guy dressed as a turtle down from the ark and passed him a lollipop from the bag of extra candy. Soon, a group of kids had gathered around him. Dan couldn't help but smile. He knew the kids were surrounding him more for the candy than for his company, but that didn't make him feel any less like a rock star.

"Bribing them again?" Dan's friend Nate, who really was a rock star—or at least the lead singer for the church's worship band—clapped him on the back.

Dan grinned. "Whatever it takes. I'd better bring some of these along to camp next month." Dan was excited to resurrect the annual trip to Camp Oswego that the church had taken when he was a kid.

"Oh." Grace popped up from the other side of the float. "I almost forgot to tell you. Cassandra Murphy said she could chaperone, so we should be all set."

"Seriously?" Dan could have hugged her. He'd been trying for weeks to find one more female chaperone. He'd asked Cassandra himself at least twice, but she'd said it'd be impossible to get time off. Apparently Grace really was a miracle worker.

"I don't know how you did it, but thank you." He pulled a stuffed giraffe off the side of the ark. "And thank you for putting this float together. It looked amazing."

Grace ducked her head. "It was nothing."

Leah bounced over to them. "What was nothing?"

"The float." His voice was guarded. The last thing he needed was for his sister to overreact to his compliment to Grace. Next thing he knew, she'd have them walking down the aisle.

But to his relief, Leah turned away from him to Grace. "Oh my goodness, yes. Thank you so much for designing it. My attempts the last few years have been kind of . . ."

"Pathetic," Dan filled in for his sister.

"Ouch." Leah swatted at him. "But yes. Pathetic is a good word to describe it." She slid the parrot wings off. "Are you coming to the fireworks tonight, Grace?"

There it was. Dan shot his sister a look, but she only winked at him.

Grace shifted the handful of stuffed animals she'd picked up from the float. "There are fireworks?"

"Oh yeah, better than the fourth of July." Leah gestured toward the sky, as if she could see them already.

Even though he knew what was coming, Dan couldn't figure out a way to prevent it. He took a step away from the float, but that didn't stop his sister.

"Actually, I know Dan is going. I bet he could pick you up on the way. He has to drive right past your house anyway."

Dan froze but didn't turn around.

After last night, Grace would recognize his sister's blatant matchmaking and say no.

Wouldn't she?

"If that wouldn't be too much trouble, I'd love to go."

"It's no trouble," Leah assured Grace, and Dan almost snorted out loud. Of course it was no trouble for her. She'd just set her little brother up on a date. He'd have to thank her later. Once he'd come up with a suitable revenge.

But for now he turned to Grace. It wasn't her fault he had a meddlesome sister. And he really did owe her after all she'd done to make the parade a success. "It's no problem at all. How about I pick you up around eight?"

Leah beamed at them both, then sashayed off, saying something about making sure everyone handed in their costumes.

"I'm sorry if you don't want—" Grace said. "I don't need to go."

"No, it's fine. I'm looking forward to it." He offered her the most genuine smile he could muster. "It'll be fun." Anyway, it wasn't like a trip to the fireworks was a marriage proposal.

He stood awkwardly, trying to figure out something else to say. Thankfully, Nate's fiancée, Violet, walked up at that moment, winding her arm through Nate's as he leaned down to kiss her forehead. Dan couldn't have been happier for his two friends, whose wedding was coming up at the end of summer.

"We'd better get going. We need to be at the airport by seven." Violet tugged Nate toward the parking lot.

Nate patted her arm. "It's only four now."

"I know, but there could be traffic, or . . ." She gave him a playful swat on the arm. "Stop laughing at me. I'm excited."

"Are you two skipping out of town? Without seeing the fireworks?" Dan's heart fell. He'd been hoping he and Grace could sit with them, so it'd seem less like a date.

"Nope." Violet's face lit up brighter than any firework. "We're going to the airport to pick up Jade."

Dan fought to keep his expression neutral, even as his heart surged at the name.

It had been eight years. He shouldn't still react that way to something as insignificant as her name.

"I didn't know Jade was coming home."

If possible, Violet's smile got even brighter. "I've been begging her for weeks to come home for the summer, and she must have gotten sick of it because she finally said yes. She's staying until after the wedding." Violet pulled on Nate's arm. "Come on. We have to go."

Nate shrugged at Dan, then followed his future wife toward the parking lot.

"Save us a seat for the fireworks," Violet called over her shoulder. "We may be late."

"Who's Jade?" Grace's question made Dan jump.

"Violet's sister." And his— His what?

His almost-girlfriend?

They hadn't dated. Not officially. But they'd spent so much time together in the last few months of high school that they'd forged a connection deeper than dating ever could.

At least that's what he'd thought.

Right up until she disappeared, leaving him only a note. He hadn't seen or heard from her once since then.

But apparently that was about to change. So he'd better get a grip on how he felt about it.

Fast.

## KEEP READING NOT UNTIL US

# More Books by Valerie M. Bodden

## Hope Springs

*While the books in the Hope Springs series are linked, each is a complete romance featuring a different couple.*

Not Until Forever (Sophie & Spencer)

Not Until This Moment (Jared & Peyton)

Not Until You (Nate & Violet)

Not Until Us (Dan & Jade)

Not Until Christmas Morning (Leah & Austin)

Not Until This Day (Tyler & Isabel)

Not Until Someday (Grace & Levi)

Not Until Now (Cam & Kayla)

Not Until Then (Bethany & James)

Not Until The End (Emma & Owen)

## River Falls

*While the books in the River Falls series are linked, each is a complete romance featuring a different couple.*
Pieces of Forever (Joseph & Ava)
Songs of Home (Lydia & Liam)
Memories of the Heart (Simeon & Abigail)
Whispers of Truth (Benjamin & Summer)
Promises of Mercy (Judah & Faith)

## River Falls Christmas Romances

*Wondering about some of the side characters in River Falls who aren't members of the Calvano family? Join them as they get their own happily-ever-afters in the River Falls Christmas Romances.*
Christmas of Joy (Madison & Luke)

## Want to know when my next book releases?

You can follow me on Amazon to be the first to know when my next book releases! Just visit amazon.com/author/valeriembodden and click the follow button.

# Acknowledgements

Forgiveness was a huge topic to write about, and I couldn't have done it if I didn't have the joy and peace of knowing God's forgiveness in my life. As ever, my first and greatest thanks goes to him—first for the forgiveness he has won for me and then for giving me the privilege of sharing the great news of that forgiveness through my books. It makes my heart full every day.

Thanks also to my husband and four children, who are a constant reminder of God's grace as they forgive my wrongs on a daily basis. What a blessing to discuss God's love with each other every day. My favorite time each day is our evening devotion and prayer time when we all open our hearts to each other and to our heavenly Father. And thanks to my parents, in-laws, and extended family, who support my books by asking about them, reading them, cheering me on, and spreading the word.

A special thank you to Jennifer Ellenson, Rachel Kozinski, Josie Bartelt, Connie, Amber G., Patty Bohuslav, Becca, Janice Petersen, and Karen Bonner—my incredible advance reader team, who gave of their time to read the book and offer invaluable insights. You ladies are a wonderful blessing to me.

And, of course, thank you to you, dear reader! You're the reason I do what I do! I hope this book has reminded you of God's great love for you.

# About the Author

Valerie M. Bodden has three great loves: Jesus, her family, and books. And chocolate (okay, four great loves). She is living out her happily ever after with her high-school-sweetheart-turned-husband and their four children. Her life wouldn't make a terribly exciting book, as it has a happy beginning and middle, and someday when she goes to her heavenly home, it will have a happy end.

She was born and raised in Wisconsin but recently moved with her family to Texas, where they're all getting used to the warm weather (she doesn't miss the snow even a little bit, though the rest of the family does) and saying y'all instead of you guys.

Valerie writes emotion-filled Christian fiction that weaves real-life problems, real-life people, and real-life faith. Her characters may (okay, will) experience some heartache along the way, but she will always give them a happy ending.

Feel free to stop by www.valeriembodden.com to say hi. She loves visitors! And while you're there, you can sign up for your free story.

Made in the USA
Monee, IL
11 September 2024

65369708R00198